SOMETHING'S GUAVA GIVE

CARRIE DOYLE

Poisoned Pen
PRESS

Published by Poisoned Pen Press, an imprint of Sourcebooks
P.O. Box 4410, Naperville, Illinois 60567-4410
(630) 961-3900
sourcebooks.com

Library of Congress Cataloging-in-Publication Data

Names: Doyle, Carrie, author.
Title: Something's guava give / Carrie Doyle.
Description: Naperville, Illinois : Poisoned Pen Press, [2022] | Series: Trouble in paradise! ; book 2
Identifiers: LCCN 2021003846 (print) | LCCN 2021003847 (ebook) | (paperback) | (epub)
Subjects: GSAFD: Mystery fiction.
Classification: LCC PS3604.O95473 S66 2022 (print) | LCC PS3604.O95473 (ebook) | DDC 813/.6--dc23
LC record available at https://lccn.loc.gov/2021003846
LC ebook record available at https://lccn.loc.gov/2021003847

Printed and bound in Canada.
MBP 10 9 8 7 6 5 4 3 2 1

To May (Merecias Gandela), who is the best!

1

PLUM LOCKHART STEPPED THROUGH THE narrow door and felt heavy, gray cobwebs wrap around her shoulders. As she squirmed to brush them off, she inhaled a strong stench of mildew. The air was stifling, heavy with heat and ripe with neglect. She squinted through the darkness, afraid someone might be lurking in the corners, but could see only murky shadows. Her heartbeat quickened.

She spun around, unable to see the person behind her.

"Hello?" Plum asked, her voice echoing around her. "Anyone there?"

"Yes," came the whispered response.

"What godforsaken place have you taken me to?" Plum demanded of her colleague Lucia, who had accompanied her into the dilapidated villa. "I can't see a thing, and if I hadn't known you were following me, I would have assumed I was being hunted down by a serial killer."

"*Cálmese,*" retorted Lucia, who flicked on the light switch. "There. Better?"

Plum blinked and glanced around the foyer, which had a grimy, linoleum floor and mushroom-colored walls that might have originally been a cool white. The light fixture above them was coated with a dense layer of dust, and a cracked mirror hung over a small console table with a broken leg.

Plum shook her head at Lucia, who was giving her an assured look from behind the thick lenses of her glasses.

"Decidedly not better," said Plum. "This place is horrible."

Lucia clucked and broke into a wide grin. "We both know that if anyone can improve and renovate this villa, it's you. And besides, you always love a challenge."

Plum didn't disagree. She was incredibly competent. But she had always considered this a secret strength, like a superpower. Yet this small, sixty-year-old grandmother had discovered it after they had only been acquainted for four months. Perhaps Plum was more transparent than she had realized.

Plum sighed. "All right, show me around."

Lucia smiled mischievously. "I thought you would never ask."

As the tall, redheaded American followed the short, gray-haired Paraison through the unkempt villa, Plum marveled at how much her life had changed. At this time last year, she had been editor-in-chief at the glamorous *Travel and Respite Magazine,* based in New York City and jet-setting around the globe on fabulous trips to five-star hotels. When that all came crashing down, she made what she assumed would be a temporary move to the small, Caribbean island of Paraiso, taking a job at Jonathan Mayhew's eponymous travel agency at Las Frutas Resort. But life wouldn't stop throwing curveballs, so the previous month, she had ultimately (and impulsively) launched her own villa broker agency: Plum Lockhart Luxury Retreats.

"This place is a dump, Lucia," marveled Plum, peering out a filmy window that overlooked an overgrown courtyard. The shaggy ground was littered with rotten guava that bore deep, brown spots. The neglected gum tree's bark sported a creeping fungus, and the drooping leaves were curled anemically.

Lucia shrugged. "We need inventory. It's April, one of the

busiest months here. We have three new clients very eager to find a place for Easter break."

A splashy article in the *Market Street Journal* by Plum's former coworker and on-and-off friend, Gerald Hand, had generated hundreds of queries, and she was now furiously working to secure more properties to manage, hence the visit to the squalid house, marketed as Villa Tomate.

"I suppose it is a good problem to have," said Plum, taking in the fractured surfaces and peeling paint.

"It is," insisted Lucia. She pulled out a notebook and began jotting down a to-do list.

"The name is kind of pathetic," said Plum. "All of the villas have fruit names, and this one has tomato?"

"Tomato is a fruit."

"Technically. But most people consider it a vegetable."

"I consider myself a twenty-five-year-old blond with an hourglass figure, but that doesn't make it true," replied Lucia.

Plum smiled. When she started her agency last month, she had been thrilled that Lucia agreed to join her (especially since it riled their former unappreciative employer, Jonathan Mayhew, and his deputy, Damián Rodriguez, who was Plum's nemesis). Plum had even offered to make her a full partner, but Lucia had owned a hardware store for years and had no interest in incurring the headaches that came along with running a business. Instead, she accepted a role as "director" (Plum was big on titles) and would work for a salary with commission. The arrangement suited both of them perfectly, as Plum did enjoy the glory of being the boss. But she also fervently admired her colleague's clarity of thought, decisiveness, and clear outlook.

"We're going to need to send in those people who clean up crime scenes in order to get this place ready," said Plum.

"Don't be dramatic."

"Never dramatic, always practical."

"Hurry up and tell me what you think you will need. We have a three o'clock meeting with Giorgio Lombardi back at the office."

"What?" yelped Plum. "Why is that at the office? We've only just moved in, the place has boxes everywhere, it's like we are living out of it…"

"You *are* living out of it."

"I know that, but it's about images and perception," explained Plum. "We need Giorgio Lombardi to support our agency, and if he thinks we're some Podunk, low-rent operation run out of a town house, he will be dissuaded."

"We *are* a low-rent operation run out of a town house," said Lucia. "But don't worry. He knows it is temporary, that you lost your housing when you left your previous employment and that this was all we could find for both office and residence at such short notice."

"Why couldn't we meet him at a restaurant?" moaned Plum. She folded her arms.

"Because we don't have the budget for all these fancy meals right now," Lucia admonished.

"That's what people do in New York."

"We're not in New York."

"No, we are certainly not," lamented Plum. "And the town house is a disgrace."

"Don't worry, he's a man. He won't even notice the decor."

When the handsome and suave Giorgio, sporting an expensively tailored, lightweight suit, entered her office and glanced around the room, Plum could swear she saw his nostrils flare in disgust. It was fleeting, though, and when he greeted her, he oozed charm.

"Plum Lockhart," he said in a suave Italian accent. He was in his sixties, with graying dark hair slicked back like a movie star, and smooth, tanned skin. A strong odor of masculine cologne oozed from his pores. He clasped her hand between both of his and squeezed. "It is so nice to meet you. They were not wrong when they said you were the image of a movie star."

Plum's pale skin flushed a deep crimson, but she remained businesslike. "You are too kind, Giorgio," she responded crisply. "I must apologize for our temporary quarters. We were inundated with work as soon as I announced the formation of my company, so I had no time to search for appropriate offices."

"It is no problem," Giorgio replied warmly, although his wary eyes darted toward the garish pieces of framed art that adorned the walls. Plum made an immediate note to throw them in storage.

After they settled into chairs, and Lucia had brought them coffee and some of her tasty *coconetes* cookies, Plum ended the perfunctory niceties and got down to business.

"Giorgio, I know that you control a vast number of villas at Las Frutas, and I would love the opportunity to represent them. My firm has the most discreet and well-heeled clientele on the island, and they are ideal renters for even the most discriminating landlord."

The last part was complete rubbish; Plum had no idea who her clients were, as she had just opened her firm, but power was perception, she knew from the vast number of marketing classes she had watched on YouTube.

Giorgio smiled, revealing unnaturally white teeth. "You must know that we have a relationship with Jonathan Mayhew, your previous employer."

"I do know that," said Plum. "But his *star* employees—myself and Lucia—have departed his agency, and I venture to say it is in a precarious state."

"Perhaps," said Giorgio. "But as you know, I am merely the president of the Fruit Corporation. The residences are the property of Alexandra Rijo, the owner of Las Frutas Resort."

"I did know that," said Plum. "I have yet to meet her, but I hear wonderful things."

"I'm sad to say she has not heard wonderful things about you," he said.

"What do you mean?" asked Plum defensively. She sat upright in her faded-yellow armchair.

"Mrs. Rijo knows everything that happens on the island of Paraiso, and especially in her resort. And she has heard that you are friends with Carmen Rijo, the villainess who stole Alexandra's beloved husband, Emilio, out from under her, who wrecked her family and thieved part of her inheritance, and who is therefore her sworn enemy."

Giorgio took a sip of his tea, keeping his eyes locked on Plum's as he did so.

Plum bit her tongue. She had to tread delicately. She would not consider herself *friends* with Carmen Rijo, but through some deception and scheming, she had been able to establish a working relationship with Carmen after exorcising the woman's enormous mansion of "evil spirits." The grateful Carmen had allowed Plum Lockhart Luxury Retreats to represent a few modest villas as a reward. Plum could not afford to alienate Carmen (especially since she was one day hoping to lease Carmen's mansion, which was the marquee house on the island), but she knew that Alexandra's rental properties were far superior, and she was itching to control them.

"I absolutely understand Alexandra's concerns," began Plum diplomatically. "But I customize my agreements with all of my homeowners, and I can assure you I would endow Alexandra with the most generous contract that I have ever made."

Giorgio nodded. "I understand the implication. And Alexandra will be very interested to know that she is getting a better deal than the second wife..."

"I didn't say that," insisted Plum.

"But you implied it. And that is very good. I will bring her this information."

Suddenly Plum was alarmed. If it got back to Carmen that she had given Alexandra a better deal, things could get dicey for Plum. "I hope you will use your discretion."

Giorgio rose and smiled smugly. "I always do."

Plum felt disconcerted when he left, and she walked over to Lucia's makeshift desk, which was really a card table set up in the corner of the room. Her own card-table desk was across from it.

"I think that went well, don't you?"

Lucia released a deep sigh. "You better hope that Alexandra doesn't go crowing to Carmen that she's getting more money out of you. It will be one more arrow in their vicious battle."

"She wouldn't do that, would she?" asked Plum with alarm.

"There is no love lost between them, so yes, I think she would."

Plum tried to shrug it off. "I'm not worried."

"Suit yourself."

Before they could continue, Plum's cell phone rang, and she quickly answered. It was Gerald Hand, calling from New York.

"You need to do me a favor," demanded Gerald, without even offering a greeting.

"Well, hello to you too," said Plum.

"This is important. My assistant, Arielle Waldron, is staying down there at the hotel with a friend. She's having an issue, and I need you to go troubleshoot."

"Me? Why me?"

"Ah, you're too fancy now?" he sneered. "Don't forget who wrote that glowing article on you and got you all that business."

Plum bit her tongue in an effort to control her terse retort. It was true, she did owe him. His article about her agency in the *Market Street Journal* had put her on the map.

"Why do you even care what happens to your assistant on vacation anyway?"

"Normally I wouldn't give a rat's ass," Gerald confessed. "But the brat's father is the owner of the publishing company I work for, and I've got to kiss her butt until she gets bored and quits or gets married to some poor sucker."

"I see."

"Yeah," he said. "And she is trouble. But you can handle difficult people—I mean, you worked with me, right?" he teased.

"True," she said.

"So, quick like a bunny, please go sort this out."

He hung up without waiting for a response.

CHAPTER 2

PLUM MANEUVERED HER GOLF CART under the canopy of palm trees and down the floral-scented road that cut through the center of Las Frutas Resort. The former sugar plantation's five thousand acres accommodated a hotel, twenty-five golf villas, two hundred houses of varying shapes and sizes, twelve tennis courts, a shooting range, a polo field, several dining options, and two spectacular golf courses. All of this was perched on the edge of the glistening turquoise Caribbean Sea.

Plum slowly traversed speed bumps and carefully avoided flocks of bikers heading to the beach and mused about how much her pace had slowed since she had moved to Paraiso. She had been impatient in the past and now considered herself completely relaxed and easygoing, although Lucia still accused her of being high-strung. She congratulated herself on adapting to a quiet life of seclusion in the tropics. In the past, a small-country life would have been an abhorrent concept to her; today, she embraced the opportunity to start anew. Ahead, Plum saw a dark patch in the road and screeched her golf cart to a complete stop. This caused the large sedan that had been tailgating her to also lurch to a halt.

Plum alighted from the vehicle and made her way over to the

dark patch, which was a turtle crossing the road. Turtles were a source of pride on the island, and every local—as Plum now considered herself despite her brief tenure on Paraiso—knew their preservation was imperative.

"Stop blocking the road!" yelled the man in the sedan, who had a sweaty face and a cigar hanging out of the side of his mouth.

"I need to make sure this little guy makes it to safety."

"And I've got a life to lead," he sneered and pressed on his horn.

Plum gave him her most withering look and stretched out her arms so no one could pass and waited until the turtle traversed the street. The odious man in the sedan treated her to a litany of profanity as she did so, but she held firm. When the coast was clear, he whipped by her, narrowly missing her with his car, and raced toward the hotel. Plum shook her head. Tourists were the worst. And he was probably from New York, she thought, noting that they were the rudest of all vacationers, while conveniently forgetting that she herself was a New Yorker who had only lived on the island briefly.

Driving a golf cart that went at a snail's pace had initially bothered Plum, but she had learned there were advantages too. It afforded a certain agility, for one thing. When she pulled into the hotel parking lot, she saw the sedan with its blinker on, waiting to turn into a spot that was currently obstructed by a delivery van. Carefully steering her cart along the path and into the grass, she tucked into the unclaimed space.

"Hey!" rumbled the man who had cursed her out at the turtle crossing. "I was waiting for that spot!"

"Sorry!" said Plum, breezing past him into the hotel. "I've got a life to lead!"

The sliding doors opened at the grand entrance of the hotel, and Plum stepped into the air-conditioned lobby, relieved to have respite from the heavy heat outdoors. Although she was becoming accustomed to the balmy weather, her blood ran almost 100 percent

Nordic and Scottish according to ancestry.com, and the humidity did not suit her fair complexion. (Not to mention that it made her red hair coil into ringlets that rivaled Little Orphan Annie's.)

The high-ceilinged lobby had a cool, black stone floor and several seating areas, where laid-back guests relaxed on wicker chairs and sofas. Caribbean music drifted out of the speakers, and the smell of coconut permeated the air. Everyone appeared to be in vacation mode, lulled by the tropical atmosphere. After making brief inquiries at reception, Plum was directed to a back office occupied by management. She looked through the glass partition and saw a pretty, young woman, with glossy, long, blond hair that hung below her breasts and darting small eyes, sitting across from Juan Kevin Muñoz, the director of security.

"Knock, knock," said Plum, opening the door.

Juan Kevin glanced up at Plum with surprise. "Miss Lockhart, can I help you?" he asked, with a formality that took Plum off guard.

She had worked closely with the good-looking Paraison the previous month to solve a murder and had developed an intimacy that Plum had thought might lead to romance. But when she had spotted Juan Kevin at a restaurant with a gorgeous woman, she had distanced herself from him, convinced that she had misread the sexual tension between them and unwilling to make herself vulnerable. He had tried to reach out to her, but they had both been busy with work and now the time that had elapsed made things somewhat awkward.

She had convinced herself that she was not at all attracted to him, but now that she was finally face-to-face with him, she realized that was untrue. Plum still experienced the crackling of sparks when she looked into his chocolate-brown, long-lashed eyes.

"My friend Gerald Hand asked me to check on Arielle. He is her employer. He said there was some sort of misunderstanding?" queried Plum, her voice faltering.

"Definitely," interjected Arielle, nodding furiously and speaking in a nasal twang. "It's a huge misunderstanding, but they won't listen to me."

Juan Kevin sighed deeply, and Plum knew him enough to grasp that he was trying to remain patient. He folded his arms on the table, and a flash of the overhead light made his cufflinks glint.

"Miss Waldron was found with several items in her possession that didn't belong to her," began Juan Kevin.

"Someone planted them," snapped Arielle. She shook her head impatiently.

"Now why would they do that?" asked Juan Kevin. He was clad in his requisite blue blazer and khakis, and his wavy, dark hair had recently been cut, Plum noticed.

A ping from a cell phone squawked, and before she answered Juan Kevin, Arielle fiddled in the pocket of her white jersey dress. She pulled out a phone with a purple case and read a message. Plum watched in amazement as the girl tapped a response. Arielle clearly was not at all flustered by the situation. She glanced up.

"What did you ask?"

"I asked why someone would plant something on you," Juan Kevin said, his voice thick with impatience.

Arielle shrugged. "I have no idea. People are weird."

Juan Kevin nodded. "People are weird," he repeated.

"You can ask my friend Jessica. She was with me the entire time and will tell you this is all a pile of crap."

A look of assurance came across Juan Kevin's face. "I did speak to Miss Morse."

"And what did she say?" sneered Arielle.

"She did not witness you taking anything..."

"There! See?" interjected Arielle.

"But security footage shows that your friend Jessica spent most of her time in the room of another hotel guest and was not always with you," said Juan Kevin, keeping his eyes locked on Arielle's.

"Proves nothing," said Arielle, nibbling at her cuticle. "She can vouch for me."

"May I ask what, exactly, you found in Arielle's possession?" asked Plum, moving farther into the room and glancing from Juan Kevin to Arielle.

When the latter didn't respond, Juan Kevin did. "Several of the guests in the pool area have reported things missing from their chaises over the past few days. Jewelry and sunglasses that they removed when they went swimming. A laptop even."

"*They* put it in my bag," said Arielle, rolling her eyes.

"Yet when we looked through the security footage, we saw *you* putting them in your bag," corrected Juan Kevin.

Arielle became suddenly enraged. "Then it was an accident! I obviously thought it was mine. Do you really think I would steal? I have more money than anyone! My God, why would I take their crap? An old computer? Junky jewelry? Do you see these bracelets and rings?" she said, holding up her wrist, where several bejeweled gold bangles hung. "They're Cartier. Worth a fortune."

Plum wasn't sure what to do. Gerald expected her to aid and abet a thief? A flattering newspaper article that was no doubt lining a soiled litter box by now was not worth staking her entire reputation on. She would leave and tell him to sort it out himself. Just as she was about to flee, she stopped. She did have to consider the future of her company and the ongoing need for publicity. It wouldn't hurt to have the owner of a publishing company be in your debt because you helped out his daughter.

"Juan Kevin, is there anything we can do to remedy this?" asked Plum diplomatically. "I assume everyone's belongings were returned."

"True. But I'm not yet sure if they want to press charges..." he began.

"That's ridiculous!" Arielle exploded.

Plum wished Arielle would shut up and allow her to handle

it, but the woman was too hell-bent on making a scene and professing her innocence. Plum ignored Arielle's ranting and stared at Juan Kevin. They exchanged a look as if to say this girl was too much, and Juan Kevin acquiesced.

"As long as she leaves the hotel, we will not press charges," he relented.

"Of course, I'm leaving this sketchy hotel! I'm going to stay with a friend of my parents' who owns a massive villa at the resort and who will be very unhappy to learn how you treated me," Arielle said, rising.

"Good luck to you and to them," said Juan Kevin, standing up. "I hope when you leave them, they don't find anything missing."

"I should sue you for slander," Arielle said, wagging her finger at him. "But you're not worth it."

Juan Kevin gave her a beatific smile but didn't respond.

"Can I have my bag now, please?" she fumed.

He picked up a large, Chanel pocketbook, the kind Plum knew sold for several thousand dollars, and handed it to her.

"I removed all of the items that belonged to other people," he said.

She sneered at him. "If I were dumb enough to ever carry cash, I'd be sure to count it. You're probably just on the take, and that's what this is all about."

"I think the opposite is true," Juan Kevin responded, nonplussed.

Frustrated, Arielle stomped out.

Plum and Juan Kevin stared at each other. It had taken an effort to keep him at arm's length, and now that she was a few feet away from him, she wondered why she had been so determined to do so. She didn't really know if he had been on a date with that woman she saw. He had told her he was having dinner with "a friend." That was harmless enough, right?

Yet it was the timing of it that rankled Plum, after they had leaned on each other through an intense murder investigation.

And it was also the fact that the friend was gorgeous. It wasn't fair; Juan Kevin unleashed feelings within Plum that she tried to keep under tight rein. He set off the retreat button in her brain and made her want to flee to circumvent getting hurt.

"You've been avoiding me," said Juan Kevin, his eyes still fixed on hers.

"What? Of course not," Plum lied.

Juan Kevin knew. And for one small second, she wanted to admit that he was right. But what would happen once she said it? She couldn't take rejection. Juan Kevin finally broke the stare.

"I'm glad to hear that," he said. "Because I thought we were friends."

Friends? He just used the same vile word she had talked herself into thinking meant nothing. With that disgusting term, he sucked all the air out of the room and caused Plum's heart to bang against her rib cage. She was deflated.

"We are definitely friends," said Plum.

"I hope so," he said. "Because your absence has been felt."

"By whom?" Plum blurted.

Juan Kevin smiled. "By me, of course."

Plum was no longer deflated. In fact, she felt a small rush of joy. She was about to make a flirty comment when Juan Kevin's walkie-talkie crackled. He ignored it, but the sound didn't stop, and he gave her a look of apology then answered it. There was clearly some incident that required his attention, so Plum took her leave. If only the moment hadn't been broken!

Plum found Arielle in the lobby on her cell phone. She finished her call as Plum approached, and Arielle began furiously storming through the lobby on her extremely high wedge sandals. Plum called to her, but she didn't stop, and Plum had to do a little jog to catch up.

"So, hey," Plum said when she reached her. She waited for Arielle to thank her profusely.

Arielle gave her a sideways look and didn't slow down. "I never should have stayed in the dumpy rooms at the hotel in the first place, but Jessica insisted because she knew Max Stylo was staying here."

"Who's Max Stylo?" asked Plum, confused.

"This loser guy she ditched me for and has been shacking up with ever since. I'm so over her. But good riddance, I'm going to Dieter's," she said, flipping her long hair behind her shoulders.

"Who's Dieter?" asked Plum. She felt as if she had come into a conversation already in progress and should know all the people referenced.

"Dieter Friedrich," she said in a tone that made it clear she thought Plum was ignorant. "He begged me to stay with him. Now I know why. These hotel people are jerks."

"Well, they're actually not really jerks," began Plum. She was out of breath from trying to keep up with Arielle.

The girl stopped and stared at Plum. Her nostrils flared. "I know bad people when I see them. These are bad people. And that security guard has a stick up his ass."

"He's actually *director* of security," Plum corrected.

"What's the difference? Still a measly employee who should be pandering to me as a guest, not falsely accusing me."

Plum wanted to slap her. How dare she talk about Juan Kevin like that? But Plum counted to three so she wouldn't freak out and give this young woman a piece of her mind. "I beg to disagree," said Plum.

"You can beg all you want," said Arielle, but suddenly her tone became pedantic. "You know, I'll give you a little inside scoop. If you refuse to take any crap from staff, they'll respect you. But if you're nice, they'll walk all over you."

"That has not been my experience," said Plum, although she wondered if it was true.

"Well, it's been mine."

In what she felt was a noble and heroic effort on her part, Plum chose to take the high road. She withdrew one of her newly minted business cards out of her Maxima cardholder handed it to Arielle.

"If you need my help, please let me know. Gerald Hand is a great friend."

Arielle's expression turned into one of revulsion as she studied the card. "Gerald told me all about you. You, like, failed as an editor, and now you're a travel agent at this dinky resort."

Plum bristled. "Absolute lies. But you clearly have a problem taking things that don't belong to you. I'll make sure to hold on to my belongings until you are out of sight!"

Arielle cocked her head to the side. "If you think I would ever be tempted by your cheesy Maxima cardholder, you are an idiot. Maxima is the tackiest brand on the planet."

"Wow, you are really something," said Plum, too stunned to come up with a better retort.

"So are you. And I'm sorry it didn't work out for you, but word of advice? Stay in your lane."

Arielle stomped away before Plum could respond. And Plum had a litany of things she wanted to say. It took all the self-control she possessed not to let this young woman ruffle her feathers further. Someday Arielle would learn the hard way, Plum hoped, although the spoiled and entitled never seemed to get their comeuppance.

But this time they did.

Within twenty-four hours, Arielle was dead.

CHAPTER 3

WHEN JUAN KEVIN CALLED TO inform Plum about Arielle's demise the following day, she couldn't help that her initial feeling was one of vindication. Only in movies did people really get what they deserved. But then Plum realized that was extremely cold-hearted and no one deserved to die just because they were a thief and a spoiled brat. Arielle was also young enough that she might have changed her ways, thought Plum, who found herself stunned by the news.

"That's terrible. What happened?" she asked Juan Kevin.

Plum stared out the window above her desk. It was the direct opposite view of the concrete jungle she had faced in Manhattan. Instead of pigeons defecating on sooty ledges, she had lizards slithering along whitewashed walls. And although her office slash living quarters were in the unfashionable town house section in the northernmost part of the resort, her property still boasted a lush garden dripping with pink bougainvillea blossoms and shaded by fruit trees. If she desired, Plum could collect a bounty of produce in her yard, enough to supply a small stand at a farmer's market. But Plum didn't have time for that, especially with a start-up.

Juan Kevin's voice was low when he responded, "She was murdered."

Plum's eyebrows shot up, and she sat erect in her chair. "Murdered? How?"

"She was strangled."

"How horrible. And strange. To think we were just with her..."

"Yes," continued Juan Kevin. "Her body was found on the beachfront belonging to Villa la Grosella Negra. She had been staying there as a guest of Dieter Friedrich."

"She mentioned him," gasped Plum. "Is he famous or something?"

"Notorious, and very wealthy."

"Did he do it?"

"I hope not. No one is being ruled out."

"Do you have many suspects?" After having met Arielle, Plum imagined there were dozens of people who wanted to strangle her.

"I can't confirm."

"You don't have to be coy with me," she retorted.

"Look, it's complicated, as you know. There is no one in custody, I can tell you that. But the reason I called is that we need to contact the family, and since you knew Arielle..."

"I had never met her before yesterday," Plum corrected. "We have a mutual friend."

"All right. Can you please ask the mutual friend for the contact information of her next of kin? The police have asked for my assistance in locating it. I would like to inform them before the press does."

"Sure."

Juan Kevin quickly hung up. She had wanted to ask him so many other questions (like when he said "her absence was felt," what did he mean, exactly, and could he break it down for her), but clearly this was not the time.

When Plum dialed Gerald's number and informed him

about Arielle's death, there was a stunned silence followed by "ohmyGodohmyGodohmyGod."

"Yes, it's very sad," said Plum, distracted. Her inbox had informed her that she had received an email from Giorgio Lombardi. She clicked on it.

"It's sad, but I hope it doesn't tank my career. I was the one who recommended the resort!" lamented Gerald.

Plum murmured a soothing noise as she scanned the email. Alexandra Rijo had agreed to meet with her to discuss business! Giorgio would get back to her with timing and dates.

"Yay! Fantastic!" enthused Plum.

"What?" asked Gerald. "Are you actually happy that I might lose my job?"

"What?" asked Plum, confused. "Oh, no, sorry. It was yay to something else. Very sad about the girl."

"Were you listening to me at all? I need you to go find out what happened."

"Me? No. I don't want to get involved in another murder."

Plum had recently been instrumental in assisting the police with solving the murder of another guest at the hotel, one who had rented a villa from Plum.

"You have no choice. It's the least you could do for me after that giant article I did promoting you."

"When is my debt going to be paid off?" she snapped.

"I'll let you know," he said briskly. "Don't be snippy. Write down Arielle's father's contact info to give to your police, and then get going to the house, chop-chop."

Plum sighed and agreed. She did slightly feel as if she had an obligation to help find out what happened to Arielle. Maybe if she had been better at smoothing things over with Arielle and Juan Kevin, the poor girl wouldn't have left the hotel and gone and stayed in the villa. She also felt a kinship to her fellow New Yorker, despite Arielle's rude demeanor. New Yorkers had to look out for one another.

As Plum still didn't know her way around the entire resort, she asked Lucia to accompany her in an effort to expedite the journey. When Plum informed her that the victim was found on the beachfront at Villa la Grosella Negra, a look of alarm flashed across Lucia's face.

"What?" asked Plum.

"There is nothing good about that place," clucked Lucia.

"What do you mean?"

Lucia made the sign of the cross. "It's always bad news."

"You'll have to fill me in on the way."

It was another cloudless day in Paraiso, with cheerful blue skies dotted with colorful birds darting between trees. Lucia had offered to drive her car, which normally Plum would have preferred, but today she declined. Much to her astonishment, she found herself beginning to enjoy the meandering pace of the golf cart as they cruised down the verdant lanes framed by lush vegetation and thickets of dazzling flowers. What was happening to her? No one in New York would recognize this laid-back version of who she used to be.

"What does Villa la Grosella Negra mean anyway?" asked Plum.

She turned down the long-melted road heading toward the iridescent sea. In the distance there were glints of the fluctuating water, as wide and gleaming as a sheet of glass, and hints of salt permeated the air.

"It means *black currant*," explained Lucia, who was hanging on dearly to the armrest in the cart. Plum was not the best driver, which was something that Lucia considered a fact and Plum considered an interpretation. "And there is definite blackness at the Villa."

"Stop being cryptic, and tell me why."

Lucia sighed dramatically before beginning to speak. "The villa was built in the 1950s by Marquis Oliver Tessle. He was the second son, the naughty rebellious one, from a very wealthy family in England. He wasn't supposed to inherit everything, but when he was a teenager, his older brother, whom everyone loved, was killed in a mysterious shooting accident. Many people believed that Oliver had shot him and it was covered up."

"Ooh, interesting," said Plum. "Go on."

"Marquis Oliver had many houses. Villa la Grosella Negra was the only one he built himself. He had come to the island as a guest of Esteban Rijo—that was Emilio Rijo's father—and he loved it so much that he decided to stay. However, his wife, the marchioness, did not like the tropics very much. You see, there wasn't much here at the time, it was very rustic—as you will recall, it had been a sugar plantation, a dark time in Paraiso's history. It took years for it to become a fancy resort, and that was done by Emilio, not his father."

"I remember you said that," Plum commented. "I know the Rijos have always been controversial."

"Indeed. And they still control the sugar industry. They just moved it away from the part of the island that was luxury waterfront."

The Rijos were a divisive element on the island. Lucia had told her before that they had done great things but also hugely benefited from exploiting the local people. Any criticism of them had to remain hushed and surreptitious due to their immense wealth and power. Plum knew that locals did not want to go on record with their thoughts on the family, and now, Lucia became quiet and pensive. Plum steered her back to the conversation about Marquis Oliver.

"What happened with the marchioness?" Plum asked.

"She stayed in England."

"Splitsville?" asked Plum.

"Yes, but she refused to grant him a divorce. Which made him very angry, especially when he found a lover he wanted to marry."

Lucia indicated that Plum should make a right turn at the stop sign. After allowing a minivan full of tourists to cross first, she turned the golf cart down the pretty road that hugged the coastline. The crystal-clear blue water lapped clutches of craggy rocks, beckoning swimmers. This street was the gold coast of the resort, where all the most-exclusive villas were located.

"I'd say good riddance. I wouldn't tolerate that nonsense," announced Plum.

"She wanted to hang on to her title and her husband. The legend is that he pretended he was going to reconcile with his wife and asked her to come down to Paraiso before he moved back."

"Then what?"

"She arrived on the island with many Louis Vuitton bags, but she herself left in a body bag."

"He killed her?" asked Plum. She turned and looked at Lucia with astonishment.

It was hard to see Lucia's wise eyes behind her prescription sunglasses, but Plum was sure they were twinkling with that look Lucia got when she was about to reveal something salacious. "It was never proven. The marquis insisted his wife was a drunk and had fallen out of bed and hit her head. There was no proof. There were no witnesses. And no one wanted a scandal."

"Did he marry the girlfriend?"

"Briefly," said Lucia. "But then he divorced her and went on to marry four more times."

"Four more times? Jeez, who has the energy for that?"

"He liked them young and perky."

"Don't they all."

Lucia pointed. "Go there!"

"Where?"

"Left!"

"Where?"

"You passed it. Back up," commanded Lucia.

Plum skeptically put the cart in reverse and pushed the peddle. The cart made that annoying beeping sound, and she kept going until Lucia again told her to stop.

"That way," she said, motioning toward a small dirt road that veered to the left. The entrance was shrouded in thick vegetation, making it impossible to see. Plum had never noticed it before.

"Are you sure? It looks as if we're driving off the cliff into the sea."

"That's the idea. Privacy is important."

Plum slowly drove down the shadowy road, where only patchy sunlight penetrated the tight thatch of casuarina trees and triple Alexander palms. It was so narrow, she was afraid of scraping her cart. After driving several hundred feet, she emerged back into the daylight and found herself steering down an exclusive peninsula she never knew existed. There was the white-capped sea on one side and a small, shimmering cove on the right.

"This is all Villa la Grosella Negra?" she mused.

Lucia shook her head. "There are two villas on this private strip. La Grosella Negra is now owned by Dieter Friedrich. He purchased it twenty years ago from the heirs to the Tessle family and knocked everything down and built his own—well, you will see. People thought it was blasphemous. La Grosella Negra was beautiful, but now..."

"Okay, now I definitely cannot wait to see. You have me intrigued."

"Yes, and the other villa down here is Casa la Manzana, which is owned by Charles Nettles."

"La Manzana! I know that one. It means *apple*," said Plum, quite pleased with herself. She had been sporadically taking Spanish classes online to master the language. Her attendance had waned as of late, due to the demands of starting a new business as well as the fact that she considered herself proficient enough, having mastered about one hundred words.

"Yes. Apple," said Lucia, nodding. "The most mundane of all fruits, in my opinion. Not unlike the owner of the villa."

"Oh, really?" asked Plum, arching her eyebrow. "What does he do?"

"He is an investor and owns a hedge fund."

"And what about the owner of the black currant? Dark?"

"You are about to see for yourself. Turn here."

4

IN HER CAREER AS EDITOR-IN-CHIEF of a travel magazine, Plum had been to a myriad of destinations and locations that ran the gamut from traditional to modern. But she had never seen anything quite like Villa la Grosella Negra.

"This is very strange," said Plum as she steered her golf cart between a Lamborghini and a Maserati.

"Just wait," advised Lucia with a smirk.

The villa—or villas—for there were several ornate structures of varying sizes and shapes, all draped in strings of lights—were evidently inspired by Mayan architecture. At the center of the property was an enormous limestone building in the shape of a pyramid. It featured elaborate, high-relief carvings of three-dimensional dragons, lions, and other such beasts and was painted in bright red, yellow, green, and blue. They walked through the large flagstone parking lot (where numerous cars had gathered, including, Plum noticed, a police car and Juan Kevin's security vehicle) toward the capacious entrance. Plum sidestepped the flock of peacocks wandering the grounds. There was a fountain spurting water out of a nymph's mouth by the front door—a dense mahogany with two glaring eyeballs etched in the front, between which hung a phallic gold gong.

"We're not in Kansas anymore," said Plum, pressing the doorbell. The first few notes of the *Jaws* theme song rang out.

"Told you," said Lucia.

The door was ultimately opened by a pretty, blond maid with exaggerated makeup: heavily rouged cheeks, false eyelashes, and dark eyeliner. She was dressed in the Halloween costume version of a "sexy maid": a tiny, black leotard with the slightest of starched skirts that flared out enough to conceal the undergarments; a small, white apron; a frilly, lace hairpiece that matched the tight, white choker strangling her neck; and fishnet stockings.

"May I help you?" asked the maid, in, true to form, a French accent. (It was hard for Plum to decipher if it was real or part of the costume.)

"We are friends of, well, not exactly friends of," began Plum, unsure how to phrase it.

The maid rolled her eyes impatiently. "Are you here for the dead lady or the party?"

Plum and Lucia exchanged glances. "Dead lady," whispered Plum.

"This way, through the temple," commanded the maid, opening the door to allow entrance.

They followed her inside as she teetered along the parquet floor in stilettos past several realistic, erotic oil paintings illuminated by fire torches. The temple was dark, but once they reached the end, they crossed a wooden plank over a moat into another structure that had a massive glass ceiling. The maid held out her arm dramatically and steered their attention to the center of the room, where a man sat on a gold throne stroking a leopard and talking to Juan Kevin.

"Oh boy," muttered Plum. It felt like an out-of-body experience already.

"That's our host," said Lucia.

As they moved closer to the throne, Plum got a better look at

Dieter Friedrich. He was in his late sixties or early seventies, with a shock of white hair worn in a mullet. His face was heavily tanned with two piercing blue eyes and a small mouth. He wore a shiny blouse unbuttoned to his navel, revealing more tanned, leathery skin, and acid-washed jeans on his skinny legs. His right hand, which was stroking the leopard, was heavily bejeweled with rings. He spoke in a thick German accent and was directing his conversation at Juan Kevin but abruptly stopped speaking when Plum and Lucia approached, allowing his unctuous to eyes slide up and down Plum's body appraisingly, like a beast sizing up its prey. His leopard gave her the same look.

"Who is zees tall drink of water?" he asked. He ran his tongue over his lips and emitted a small hiss. "Very nice."

Despite herself, Plum's chalky, white skin became enflamed with a blush. She felt suddenly naked in her light-blue linen suit, worried that her skirt was too short and she was showing too much leg. She quickly responded, "I'm Plum Lockhart, and this is my colleague Lucia Garcia. We are friends of, well, our friend is a friend of Arielle..."

Why was she stuttering? This was so not like her. And to add to her irritation, a look of amusement fluttered across Dieter's face.

"Do not worry," he commanded. "Vee do not bite."

The leopard endowed her with a petulant glance, as if to say his master should speak for himself.

Plum took a deep breath and composed herself. "I apologize. It's that my relationship to the victim is tenuous at best. I only just met her. But I promised her friend I would check in and give you my card, in case there is anything I can do to be of help."

Plum held out her business card, and Dieter stared at it, not making any sort of move to retrieve it. She moved closer, awkwardly pitching her body toward him all the while trying to avoid the leopard. What if he attacked her? The leopard appeared bored and not as if he would pounce, so she inched forward to Dieter.

Again, he merely stared and didn't extend his hand. Frightened to make any more moves, she stopped and put her hand down. Her debt to Gerald Hand was not worth losing an arm.

Juan Kevin came over to Plum, took her card, and handed it to Dieter, sticking it in his face so he had no choice but to claim it. The leopard did not stir.

"Mr. Friedrich, let's cooperate," Juan Kevin reprimanded.

Dieter scanned the card and then put it in the pocket of his shiny blouse. "I am the most cooperative person on this island."

"Excellent," said Juan Kevin. "That will make everything move swiftly. Right now, the police are securing the crime scene, and the body will be removed as soon as possible."

"I do not like this phrase *crime zeen*," protested Dieter. "Tacky. Zees is my home, my loving, special home, a place where zere is nothing bad, only love and peace."

"I'm sorry to say that was not the case last night," said Juan Kevin. "Your loving, special home was the location for the murder of a young woman."

Dieter sniffed dismissively. He waved his hand in the air. "We do not know that. Accident."

Juan Kevin shook his head. "She was strangled from behind. It was no accident."

"Kinky," said Dieter. "Autoerotic asphyxiation."

"Impossible," corrected Juan Kevin. "This was murder."

Dieter moved his shoulders up and down and rolled his eyes dramatically. "Zees very sad..."

"Yes," agreed Lucia. "She was very young."

"Sad that I have to go through zis," corrected Dieter. "I do not deserve a scandal. I have a beautiful, loving home. I welcome all people. She should not have gotten herself killed. Tacky."

Plum, Juan Kevin, and Lucia all exchanged incredulous looks. Finally, Plum spoke. "Did you know Arielle?"

"Who?" Dieter asked.

"The victim," Juan Kevin, Plum, and Lucia all said in unison.

"Oh, no," Dieter said.

"How did she end up staying with you?" asked Plum.

Dieter shrugged. "I am very generous. I know many people. I have the largest acid-washed jean company in the world. I have no rivals. Her father is in publishing, and he always wanted to feature my beautiful clothes. I am sure zat I said, come to my island. I have beautiful women. I have love. I have my own personal casino and zoo. I have paradise on Paraiso."

"The invitation extended to his daughter Arielle as well?" asked Juan Kevin.

Dieter scratched his leopard under the chin and addressed the animal rather than his inquisitors. "Everyone wants to come to my beautiful villa. Strangers come all the time. When zey come, zey are my friends," he boasted.

"But did you actually meet Arielle last night?" asked Plum, after he had finished his laudatory speech about himself.

"She came in. I was having my card games with my guests. I said make yourself at home. I always say zat, I am very generous."

"Yes, you mentioned that," said Plum.

A flash of anger crossed Dieter's face, and he glared. "She was a foolish girl. She wanted to be part of the game. She wants to be the center of attention, very rude. It disturbed my guests. She made a scene. Tacky. I had to have her removed," he said.

"Removed?" asked Juan Kevin.

"Yes, taken out of the card room," said Dieter. "I have famous friends, she bothered them. Obviously, she wanted to stay. Everyone wants to be with me and my friends. We are kings. But no, no, no," he said, clucking his tongue.

"So she was escorted out?" Juan Kevin clarified.

"Yes," Dieter confirmed.

"Do you have any idea if she spent time with any of your other guests?" asked Plum.

"I do not know. I do not keep track. You may ask zem. I have no secrets here."

"Where can we find them?" asked Lucia.

"Zey could be anywhere. My estate is four acres. I have so much entertainment here, so much. People do not want to leave. They say, 'Dieter, zis is the best place in the world. I do not want to leave.' And I say, 'Yes, it is. I understand. I do not want to leave either.' Many people stay long. You may find zem anywhere on my enormous property. But you maybe start in the pool. Zey like to swim with zee sharks."

After Juan Kevin told him he would be back to continue their conversation, Plum, Juan Kevin, and Lucia walked wordlessly outside of the throne room through the back door, along a mossy footpath, which led into a small meditation garden. There was a bubbling birdbath on one side, a koi pond with a tiered waterfall running along the southernmost part, and a large stone statue at the center. At first glance Plum thought the statue was of Buddha, but upon closer inspection, it was evident it was Medusa. She had an angry expression carved into her face, similar to the one etched into faces of the snakes in her hair.

After clearing the garden, the trio found themselves traversing a wooden tiki bridge that arched over an intricate blue lagoon. They stopped in the middle of the bridge, which afforded the best view of the entire estate. Like a "lazy river," the lagoon had estuaries all over the property, creating an intricate maze that dead-ended in various spots. It ran between several other outbuildings, including one that was a thatched-roof pool bar with a uniformed bartender standing idle, ready to serve customers.

"What did he mean, 'swimming with sharks'?" asked Plum. "Usually I would think someone was being hypothetical when they said that, but I'd believe it here."

"And you should," said Lucia, pointing down into the water. Plum had not initially noticed, but parallel to the lagoon ran another body of water, separated only by glass, where several sharks were swimming.

"Oh my," said Plum.

"Yes," said Juan Kevin. "He was being literal. These are bull sharks, sandbar sharks, and sandpiper sharks. You swim on one side, they swim on the other."

"And you better pray the glass never breaks," added Lucia.

They watched in silence as the sharks swam their continuous, circular path. Plum felt there was something hypnotic about their endless journey but also something very cruel about keeping them contained. This Dieter clearly felt empowered by capturing and containing wild animals, she thought. Someone like that was heartless. She wondered if he was heartless enough to commit murder. But then, what was the motive?

"Let's go talk to them," said Juan Kevin, pointing to a couple lying in chaises overlooking the sea.

The path to the guests was not straightforward, and they had to navigate a drawbridge and a bamboo path and pass through a beach cabana stacked with boogie boards. At one point they walked by a giant cauldron that began spurting flames as soon as they passed, so suddenly that Plum jumped. Much to her annoyance, she grabbed at Juan Kevin like a damsel in distress. She quickly apologized. Plum did not want him to believe that she was making romantic overtures. To her surprise, he placed a tender hand on her lower back to guide her past the fire. She felt more heat coming from his hand than the fire and wished he would keep it there.

When they reached the lounge area, the couple came into clearer view, Juan Kevin dropped his hand, and Plum inwardly groaned.

"Plum Lockhart, is that you?!" boomed the woman. "Gary, Gary, look who's here, it's Plum Lockhart!"

"Hello, Hallie," Plum said, mustering her most polite voice. "How very nice to see you."

Hallie Corona was in her early fifties, a tall, faded, once-pretty blond with watery blue eyes. She had patrician features and, to her credit, disdained plastic surgery, Botox, and anything that would remove her wrinkles and jowly chin.

"Well, hello, yourself! Babe, Plum was editor of *Travel and Respite*. I wrote that hilarious monthly column for them, remember?" Hallie asked her husband.

"Oh, right," Gary Grigorian responded blandly.

Hallie Corona was a "comedienne." At least that's what she called herself. Plum thought she should really describe herself as a star-you-know-whatter, a wannabe, a sycophant, and a social climber. Brash and outspoken, she thought herself very amusing and somehow had wrangled her way into writing a "funny" travel diary for the magazine. But she had been a pain in the derriere who never completed her work on time and needed heavy editing. The column eventually disappeared after Plum told the publisher she was tired of wasting her time on a Z-list celebrity's musings.

For the past decade, Hallie had been married to Gary Grigorian, the diminutive former weatherman turned game show host, who was also relentless in his ambition for fame, but not as blatant about it as his wife. He attempted to appear aloof, but his strategic black eyes were continuously darting around trying to locate people from whom he could benefit. Plum couldn't understand how he was able to maintain a nice-guy, positive public reputation as an "everyman" and "America's host" when he had basically stolen his game show gig from the iconic host who launched the program. To secure the gig, because his job predicting the weather had become mundane, Gary had engaged in a whisper campaign on talk radio that the older host of *Who Wants to Make Money?* was losing it, and that Gary would like the position. He ultimately received it. Somehow the public forgot that he had pushed aside the previous host, who died shortly after, many said of a broken heart. The word on the street in New

York was that Gary was cold and calculating in the most vicious, underhanded way.

Plum introduced the couple to Juan Kevin and Lucia. If the Paraisons recognized these minor celebrities, they gave no indication. Plum had dealt with Hallie Corona enough to know that it infuriated her.

"What brings you to Dieter's?" Hallie asked in her plummy voice. She continued without waiting for a response, "He is a *huge* fan of Gary's, watches *Who Wants to Make Money?* every single night, and has been begging us to come down to visit him. It was so difficult to find the time—I just finished up a three-episode arc on *Law & Order: SVU,* and I'm about to start shooting a new series for Gotcha network, and we are so busy. But we finally made it!"

Plum set her mouth in a flat line and nodded. "It's unfortunate that a murder took place during your vacation. Did you meet Arielle?"

"For like a hot minute," answered Hallie, blowing a wisp of blond hair out of her eyes. "We didn't even talk to her. Although she wanted to talk to us. Was desperate to be with us. Thankfully, she was not allowed."

"She came in late last night," Gary explained. "Hallie and I were playing poker with Dieter and Johnny Wisebrook."

"The singer?" asked Plum.

"Of course. Johnny Wisebrook is so divine," said Hallie. "Although very naughty. He literally had me smoking cigars! Sometimes, hanging out with the boys means too much smoking and too much booze. But I would totally take the company of men over the company of women any day of the week. I'm a guy's girl."

Hallie looked around the group for validation, but no one responded to her assertion. Gary ignored her.

"Johnny's going to have a concert down here on Friday," said Gary, running a hand through the thick, salt-and-pepper hair he wore in a bowl cut. "I haven't seen him play in years. Last time was in the Garden when I was with Kevin Costner."

"Johnny performs here every year," interjected Juan Kevin. "He resides at Las Frutas, and we consider him our local celebrity. He's a wonderful man, always on the golf course, very approachable."

Hallie and Gary looked momentarily deflated, as if the fact that other people knew Johnny made him, and therefore them, less famous.

"We're going on his yacht tomorrow," boasted Hallie.

"Exciting," said Plum flatly.

Juan Kevin cleared his voice. "You perhaps have to run your plans by the police. They will want to make sure they interview all of the people who were in the villa when the murder occurred."

"They can't detain us," snapped Gary, ruffled.

"They cannot," said Juan Kevin. "Paraison law does not allow it. However, we can request you remain."

"We had nothing to do with the girl's murder!" said Hallie. "I don't want this to be some giant thing where we're stuck down here."

"I am sure that will not be the case. Everything in Paraiso is done very discreetly, and we find justice as expeditiously as possible," said Juan Kevin.

Plum gave him a sideways look, but he refused to meet her gaze. It was wishful thinking on Juan Kevin's part. Things were done very slowly in Paraiso, and the last case had only been solved in this century because of her help.

"I don't know... This is sounding more serious than I thought," said Gary. "I'm not sure I want to be mixed up in this. Could be bad publicity."

"Although..." said Hallie. She gave her husband a look then turned to the others. "Do you mind if we confer a minute by ourselves?"

"By all means," said Juan Kevin.

Hallie and Gary walked over to the other side of the pool and bent their heads close together, murmuring.

"What do you think they are talking about?" asked Lucia.

"They're deciding if it is better for their careers to remain in Paraiso at the center of this investigation or to leave," observed Plum, as she watched the couple engage in a heated conversation.

Lucia watched them carefully. "I don't like his show," she said, her eyes fixed on Gary. "He's very patronizing to the contestants."

"I've only seen it a few times, but he appeared completely bored," agreed Juan Kevin.

"They're both fake and overly ambitious," said Plum.

Hallie and Gary came to some sort of decision and walked back toward the others, holding hands.

"We think it's really important to do anything we can to help," said Gary, a pleased smile on his face. "That's just who we are."

"Yes, and since we are literally staying here and just spent the evening with the victim, no one is in a better position," added Hallie.

"I thought you said you didn't even talk to Arielle?" asked Plum.

Hallie gave her a phony smile. "I think it's best if I only share my information with the police."

And probably your publicist, too, thought Plum, but she bit her tongue.

"If you'll excuse us, we need to go find the person in charge of the investigation," said Gary.

"That will be Captain Diaz," said Juan Kevin.

Plum turned and grimaced at Juan Kevin. "Really?"

Juan Kevin nodded. Plum had dealt with Captain Diaz on a previous case and did not think very highly of him. Nor did he think highly of her, for that matter.

"We'll find him," said Hallie. And then she turned to Plum and took Plum's hands in her own. "Let's catch up later? I have a book idea; you can ghostwrite it for me!"

5

WHEN THE LOW-LEVEL CELEBRITIES HAD departed, Plum, Juan Kevin, and Lucia hung back, staring out to sea. Juan Kevin walked slowly to the edge of the cliff and peered down. His gaze remained fixed below. Plum and Lucia quietly followed him. When Plum glanced beneath her, she shivered, and Lucia emitted a small gasp. Arielle Waldron's body was still splayed on the beach, her blond hair fanned around her like a halo and her gauzy slip dress fluttering in the breeze. The small waves were beginning to lap at her head. A police photographer was snapping pictures, and a man with a notebook was measuring the distance between her toes and the closest boulder. Plum couldn't help but think she looked peaceful, almost as if she were posing for a photo shoot for a fashion magazine or the cover of a record album. It would all seem very normal if not for the dark contusions around her neck.

Lucia clucked and made the sign of the cross again. "I will pray for her."

"Me too," said Plum, although she had never prayed a day in her life and wouldn't know where to begin.

They watched as Captain Diaz, a short, bald man with two upside-down *v*'s for eyebrows, barked out commands to his deputies, who were clustered on the private strip of beachfront. A small rowboat, anchored just off the shore, bobbed gently in the water. A sleek, fifty-five foot VanDutch motorboat was tied up to the dock. In the distance, people on Jet Skis frolicked and screamed in the surf with gleeful animation, oblivious to the horror that had transpired at Villa la Grosella Negra.

As they watched, Hallie and Gary walked down the steep stone staircase to the beach. The couple held on to the precarious, cold metal railing as they navigated the narrow steps. When they landed on the shore, Captain Diaz walked over to the couple and put his hands up to block them from coming closer.

Juan Kevin, Plum, and Lucia stepped back from the edge and the gruesome scene.

"Who found Arielle?" asked Plum.

"She was spotted by the gardener this morning at around nine a.m. It was high tide at six thirty-three a.m. this morning, but she wasn't wet," said Juan Kevin. "They believe she was killed between seven and nine a.m."

"Do they have any suspects?" asked Plum.

"It's too early," said Juan Kevin.

"What about motive?" asked Lucia.

Juan Kevin shook his head. "I don't know, but after meeting her...well, I should not speak poorly of the dead."

"I will," volunteered Plum. "Arielle was a spoiled brat Juan Kevin had to kick out of the hotel for stealing."

"I thought she was very wealthy," said Lucia.

"It didn't stop her from being a kleptomaniac," said Plum.

"She was also rude. The staff at the hotel were subjected to many tirades during her brief stay. They were very happy to have her leave," said Juan Kevin.

"But let's be honest, people don't generally get murdered for being rude," said Plum. "There has to be another reason. Did any of the other guests have prior relationships with her?"

"No one will admit to it," said Juan Kevin. "Dieter and his girlfriend Shakira Perez, Hallie Corona, and Gary Grigorian all say they never met her before yesterday. Ditto the staff of the house. But it is still early. There are many more people to be interviewed."

He rubbed his eyes, and Plum noticed he seemed tired. She felt a pang of compassion, believing that perhaps he was working too hard. But that was quickly replaced by the thought that perhaps he had a woman who was working him too hard in the bedroom, and she felt suddenly jealous.

"I suppose Lucia and I should head back to work," said Plum briskly. "There's really nothing for us to do here. I don't want to get involved in another murder."

"Yes, that's for sure," remarked Juan Kevin, starting to walk toward the direction of the exit.

She stopped. "What's that supposed to mean?" asked Plum.

He glanced back at her. "I was agreeing with you."

"Huh," she said. As she and Lucia began to follow him out, she wondered if it was meant to be a slight. "You know I single-handedly solved the last one."

"You were instrumental," he said, without looking at her.

"Oh, come on, give credit where credit is due," insisted Plum, teasing only somewhat.

"Your help was noted," he said.

"Noted?" she exclaimed with exasperation.

Juan Kevin turned and stared at her with a serious face. Finally, he broke into a smile. "Okay, yes, Plum, you were essential! The murder would have gone unsolved if not for you."

"That's better!" said Plum playfully.

Plum watched Lucia's horrified expression as they passed the giant nude statues that dotted the property. The grotesque renderings of buxom females performing cartwheels and other gymnastic endeavors was jarring. Plum felt as if she were in a theme park at the Playboy mansion.

"How can he live with these disgusting statues?" mused Lucia, her head craning up to stare at a particularly vulgar depiction of a naked woman in repose.

When they reached the main building, they saw Dieter striding hand in hand with an attractive woman. He stopped to introduce them.

"Zis is Shakira Perez," he announced. "She is my favorite girlfriend."

Pleasantries were exchanged while Plum studied the woman. Shakira was in her early thirties, with a fantastic body, long, brown hair with blond highlights, and thick eyelashes. She wore a tasseled string bikini with a diaphanous cover-up around her waist. Her beauty was undeniable, and Plum could not for the life of her understand why such a knockout would date a creepy geezer like Dieter. True, he was loaded, but someone as gorgeous as Shakira could certainly find someone wealthy and age appropriate.

"Are you staying for lunch?" asked Shakira, in accented English.

"Yes, you must stay for lunch," said Dieter. "The chef is making a fabulous pig roast. It is delicious. I have the best chef on the island."

"No, we're on our way out," said Plum.

Shakira frowned. "That's a pity, we love meeting new people."

"I would assume you are probably busy with the murder investigation that's taking place here," said Plum.

Shakira ignored the statement. "You must come to our disco tonight. *Sí*, Dieter?"

"Yes, you must come. I have my own disco. It is very special. You will have zee most fun of your life. I have zee best DJ," he boasted, his voice ripe with certainty.

Plum murmured some excuses, as did Juan Kevin.

"My disco days are long behind me," said Lucia firmly.

Dieter and Shakira were having none of it. Plum and Juan Kevin finally agreed just to escape, and Lucia had to promise to reconsider after Dieter told her he would love to see her boogie on the dance floor.

The trio conferred on the driveway before Juan Kevin had to return to the crime scene and reunite with the police.

"What about Jessica? Do we know where she is?" Plum asked.

Juan Kevin turned and glanced at her, as did Lucia.

"Jessica?" asked Lucia. "Who's that?"

"Arielle told us she was here with her friend Jessica," Plum said, turning to Juan Kevin. "Don't you remember? Jessica Morse? Her friend who was staying at the hotel?"

Juan Kevin slowly nodded. "That's right. I'll tell Captain Diaz that he needs to reach out and inform her of her friend's death."

"Maybe I should do it," said Plum.

"You? Why?" asked Juan Kevin.

"You know, I'm a woman, I have a soft touch," said Plum. She was irritated to see a flicker of amusement cross Juan Kevin's face, so she continued, "What? I do have a soft touch."

Juan Kevin said, "Soft touch? You are as blunt as they come."

"I don't think that's true," said Plum, wondering if it was true.

"It is true, and don't get offended, it's not a bad quality. I quite like it when people are straightforward."

"Thank you," said Plum.

"However," warned Juan Kevin, his voice firm. "We need to let the police handle it."

"Yes, don't get involved," warned Lucia.

That didn't sit well with Plum. "Jessica might feel less threatened if it comes from me. And let's face it, the Paraison police will bungle it."

"You must trust them," chided Lucia. "There is a saying in Paraiso, 'Our way isn't the wrong way, and it will end up rewarding you with a payday.'"

"I sincerely doubt they will be able to reward anyone with anything, judging by what I have seen in the past," Plum contested.

Juan Kevin shook his head. "Plum, there's a murderer out there. It's dangerous. Leave it to the police."

"Then it will never get solved," she insisted.

Juan Kevin's voice was unexpectedly stern. "I would like you to please let the authorities handle it."

Juan Kevin's eyes remained fixed on hers. Plum momentarily wavered, realizing she was being irrational, but then she decided not to back down. *He's just being protective,* her inner voice screamed. But then another voice yelled back that he was trying to control her. She wasn't used to men doing the former, so she assumed it must be the latter. She raised her chin and kept her eyes on his.

"I can't promise anything," said Plum defiantly.

"I wish you would," said Juan Kevin. "I don't want you to be the next victim."

So he was being protective, thought Plum, secretly pleased. It wasn't a control thing at all. But that didn't change her mind.

"I will never be a victim," announced Plum.

"We should go. We're going to be late," interjected Lucia.

Plum and Juan Kevin broke their standoff, said their goodbyes, and headed to their respective vehicles. Juan Kevin drove off first.

"Don't do it," whispered Lucia as they settled into the golf cart.

"Do what?" asked Plum, feigning ignorance.

"You know," said Lucia. "Go find that Jessica."

Plum snorted as if the thought were ridiculous. But she didn't have to share her every move with Lucia.

There was a large oil truck barreling down the narrow road, heading toward Dieter's driveway, so rather than make a right, Plum had to turn left to allow him entrance and avoid being flattened like a pancake. The vegetation was so thick, there was no proper place for Plum to flip a U-turn, so she continued to the end of the short road, which came to an abrupt stop in front of a metal gate.

"What's this?" asked Plum.

"This is Casa la Manzana. Charles Nettles's house," said Lucia.

Plum squinted but was unable to see anything but a driveway through the gates. Almost immediately, a security guard with a clipboard emerged from the small hut adjacent to the entrance.

"May I help you?" he asked politely. He wore an immaculate uniform and a blue baseball cap with an apple etched on the front.

"We're just trying to do a U-turn," said Plum.

"You'll have to back up."

"Do you know anything about what happened last night? You know, the murder next door?"

"No, ma'am," said the security guard, all business. "I'm afraid I'm going to have to ask you to turn around. I need this driveway clear."

"I heard what you said, and I will," said Plum.

The security guard assisted Plum as she negotiated a tight circle in the constricted area. She had to do a clumsy eight-point turn, reversing and going forward then reversing, all the while with that annoying beeping that accompanied the reverse signal. He watched patiently, a neutral expression on his face, until she was successful.

"He could have let me through the gates to turn around," fumed Plum.

"No, he couldn't have," said Lucia. "It's his job to protect the villa."

"But do I look like a serial killer?" asked Plum, putting her hand to her breast in mock horror. "I mean really."

"Someone was murdered next door only yesterday," said Lucia.

"That's true, but they didn't install those gates and hire that guard this morning," said Plum.

"There's bad blood between Charles Nettles and Dieter Friedrich. They hate each other and have accused each other of terrible things. They each claim the other has tried to kill him."

"Really?" said Plum, turning away from the wheel to glance at Lucia. "Why?"

"It started with a noise complaint. Dieter enjoys hosting many loud parties and concerts. Charles Nettles enjoys solitude, peace, and quiet. He became exasperated and reported Dieter to the Las Frutas management. They gave Dieter several warnings and then started to fine him. It escalated from there."

"How do you know all this?" asked Plum with amazement.

"*Chisme*," she said.

"What's that?" asked Plum.

"It's a newspaper...more like a gossip magazine. That's why it is called *Chisme*, which means gossip. No one knows who writes it, but every Las Frutas resort worker reads it. There are lots of stories on squabbling villa owners, and they keep a running list of who are the worst people on the island to work for. Once you are on that list, good luck finding a staff for your villa!"

"Fascinating."

"It's my guilty pleasure. They had extensive coverage of the Rijo divorce—with opinion pieces on both sides. Some favored Carmen, and some favored Alexandra. Whoever is behind it knows a lot."

Plum was pensive. She hoped she never made a cameo appearance in *Chisme*. She wanted to ask Lucia if she had yet, but she decided she wasn't sure she wanted to know the answer.

"What do they say about Charles Nettles?" she asked instead. "What is he like?"

"The exact opposite of Dieter. Reserved, conservative, and careful."

"Would he be the type to kill a woman at Dieter's house? Maybe he was too irritated about the noise?" asked Plum.

"I don't think so. He's very measured. But that's not to say that he wouldn't hire someone to do it, like a contract killer."

"Really?" exclaimed Plum.

"No, not really," said Lucia. "But people with lots of money are irrational and can be dangerous. They think they are immortal. And untouchable, which is even worse."

Plum thought about this. She turned right out of the private road and coasted along the sunny street behind a souped-up golf cart. She had seen that golf cart before: it belonged to Martin Rijo, the son of Alexandra and the late Emilio Rijo. Even though she only viewed him from behind, she recognized him by his muscular shoulders nestled snugly into an extremely tight T-shirt that accentuated their size. He was driving with a blond woman who was running her fingers through his syrupy-black hair. Plum was no fan of his. In fact, Lucia's words rang truer than ever when she thought about it. People with lots of money can be dangerous.

6

PLUM HAD NOT CHECKED HER phone during her excursion and was irritated to find several emails from Gerald Hand, which became increasingly threatening and demanding due to her silence, an act that he perceived as aggressive stonewalling. She was dismayed that the most recent missive informed her he was on a flight to Paraiso and expected her to host him. She glanced around the town house in dismay. With the entire first floor used as an office and only two bedrooms upstairs, one of which Plum had turned into a makeshift storage room for all her belongings, there was simply no space for Gerald. He would have to find his own place to stay.

"I received the contract for Villa Tomate," said Lucia, who had already situated herself behind her desk and was wading through paperwork and mail. "I've called the contractors, and I'll meet with them this afternoon. I also need to go by Villa Fresa. The renters are having trouble figuring out how to use the remote control for the television."

Villa Fresa was owned by a former childhood classmate of Plum's, Brad Cooke, and it had been the first property she had secured to represent when she set out on her own. It was beautiful and subtle, and it was actually her dream house. One day, Plum thought, if her business took off, she would try to buy it herself.

"What is it with renters and remotes?" asked Plum. "They need tutorials."

Lucia nodded. "It's too much effort to press buttons. They want you to do it for them. Especially when they are on vacation."

"How in the world did I get myself into this business? I was traveling all over the world, dining at five-star restaurants," began Plum.

Lucia had heard this pity-party rant many times before and put her fingers in her ears. Plum stopped talking.

"I know, I know."

"You never know where your life will lead you. You just have to take your blessings as they come," admonished Lucia.

"True," agreed Plum.

"And stay out of murder investigations. Don't go see that girl; it will only lead to trouble."

After Lucia left, Plum realized that she was hungry and had not had lunch. She wandered over to the refrigerator. Although there were bread and cold cuts, fruit, and vegetables, Plum decided that there was absolutely nothing to eat. She would head to the food truck near the hotel and pick up a taco. And then, if time permitted, she would wander over to the hotel to see if she might bump into Jessica Morse. *Just being in the same building was not leading a murder investigation,* she told herself. Lucia didn't know everything.

The line was long at the food truck, and the servers were extremely slow. Plum began to be irritated, especially since she could feel the sun sizzling her flesh as she stood in the unshaded queue. The pace at which things happened in Paraiso especially irked Plum when she was hungry.

"Nothing will stop you from eating! Not even a very long line."

Plum turned and was face-to-face with her nemesis, Damián Rodriguez, who was giving her a crocodile smile, affording her a good view of his gleaming, overly white teeth. She was several inches taller than Damián and stared down at the muscular, dark-haired man, who she loathed to admit was good-looking. He held a plate of tacos in his hand.

"The same could be said for you," snarled Plum, motioning toward his food.

He glanced down at his plate then gave her the once-over. "True, but I'm a man and I work out, so I don't need to watch what I eat. I don't gain weight easily. I feel terrible that you don't have the same privilege."

Plum was enraged and was about to give him a piece of her mind, but fortunately a wave of reason enveloped her. She didn't have to go head-to-head with Damián. He had nothing on her.

"Enjoy your meal," she said breezily.

He eyed her suspiciously, surprised that she had not engaged in a sparring contest. Then he hesitated, as if unsure if she was making fun of him in some way or planning a stealth attack, but when she remained silent and unemotional, he walked away.

Plum was thrilled with the way she had handled the situation. There was no use bickering with Damián. She would win by being more successful. It had been her strategy during her miserable high school years when she was unpopular and ridiculed, as well as when she climbed the corporate ladder. She already had customers after only recently opening her agency, and she had a meeting on the books with one of Damián's biggest clients! Life couldn't be better.

After indulging herself in the most delicious freshly pressed tortillas stuffed with cumin-and-pepper rubbed steak with a relish of charred onions and smoky chipotle sauce, Plum felt properly sated. She washed her food down with a pomegranate soda. Although, yes, she moaned that she was no longer eating at five-star restaurants in Europe and New York, she had to admit that

Paraiso had some of the best food she had ever eaten. With the bounty of fresh produce and spices, as well as the proximity to the community farms, she was experiencing a food revolution all on one tiny island. And it was definitely worth the wait.

Plum reassured herself that it would do no harm to pop by the hotel. Ultimately, she owed it to Gerald to try to find out more information about his boss's daughter's demise. She was acting as an agent. It was a free country, after all. Although she actually wasn't sure of that. Was Paraiso a free country? Probably. She felt free.

She recognized the receptionist at the front desk, and after the woman asked her how she was doing, Plum took that as a sign from the universe that she should proceed. She told her she needed to find Jessica Morse. After what felt like hours, she was able to find out what room Jessica was in and decided to see if she was in residence. The girl probably wasn't even there, but it was worth the effort. It was only a short elevator ride to the third floor.

"Hello?" asked the small brunette who answered the door.

"Jessica Morse?" Plum queried with disbelief.

"Yes?" said the girl.

"Jessica Morse, who is a friend of Arielle's?"

"Yes, that's me," repeated the girl.

Plum tried to hide her astonishment. After meeting the style-conscious Arielle, Plum had not expected Jessica to look like the mousy, bespectacled creature who stood before her. The girl's shoulder-length hair was limp and unstyled. She wore a dowdy and shapeless blue T-shirt dress with a boat neckline and Birkenstock sandals of the sort hippies wore. The scent of patchouli wafted from her.

"I'm Plum Lockhart. A friend of, well, a friend of a friend of Arielle's."

"Oh, can I help you?" Jessica asked, opening the door. "Arielle's not here. She went to stay with a family friend."

Plum's stomach lurched. Jessica had no idea her friend was dead. She should have listened to Lucia and not interfered.

Instead she said, "I think it's best that I come in."

Jessica took the news calmly, much to Plum's relief and surprise. It had been difficult to start the conversation, and Plum was certain that the young woman would not be able to control herself when she learned her friend had died. At first Plum had wanted to take her out to the balcony so her inevitable wailings would not disturb guests in their rooms, but then she had visions of the girl thrusting herself over the ledge into the pool area and decided that was a bad plan. After closing the sliding glass doors, she ultimately insisted that they sit across from each other in the deep, upholstered chairs by the windows, and she kneaded her hands while she came up with the best way to proceed.

"Did she suffer?" asked Jessica, after what seemed like a long silence. She kept her gaze at the sisal area rug that partially covered the white tiled floor.

"Absolutely not," said Plum with certainty, despite having no idea if that was true.

Jessica nodded. "That's good. Arielle wouldn't have wanted to suffer."

Plum restrained herself from saying, "Who would?" and instead said, "Do you have any idea who would do this?"

Jessica glanced up. Her glasses were steamy, but Plum wasn't sure if it was from tears or the fact that the well-appointed room was quite hot with the windows closed. In fact, it didn't even feel like the air conditioner was on.

"I don't know," said Jessica carefully. "This is going to sound really unbelievable..."

"Go on," Plum prompted.

"But, Arielle...well, she could make people angry."

Plum restrained herself from making a snarky retort like, "No, duh!" so she instead murmured vaguely, "Oh, really?"

"Yes. She had that way about her. Don't get me wrong, it

doesn't mean that she wasn't an amazing person, but she could be impatient, and entitled, and arrogant."

"Hard to get along with people like that," said Plum, quite forgetting that Jessica could be describing her.

"Yes," agreed Jessica. "But I don't know why anyone would kill her. She wasn't evil or anything."

"Of course not," said Plum, before adding almost as an aside, "She did steal, however."

Jessica's eyes widened from behind her lenses. "You know about that?"

"She had a record here at the hotel."

"But I'm sure it was an accident."

Plum leaned back in her chair and crossed her legs. "How so?"

"I mean, she just would grab stuff and put it in her bag, thinking it was hers or mine. It wasn't calculated, she just has a lot of stuff! How could she keep track? Back home in New York, people always gave her things. Because she was so pretty and popular, they all wanted to be her friend. It wasn't her fault."

Plum noticed that Jessica's neck became red as she grew angrier. She wondered if the girl could really be that naive or if she was simply very loyal.

"Why didn't you move with Arielle to Dieter Friedrich's villa?" asked Plum, thinking she knew the answer.

This time, Jessica's entire face flushed. She picked up a lock of her mousy hair and bit on it. "I, um, well, I started seeing, well, I have a friend here. It's a guy actually. Max Stylo. You have probably heard of him, he's a photographer."

"No," said Plum.

"Max Stylo," she repeated, as if Plum hadn't caught his name the first time.

"Never heard of him. Well, not professionally, anyway. Arielle *had* mentioned his name yesterday and said you were spending time with him."

"She did? Well, yes, anyway, he and I," she stammered. Her eyes flicked around the room as if desperate for someone else to fill in the blank. Plum did the honors.

"Are together?" prompted Plum.

"Yes," said Jessica, emitting a loud sigh. Her face immediately changed from despondent to enraptured. "He and I go way back. Actually, and this may sound weird, but he used to date Arielle a few years ago."

"Really?"

"Yes, but she wasn't really that into him," Jessica quickly added. "And *I* always had a crush on him. A month ago, we hung out at a party, and when I found out he was coming here for vacation, I convinced Arielle to come with me. It sounds like I was chasing him, but it totally wasn't like that at all. In fact, it was all his idea for me to come. When he told me about Las Frutas, I said that it sounded amazing, and he sort of said, hey, it would be cool if you came down, so here I am."

Plum nodded. "And Arielle didn't mind that you were hanging out with her ex?"

Jessica shook her head. "Not at all. She told me to go for it. There was actually someone else she liked that she knew would be down here too, so she was pretty focused on that."

Plum's interest was piqued. "There was? Who was it?"

Jessica shrugged. "She wouldn't tell me. She called him Mr. Big, like, you know, Mr. Big from *Sex and the City*. Arielle wanted to be cryptic and mysterious, and I was okay with that. She couldn't keep a secret for long, so I figured she would tell me. And honestly, I didn't want to push it, in case it didn't work out and she was suddenly interested in Max again."

"But you told me she was over Max."

"Yes, she totally was," insisted Jessica, shaking her head. "It's just, Arielle always liked to have a guy. I really encouraged her to pursue Mr. Big so that she would be happy."

"And not take your guy."

"I guess," said Jessica, a guilty look on her face. "But is that so bad? I mean, Arielle could get anyone. It's harder for me. And I really like Max."

Plum felt compassion for the girl. She was sure it was hard for someone like Jessica to get a man, especially in New York where a single, straight man was a unicorn despite a population of eight million people.

"I get it," Plum conceded. "Tell me, what did Max think of Arielle?"

"I can tell you myself," a voice boomed from the doorway. Plum swung around, practically leaping out of her chair from shock. She hadn't heard the door open, and all this talk of murder made her a bit jumpy.

"Max!" squealed Jessica, fully animated. She vaulted up and kissed her new love's cheek.

"Who's this?" he asked.

It took a second for Plum to register that he was talking to her because she was so taken aback by Max Stylo's blazing good looks that she felt as if she would faint. The young man, with tousled golden hair, a bronzed, well-sculpted body, and a row of perfectly straight teeth framed by plump lips, was like an Adonis come to life. He wore a bathing suit but no shirt—his six-pack on prominent display—and was possibly one of the most handsome men Plum had ever seen. Her eyes slid from him to the plain, lumpy girl grabbing his hand, and she felt as if the universe were playing tricks on her.

"This is Plum Lockhart," said Jessica, staring up into his eyes. "She just told me that Arielle's dead!"

"Oh no," said Max. He folded Jessica into his arms and hugged her, before pulling back and swiping a lock of hair away from her eyes. "Are you okay, baby?"

"I'm sort of in shock," said Jessica.

"Me too," murmured Plum. She couldn't believe that she wasn't being pranked by a reality show. Could these two really be an item? She knew she was being unkind, but she had never seen such physical disparity in a couple.

"What?" asked Max, turning his attention to Plum.

She stood and straightened her posture, pulling down her skirt and adjusting her blazer. "I just mean it's shocking. Arielle's death is shocking."

Max nodded. "This is bizarre. Do her parents know?"

"Yes," said Plum.

"When's the funeral?" he asked. He wrapped his arm around Jessica and stroked her hair.

"Um, not sure," mumbled Plum.

"Well, please keep us posted," said Max. He pulled away from Jessica then walked to the door and held it open.

"Yes, thanks so much for telling me," said Jessica. "I can't imagine how hard that was."

"It was," said Plum.

"Goodbye then," said Max before she was ushered out.

It was only after the elevator doors had opened upon reaching the lobby that she realized Max hadn't asked her how Arielle had died. Very odd.

7

GERALD HAND HAD ENOUGH LUGGAGE to set sail on the *Queen Mary* for three months. He hadn't bothered to move it past the front hall of Plum's town house, and Plum had to wade through the tower of monogrammed suitcases in order to enter the living room. He even had a hatbox. *A hatbox! Who carries one of those?* Plum thought. She wasn't even sure she had ever seen one in real life, only in movies or TV shows.

"You have nothing to eat," Gerald announced when she entered the kitchen and found him riffling through the fridge.

"That's not true at all. You are just spoiled," said Plum, pushing him aside and pointing. "I have cold cuts, I have bread, eggs, produce."

He shrugged dramatically. "Everything you have requires compiling or some sort of effort. They didn't serve us anything on the plane, and it was absolute rubbish in the airport. And don't tell me that you don't go out to eat for every meal."

"Of course, I don't," Plum replied sanctimoniously. "I almost never go out."

"Well, I'm famished," he said, plopping down into the stool propped by the island and staring at her over that pointy nose of his. "Please help."

Plum eyeballed her frenemy. Gerald Hand was meticulously dressed as usual, clad in the latest designer getup, which included a jaunty striped blazer and tight, blue pants. Although not very tall and prematurely balding, he had a good jawline, attractive features, and didn't have trouble finding romance when he hit bumps in the road with his on-again, off-again boyfriend, Leonard.

"Fine," said Plum.

She popped two pieces of bread in the toaster and set about slicing tomatoes and avocadoes. She pulled roast chicken out of the fridge and chopped it up, adding mayonnaise, salt and pepper, and a dash of local spices.

"I love to watch you cook," he said mischievously.

"You love to watch anyone wait on you," she corrected.

"Guilty."

When she finished, Plum slid the plate across the counter, took a pitcher of hibiscus lemonade out of the fridge, and poured two glasses with ice.

"You know you can't stay here," she said. "I have no room."

"I don't take up much space," he protested. "I travel light."

She glanced over at his stack of luggage at the front door and sighed. "Let's go out on the balcony," she said, carrying the drinks.

Gerald picked up his plate and a napkin and followed her through the kitchen to the "living room." He eyed the place with incredulity.

"You've downgraded," he remarked, staring at the junky furniture and the cluttered tabletops. "How is that possible?"

"It's temporary," insisted Plum. "It's high season, everyone is subletting their places, and there is no inventory."

"All the more reason I should stay here," he interjected. "I'd never find a room."

She ignored him and continued, "As soon as it gets too hot for the tourists, I'll find a desperate landlord who wants a year-round rental and make my move."

Gerald gave her a skeptical look before sliding open the screen doors.

The temperature had cooled and there was a gentle, late-afternoon breeze ruffling the leaves on the trees. They sat down at the patio table, and Gerald went to work on his sandwich.

"Not bad," he said.

"You're welcome," she said, taking a sip of her drink. "Now please tell me all there is to know about this Arielle Waldron and why it so happens that they sent you down here to deal with it. Are you even close to the family?"

"Glen Waldron is my boss. He owns the company, so I have to ensure that he loves me at all times, with the current state of publishing being what it is. I need to make myself an 'essential worker,'" he said, nibbling on his sandwich.

"I know better than anyone the current state of publishing," said Plum. "But still, it seems unusual that he'd send you down here."

"Oh, I volunteered. As soon as he found out, I said I would do anything I could to help. Also, I really needed a vacation," he said.

"A vacation? You were just here a month ago," exclaimed Plum.

"I've been working very hard," he said.

Plum shook her head. She knew that his work ethic was erratic at best. Gerald saw that she had called his bluff, and he slumped in his seat.

"Truth is, I can't stand my job. With the magazine world crumbling, you have to perform like a superhero and work day and night, and everyone is after your position. I never realized how good I had it working for you," he said.

Plum was gratified. Their work relationship had not ended on a positive note. "Thank you for saying that. And I'm sorry I fired you."

"Ah, I shouldn't have blamed you. I was a bit checked out and very distracted by my relationship with Leonard."

"How is he, by the way?" asked Plum, taking a sip of her drink.

"Don't ask," said Gerald, waving his hand in the air. "My problem is I am such a romantic. But let's not talk about that. I would rather return to the topic of murder—it is far more pleasant than my love life."

Plum smiled. "Fair enough. So, what are your duties while you are here? Do you need to identify the body? Bring it home?"

Gerald shuddered. "God, I hope not."

"Is the family coming down?"

"No..."

"Then you *will* have to do that," insisted Plum.

Gerald's face drained of color. "Eeks, that never occurred to me. I just fancied myself asking a few hard-hitting questions and pushing the police to make an arrest. I told Mr. Waldron that the Paraison police were completely inept and you'd had to solve the last murder. Then he sort of became angry that I had suggested Arielle come down to a resort where there was a recent murder, and that's when I said I'd help."

"You overpromised," chided Plum. She took a deep breath. "I'm not sure if they have suspects, but what can you tell me about Arielle? Did you know she was a kleptomaniac?"

"Of course. Everyone did," he replied, finishing the last piece of crust and pushing his plate away. "We thought it was sort of charming, or at least, we had to think it was charming because her dad was the boss. He knew about it as well and just said, 'Please make a list of what she steals and send it to me every month, and I will reimburse people.' Apparently, he had tried several times to get her help, and it didn't stick."

"Jeez."

"Yes. She was something. She was actually smart, and if she weren't so troubled, she would have been successful."

Plum leaned forward in her seat. "How was she troubled?"

"Along with the stealing, she had a bit of a stalking problem.

She'd become obsessed with celebrities or prominent social figures and turn up at their houses or follow them to restaurants. I think Robert Pattinson had to get a restraining order against her."

"Wow," said Plum, her mind racing. "You know Gary Grigorian and Johnny Wisebrook were both at Dieter's house the night she died. Could she have been stalking them?"

"It's possible," Gerald responded. "But she also stalked women as well. Not in a romantic sense but wanting to be their best friend."

"Then she could have been stalking Gary's wife, Hallie Corona."

"Do we really consider her a celebrity?" he sneered.

Plum smiled. "Ha, I think the same thing. She's so annoying."

"I agree." He shuddered. "I can't see Johnny Wisebrook killing Arielle, though. Isn't he like a hundred years old?"

"He's been rocking and rolling for decades, that's for sure," agreed Plum. "But maybe she enraged him. She did seem like a little word that rhymes with rich."

"She was," said Gerald. "Irony is, if it was one of them—a celebrity—that killed her, she would have relished it. I can only imagine the social media posts! How can we find out?"

"Actually, I was invited to a disco at Dieter's tonight. I wasn't going to attend, but maybe we should..."

"Absolutely!" squealed Gerald. "And to think, I almost didn't bring my leather pants. That would have been such a missed opportunity."

Plum's eyes widened. "It's the tropics. Don't you think you'll get a little hot?"

"I'm cold-blooded," said Gerald smugly.

"What was I thinking wearing these pants?" moaned Gerald a few hours later. "I'm sweating like a pig."

"Told you," Plum retorted.

"Well, you should have been more insistent," he barked. "You're the local."

Plum was secretly pleased that he had noticed how well she had integrated into the local population.

They were in Plum's golf cart, driving to Villa la Grosella Negra. After Gerald's afternoon snack, he had insisted they head down to Playa del Sol for a dip in the sea. At first Plum tried to beg off, claiming she had legitimate work to do, but Gerald was persistent and ultimately Plum was grateful that he was so pushy. Despite living on Paraiso for four months, she realized she did not make it down to the beach as much as she would have liked. As they floated in the warm, crystal-clear water with the white sand underneath, she felt a sense of calm she had never felt anywhere else in her life. There was something so restorative about the Caribbean, as if all her worries drifted away with the baby waves.

After returning home salty and sandy, they each took a brief siesta before preparing to head out to the disco. Following her shower, Plum initially threw on a casual sundress and knotted her damp hair into a loose bun, too lazy to blow out her curly locks. When she informed Gerald that she was ready, he squawked and told her in a horrified voice that she had become self-hating and needed to make an effort. Plum went back to her bedroom and changed into an elegant, red, A-line midi-dress and stood in front of her bathroom mirror, painstakingly straightening her hair, clump by clump. By the time they had left the house (Gerald took forever to primp) her actions had proved futile and her hair was already frizzing up into a puffball. Gerald threw up his hands in defeat.

"Wait until you see this house," said Plum, attempting to change the subject from Gerald's hot pants. "It's Disneyland on acid."

"Oh, goodie," said Gerald. "I've always wanted to see Villa la Grosella Negra."

"You've heard of it?" asked Plum, giving him an inquisitive look.

"Of course," said Gerald. "*Vanity Fair* did a huge article on it. All about Dieter Friedrich and his battle with his neighbor, Charles Nettles."

"Why am I the last to hear about this?"

"Maybe you've had your head buried in the sand, literally," he said. "I've followed it on *Page Six*. Charles Nettles is being investigated for insider trading. He claims it's all rubbish, that Dieter's trying to set him up and paying off people to lie about it."

"And this is all over a noise complaint?" asked Plum.

She made a wide turn in her cart to overtake a slower golf cart being driven by an elderly woman.

"Not only the noise. Actually, there was a suggestion that it actually is over a woman," said Gerald. "There was some sort of love triangle between Dieter and Charles, but no one is really sure what happened. Dieter is not married, so maybe it was a girlfriend of his, and Charles has been married forever. Some have suggested that Charles's wife, Wendy, used to date Dieter, but no one knows for sure."

"I wonder if that is at all connected to Arielle's murder?" mused Plum.

"Anything is possible."

CHAPTER 8

IN THE GLITTERING CARIBBEAN STARLIGHT, Villa la Grosella Negra took on an entirely new identity. Although it was still gaudy and vulgar, an example of when someone has too much money and entirely no taste, the tiki lights festooned around the disparate structures gave it a hint of the ethereal. Combined with the fake volcanoes, the plethora of firepits, and the massive cauldrons spouting flames, the property emitted a mysterious and tantalizing vibe.

Gerald was in heaven. "This place is incredible," he gushed, as he glanced around the exterior.

"Yes, it is," said Plum, although she was certain that they had different definitions of *incredible* in this case.

The maid who had answered the door (not the same as earlier, this one was older, but was also dressed like a male fantast) appeared confused when they informed her that they were there for the disco.

"It's nine o'clock," she said.

"Yes, we weren't sure what time it started..." began Plum.

"Not for hours," said the petulant maid in a tone that suggested they were idiots.

"We don't have mental telepathy," Plum said fiercely. "It would have been nice if our hosts had designated a time. Especially when it is outrageously late."

"Don't mind her," said Gerald, to the maid. "Shall we come back?"

"No, I will tell Monsieur Friedrich that you are here. In the meantime, you may stroll the property or wait at the pool bar."

"Thank you," they said in unison.

During their leisurely jaunt to the pool bar, Gerald gleefully snapped pictures on his phone and made exclamations about everything they passed. Just when he announced that something was "the most outrageous thing he had ever seen" (a nude portrait of Dieter that Plum had not noticed on her previous visit), they would stumble upon something equally delicious (a polka-dotted zebra foal sharing a cage with a short, stocky giraffe) that would usurp the previous award winner. Gerald had already inundated social media with dozens of posts by the time they made it to the bar.

The bartender was a middle-aged man with a fleshy nose and thinning, gray hair swept back so his pink, sunburned scalp was visible. His shirt was strained over his potbelly, and he chewed on his thumbnail in a bored manner. Since the bar was situated in the center of the pool, they had been forced to use a raft and oars to reach their destination, under the amused gaze of the bartender. They squabbled about who was not doing their part in the rowing, each accusing the other of being lazy. When they extracted themselves from the flimsy vessel and alighted onto the deck (with Gerald complaining that he better not fall in because his pants were worth an exorbitant amount), they heaved themselves into the barstools with effort. Plum mused that they were both so out of shape, it was as if they had crossed the English Channel.

"If I had to row myself to the bar every day, I would quit drinking," complained Gerald. He rubbed his sore arms.

"I concur. I'd be a total teetotaler," agreed Plum.

The bartender had the cloudy smell of cigarette smoke clinging to his clothes. He wore a name tag that identified him as Michael and slapped two cocktail napkins in front of them from behind the sunken bar.

"You could have walked over the bridge," he said, motioning toward the other side of the pool.

Plum and Gerald followed his gaze and saw that there was indeed a bridge that made access to the bar decidedly more attainable. "You could have mentioned it," said Plum curtly.

Michael smirked but didn't answer her. "What can I get you?"

"A white wine, please," said Plum.

"Daiquiri for me," said Gerald. "And a heavy pour."

Plum gave him a look. "We aren't here for pleasure," she reprimanded.

"I'm only having *one*," insisted Gerald.

She returned her attention to Michael, who was uncorking a bottle of wine.

"I'm Plum, and this is my friend Gerald. We're here because Gerald was friends with Arielle Waldron, the girl who was murdered this morning."

Michael wordlessly placed the white wine in front of Plum and then turned back to the bar to make the daiquiri.

"Did you happen to meet Arielle?" asked Plum.

Michael pressed a button on the blender, which began emitting a loud, rocket-launching sound while the pineapple, coconut, banana, ice, and alcohol danced together until they were decimated into oblivion. Plum and Gerald waited for him to answer, but when the blender finished, he still didn't say a word and instead poured the iced, yellow liquid into a large glass and garnished it with a cherry, a slice of pineapple, and a little pink umbrella.

"I asked if you happened to meet Arielle," repeated Plum.

"I'd have to jog my memory," said Michael. He put the glass in front of Gerald. He looked at them expectantly.

Plum kicked Gerald under the table, and he yelped and rubbed his leg. He gave her a withering look. "Ouch!"

Michael turned his back to them to rinse out the blender. Plum leaned over to Gerald. "You should give him some money," she whispered.

"Why?"

"Can't you tell that he's hinting for it?"

Gerald frowned and reached for his wallet in his pants pocket. "I'll have to figure out a way to expense this."

Extracting his wallet from his tight pants proved to be a larger endeavor than Gerald had estimated. The leather ferociously clung to his skin, and the small slit for a pocket gave little way for the fishing expedition. Gerald ultimately had to stand up and wheedle his hand in and out, hopping up and down, before pulling out a monogrammed leather wallet and removing a one-hundred-dollar bill.

"This better be worth it," he hissed at Plum.

"It would have been much easier if you didn't wear those hideous pants," remarked Plum.

Michael the bartender feigned obliviousness during the entire exercise, but Plum scrupulously eyed him and determined that he was well aware of what was transpiring.

"Would this help jog your memory?" asked Gerald, waving the bill in Michael's direction.

"You could be subtler," murmured Plum.

But Michael didn't appear to care that Gerald was brazen. He greedily took the money and put it in a small leather bag in a cabinet under the bar. He stood now in front of them, finally maintaining eye contact.

"Yes, that girl Arielle was here. I try to mind my own business, but she wouldn't let me and talked my ear off," he said, a note of disdain in his voice.

"Oh?" asked Plum, brightening. "How was that?"

"I think she expected some sort of hero's welcome when she showed up. But Mr. Friedrich and his guests were in the middle of their poker game, and although he is a gracious host, that is one time he doesn't enjoy being interrupted. He had Jeremy take her to her room…"

"Who's Jeremy?" interrupted Gerald. He removed his lips from his straw long enough to ask the question then returned to sucking down the sugary drink.

"Jeremy Silver is Mr. Friedrich's right-hand man. He's in charge of everything," said Michael.

Michael watched the rate at which Gerald's drink was becoming lower in the glass. He pulled out a dish of fried plantains from behind the bar and set it in front of them.

"We haven't met Mr. Silver yet," said Plum.

"You will," said Michael with confidence. "He's always here. Mr. Friedrich has a ton of guests coming and going, and Jeremy manages it all as well as his business. It's not an easy job. There are a lot of demanding people who turn up, not to mention the atmosphere is always festive, and with the parties come the day after the parties."

"You mean people get hungover and stuff?" asked Gerald.

"You could say that," said Michael. "I would describe Jeremy as not only a manager but cleanup crew. And I'm not talking about mopping floors or wiping toilets. He has to clean up a lot of messes."

"What sort of messes?" asked Plum.

"Not everyone behaves very well," said Michael cryptically. "There have been some girls who were harassed. Not by Mr. Friedrich of course, but with other guests."

"Was that the case last night?" asked Plum.

"I don't think so," said Michael.

Gerald noisily slurped the last of his drink and took a bite of the pineapple.

"You want another?" asked Michael.

"Yes," said Gerald.

"Remember, we haven't eaten dinner," advised Plum.

"I'll be fine," said Gerald, waving her away.

"Oh, for the love—please have a plantain," she implored. "Something to sop up all of the booze in your belly."

"Fine," he said, picking one up and popping a piece of plantain in his mouth.

"Do you happen to know which room Arielle was staying in?" Plum asked Michael.

"Yes," said Michael, and he pointed to a low, thatched-roof bungalow with teal trim situated on the edge of the property next to the hot tub. "Over there."

Anyone sitting at the bar would have a very good view of people entering and exiting Arielle's bungalow.

"Did you see Arielle again after she had been sent to her room?"

"Yes," he said, plunking in the fruit and liquor before pressing the button on the blender. They again waited until the whirling sound stopped drowning out the conversation and Gerald had his new drink. "After Arielle did whatever in her room—unpacked, changed, I have no idea—she came over to the bar. She started complaining about everyone and was furious at Jeremy for forcing her to leave the card game."

"Makes sense," said Plum.

"And then she started in on everyone. Someone at the hotel had wrongfully accused her of some crime and pissed her off."

"Juan Kevin," murmured Plum.

"Then her friend was annoying her because she was lusting after some guy who was Arielle's ex-boyfriend..."

"Jessica and Max!" said Plum. "What did she specifically say about that?"

Michael refilled Plum's wineglass, despite it being half-full. "Arielle said that her friend was delusional that this hot ex-boyfriend—her words, not mine—was still in love with her. She said it was obvious to her he was hooking up with her friend just to make her jealous. Arielle claimed it wasn't worth it and it was just weird, but she sounded annoyed."

"Interesting," said Plum. "What else did Arielle complain about?"

"She said there was someone here at the Villa who wasn't taking her seriously and would have to pay big if he didn't."

Plum's interest was piqued. "Did she say who?"

He shook his head. "Nope. She wanted me to ask, but I was not interested."

Gerald's straw slurped, and he moved it around, trying to ingest the coconut dregs at the bottom of his glass. Plum gave him a withering look.

"Who do you think Arielle was referring to?" asked Plum.

"No idea," said Michael. "I'm not here to ask questions. I'm here to listen and serve drinks."

"Was that the end of the conversation?" asked Gerald. "And can I please have another?"

Plum put out her hand. "Before you make it, please answer the first question."

"She rambled on about how that person would get their comeuppance and drank a lot of margaritas, and then Mr. Grigorian and his wife, Miss Corona, came over, and Arielle perked up. She was effusive about what a big fan she was. Mr. Grigorian was lapping it up, but Miss Corona seemed annoyed and kept trying to get her husband to leave. But he didn't want to, so Miss Corona left without him."

Michael looked about to say more but suddenly straightened up and turned back to the blender to prepare a third drink for Gerald. Plum glanced behind her.

"Speak of the devil..." she muttered.

Gary Grigorian and Hallie Corona were walking over the

bridge, arm in arm, with Hallie's head resting on her husband's shoulders. He said something to her, and she threw her head back and laughed dramatically. If Plum hadn't known they had been married for ten years, she would have assumed they were newlyweds.

As they walked closer to the bar, Hallie's eyes widened, and she waved at Plum. "I had no idea you were here!" she boomed, although Plum suspected that wasn't true and the lovey-dovey display was all for her benefit.

"I'm here!" said Plum lightly.

After introductions were made between Gerald and the happy couple (during which Gerald went head-to-head with Hallie on the New York name game, an exercise Plum found inane, although she had been guilty of engaging in it only a month prior), they ordered drinks. Michael retreated to his post in the back of the bar, and Plum knew that they had gotten everything out of him that they would. While Gerald tried to butter Gary up, Hallie sat down on the barstool next to Plum, maneuvering her legs so that her way-too-tight, sparkly dress wouldn't reveal too much.

"Are you excited for the disco?" asked Hallie. "It's so much fun! I love dancing, don't you? Gary is the best dancer in the world. He should be on *Dancing with the Stars*. I keep suggesting that to the network, and I think they are really waiting because they probably want him to host it one day. He would be such a great host. He's so great with people."

"Right," said Plum.

"It's funny because Gary says *I* should be on *Dancing with the Stars*."

She gave Plum an expectant look, but Plum didn't respond. She was remembering one particular column Hallie wrote for *Travel and Respite* where she talked about a visit to an orphanage in Burkina Faso and said that she related to the children there because she had also not eaten that day and Gary had not accompanied her, so she was both starving and lonely. She had also mentioned that she had thought about adopting a child herself, but when she met the children, she decided they were too old. Plum had edited that part out.

Hallie took a large gulp of her whiskey and soda. "I need this drink like you wouldn't believe. They grilled me and Gary all day about that girl's murder. It was so annoying."

Plum decided to appeal to Hallie's enormous ego. "But you're so perceptive, I'm sure you had a lot to tell them."

Hallie fondled the rim of her glass with her index finger as if conducting an internal debate. Then she turned to Plum and said in a conspiratorial tone, "It's true. I have always had the ability to gather information in a short amount of time. That's initially why I wanted to be a reporter, but then the the-a-tah called. Well, first theater, then Hollywood. Big screen, small screen."

Plum nodded. "I'm sure being astute is what makes you a great actress. Have you ever played a detective?"

"Tons of times. And yes, you are correct. My deductive skills are tremendous."

"You must have had some helpful information for the police. I bet your recall is great," said Plum. She almost wanted to barf with all the hollow compliments she was feeding Hallie. Mercifully, Hallie didn't even seem to notice that she wasn't being genuine and was lapping them up.

"I was able to really set the scene with the police," she explained. "I told them how we were all playing cards when Arielle arrived. Me, Johnny, Gary, and Dieter. It was an intense game; we had a lot of money riding on it. I mean, we can, of course, afford to lose money, my husband and I do very well, but it's better to win, right?" she said, adding a fake laugh.

"Always," prompted Plum.

"Arielle was fed up that none of us gave her the time of day. I mean, really, can you imagine the ego?" she asked rhetorically.

Yes, thought Plum.

Hallie continued without waiting for a response, "And Dieter just kind of waves her away, and Jeremy shows her out. But after that, Shakira comes in and whispers something in Dieter's ear. I heard her say 'Arielle' and 'working with Nettles.' He glances up, and his face becomes angry. He's usually a fairly easygoing guy, so it was noticeable."

"Nettles? Did she say Charles Nettles?" asked Plum.

"I didn't hear her say Charles, but then I couldn't hear everything. I just heard Nettles. And of course, I know all about the bad blood between Dieter and them. They are apparently horrible neighbors."

Plum wondered what Arielle's connection was to Nettles. "Then what?"

"Then he told Shakira to go deal with it and get rid of her. I didn't see her again."

"Not even after the card game?" asked Plum, remembering that Michael had said they got drinks at the bar.

"No," said Hallie. She paused. "My husband and I stopped by the bar for a hot minute and saw her there but quickly retired. I mean, anyone who knows me and Gary knows that we have a very vibrant sex life. We're insatiable. Only with each other, obviously," she said, proudly. "He never even looks at another woman."

Plum tried to adopt her most casual tone. "Someone mentioned that Arielle was aggressively flirting with him at the bar."

Something dark flashed across Hallie's shiny face, but she took a sip of her drink to bide her time and then played dumb. "Oh, really? I don't know anything about that. *So many* women worship my husband."

"But wasn't she throwing herself at him?" pushed Plum.

"I have no idea!" said Hallie, throwing up her arms. "I'm just numb to it, because he is such a hot commodity, and everyone wants a piece of him. I don't care at all, because our marriage is rock solid."

"That's wonderful," said Plum. "But did you get any sort of stalker vibe..."

Just as Plum finished her statement, a dwarf dressed in a *Game of Thrones* costume appeared on the other side of the bridge and banged on a large, bronze gong. Everyone fell silent.

"Disco has commenced!" he announced.

CHAPTER 9

I LIKE TO MOVE IT MOVE IT. I LIKE TO MOVE IT MOVE IT.

The music thundered through the disco, a combination of pop and rap, with songs overlapping other songs. While strobe lights bounced across the walls, the DJ held on to his earphones and spun the records. Plum nursed a wine spritzer with extra ice and swayed to the music as she stood off to the side, trying to decipher if any of those present were homicidal maniacs.

Gerald, who was completely inebriated, boogied in the center of the room with Shakira, Dietrich's girlfriend. They were both remarkable dancers, full of rhythm and timing. Shakira wore a shimmering silver gown that plunged down to her navel, her amble bosom on full display. Gerald's leather pants were having their moment as he dipped and spun his partner around the floor.

Hallie Corona was grinding against Gary. She seemed a bit drunk, but they were both so conscious of who was watching them and how they appeared that it seemed like it was all an act. Plum actually caught them admiring themselves in the mirror and concluded that they were their own favorite audience.

There were a few other guests on the dance floor who were excellent dancers, but they didn't interact with anyone else, and

Plum wondered if they were professionals hired by Dieter. They appeared joyless and robotic in their performance, as if they were working a shift and couldn't wait to get home. Dieter sat in a low balcony on another throne, watching the dancers and eating caviar and drinking champagne that two perky brunettes were fetching for him. There was a thirtyish man with dark hair, a neat beard, and dark eyes set close together who would appear every now and then and whisper something to Dieter before disappearing. He had good posture and strode with his shoulders back and his head held high. Plum wondered if he was Jeremy Silver.

"I didn't expect to see you here."

Plum spun around. It was Juan Kevin. And he looked particularly handsome this evening. He had forgone his usual blazer and was wearing a short-sleeved shirt that accentuated the cut of his muscled arms.

"I didn't expect to see you here either," said Plum.

He raised his eyebrows. "I'm here in a professional capacity. I want to see if I can do anything to assist the police."

"So, you can assist the police, and I can't?" Plum blurted before she could stop herself.

Instead of annoyance, amusement flickered in his eyes. "Plum, I'm in resort security. It's my job. It's not your job to solve murders."

She was about to protest but stopped herself. Why antagonize the man? "Are you planning on dancing?"

"Are you planning on asking me?" he asked, arching an eyebrow.

"Sure," she said.

"Wonderful," he said, taking her arm and leading her toward the center of the room. "I didn't think you liked to dance."

She gave him a quizzical look. "I love to dance. Why would you think that?"

"No reason," he said quickly.

Plum wondered how Juan Kevin could have come to that conclusion.

It was one of Plum's favorite songs, and she began to shimmy. Juan Kevin was an excellent partner. He held the small of her back and led her around the dance floor with ease. As the music became faster, she struggled to keep up with him, but he deftly maneuvered her and spun her. He held her hands and drew her close to him so she could feel his breath on her face. Plum knew she didn't have the same talent as Shakira and Gerald, but she loved to feel the beat, sway her hips, and let her hair loose.

The dance felt intimate, almost as if they were the only two people in the room. As she watched him, she started fantasizing about what he would be like as a lover then a husband. And a father. What was happening to her? Why had she mapped out their entire future? Maybe she was tipsy from the wine? Michael did pour a large glass.

Suddenly, out of nowhere, Shakira cut in between Plum and Juan Kevin and pulled him into a clutch. She gyrated against him in a very erotic manner. He gave Plum an apologetic look, but before he could return to her, Gerald grabbed Plum's hand and spun her away, dancing her into the corner.

Gerald bent toward her and whispered in her ear, "Honey, if you like that man, stop what you are doing right now," he said, a Cheshire grin on his face.

"Huh?" she said, as she threw her fists in the air and shimmied to the beat.

"I'm serious, time to evacuate," he hissed.

She stopped and turned toward him. "Has something happened?"

"Yes," he said. "And please remember that I am saying this with love. You have just exposed yourself. You're the worst dancer I've ever seen in my life. That overbite and those off-tune spasms are doing you no favors. Abort!"

Plum stared at him with astonishment. No one had ever told her she had no rhythm. Was he joking? She glanced back at Juan

Kevin and Shakira, who were dancing as brilliantly as Danny Zuko and Cha-Cha in *Grease*, and she felt exactly how Sandy did. She wanted to run off in tears like her celluloid twin.

She walked out of the disco, leaving the thumping music behind, and into a courtyard. Dieter must have soundproofed the disco after his run-in with his neighbor, because it was impossible to hear anything from the outside. The only noise was the dribbling water from the fountain. Plum sat down on one of the stone benches.

Gerald's criticism of her stung. Although she was a strong woman, often people misconstrued that quality for being heartless or cold. On the contrary, Plum frequently felt vulnerable and misunderstood. She spoke her mind, but it didn't mean she didn't want to be liked. Or loved, for that matter.

"Having too much fun?" came a voice from across the courtyard.

Plum was so startled, she actually flinched. She glanced around the shadowy area.

"I'm sorry. I thought you saw me there."

The man she suspected might be Jeremy Silver stubbed out a cigarette on the stone path, pocketed the filter, rose, and strode toward her. He wasn't very tall, but the way he moved made him appear taller than he was.

"I'm Jeremy Silver," he said. "I didn't mean to scare you."

"It's fine. I'm just getting a little air," she said, using her hand as a fan to cool herself down. "I'm Plum Lockhart."

"Yes, I know," he said, eyeing her carefully. "I saw your name on the guest list."

"You work with Mr. Friedrich?" she asked, knowing full well he did.

"I do. I'm his executive. I know, it is an odd title, but I don't want to be called executive assistant, because it makes me sound like I'm a secretary. I'm much more than that, so we came up with this designation."

"I like it. It's all-encompassing," she said.

"Exactly."

He made a motion as if he was about to leave, so Plum gestured to the bench. "Please sit for a minute. I could use the company."

Jeremy hesitated but then sat down. His shrewd, dark eyes turned and surveyed her. "I could use a rest myself."

"Yes, it appears that you work very late. What 'executive' functions do you perform in the evenings?" she asked, adopting a casual tone.

"Mr. Friedrich has business all over the world. His garment company is flourishing, and we have offices on four continents. I am the gatekeeper between him and all of his satellite offices."

"And are you also the gatekeeper here?"

Jeremy shook his head a little as if to imply yes and no. "I assist Mr. Friedrich on all affairs."

"Including Arielle Waldron?" asked Plum, staring straight at him and trying to gauge his reaction. "What do you think happened to her? Any idea?"

She couldn't swear it, but she thought she saw a steeliness flicker in Jeremy's eyes. Then it passed. He paused to assemble his words before he spoke. "I don't know. But I am confident the Paraison police will find out right away."

Plum snorted. "But do you think there is a killer on the loose? I mean, why are you still having discos? I'm not sure why the guests are still here also. Shouldn't everything be cordoned off?"

"I agree it's strange," said Jeremy. "But there is no danger. I am certain it was someone who came off the water and killed Arielle. I don't think it had anything to do with Mr. Friedrich or his guests. And I believe that's what the police think also, or else they would have made this a crime scene."

"But that doesn't make any sense," said Plum. "Why would someone randomly come and kill her?"

"Maybe it wasn't random," said Jeremy, rising.

"Did she give you any indication that she felt threatened when you talked with her?"

"On the contrary, she was the one who appeared combative. She was unhappy that she was not invited to play poker with Mr. Friedrich and his friends because she was determined to talk to one of his guests."

"Which one?"

"Johnny Wisebrook. She implied that they had a past."

"What kind of past?" asked Plum.

He hesitated. "I suppose I can be candid because she is dead, and I already told this to the police. Arielle announced that she had been Johnny Wisebrook's lover and she refused to allow him to discard her. She made a scene, and unfortunately, Mr. Wisebrook had to leave just to avoid her. Now I really shouldn't say any more, and I need to return to the disco."

After Jeremy had left, Juan Kevin wandered into the courtyard. He was flushed from dancing, his forehead gleaming with sweat, but his eyes were sparkling. If he had felt at all indisposed for dancing with Plum, his manner didn't show it.

"There you are," he said with a smile. "I'm sorry that we were interrupted. I wish you hadn't left."

"I didn't want to bring you down," said Plum in a rare moment of openness. Then realizing she had exposed herself, she said, "Just kidding."

"I hope so," he said, sliding onto the bench next to her. "Because you could never bring me down."

It was the perfect answer, and Plum didn't know how to respond. It made her somewhat breathless and burn with excitement. She turned to look at him. They stared in each other's eyes under the moonlight for what felt like a minute but was probably only fifteen seconds. They slowly started to move toward each other.

"Plum!" Gerald roared, stumbling out toward them, a

half-drunk piña colada in his hand. "You have to come back inside! Johnny Wisebrook is here!"

The moment broken, Plum sighed. On the one hand, she wanted to throttle Gerald, who was drunk as a skunk, but on the other hand, she was grateful. It wouldn't be a good idea to kiss Juan Kevin. It would just make things complicated. *It would be amazing!* screamed her inner voice, who was dying for romance. *It would be messy!* a practical voice retorted in a know-it-all tone. Oh well, it wasn't like she had the option anymore, thought Plum as she followed the others back into the disco.

She had seen Johnny Wisebrook once from a distance, at Coconuts, the beach bar, the previous month. But standing within ten feet of him was an entirely different experience. He exuded charisma and possessed that glossy aura that encapsulates people who have been celebrities for decades. Now in his late sixties, the whippet-thin Australian lead singer of the Moving Targets was full-lipped, with large, blue eyes, a mop of brown hair, and an elastic body. A legendary lothario with raffish charm, Johnny had a flock of young women surrounding him as he danced in the center of the room.

"He has a lot of energy for his age," said Plum.

"He has a lot of energy for any age," confirmed Juan Kevin, who was standing next to her, surveying the scene.

"I'm not sure I'd want to go to discos when I'm in my sixties," said Plum. She watched as Johnny spun a young blond around and dipped her so that her hair swept the floor.

"I'm not really big on discos in my forties," said Juan Kevin.

"But you're such a great dancer," she said.

"When I have the right partner," he said carefully. Plum burned with pleasure. Did he mean her?

They stood watching as Gerald approached Johnny and attempted to engage with him. He put a heavy, drunken arm over Johnny's shoulder and whispered in his ear. Plum grimaced with embarrassment for Gerald. Johnny, evidently used to sycophants and fans, gave him a dazzling smile before smoothly leading him over to dance with one of the suspected professional women, who, as if understanding, took Gerald's hand and dragged him away.

Dieter remained watching and clapping from his throne, although now he was joined by Shakira, who had usurped the other female admirers. Dieter was left to serve himself caviar. Shakira's face appeared canny as she scanned the room. She would beam at Dieter when he glanced in her direction, but then her face would fall into a more baleful expression when she watched the others. Plum made a note to talk to her further.

"I'm showing my age, but this music is giving me a headache," said Juan Kevin.

"Maybe we can slip away and do some snooping?" asked Plum.

She waited for Juan Kevin to don a disapproving look, but he surprised her by nodding. "Good idea."

10

NIGHT HAD SETTLED IN, WITH the moon launched into the sky. Puffs of sea-scented breeze were coming off the swath of water below. Plum and Juan Kevin walked quietly along the paths and over bridges, careful to remain in the shadows. It was a warm, romantic night, and Plum wanted to forget about snooping and kiss Juan Kevin under the stars. But this wasn't the right moment. They had a chance to case the property.

Although they had not verbally agreed on what direction to take, it was evident they were heading toward Arielle's bungalow. This route involved avoiding detection from Michael, the bartender, who was still at his post, listlessly washing glasses with a dishrag.

"This way," whispered Juan Kevin.

Instead of walking on the direct path, Plum followed Juan Kevin to a small pebble footway that went behind a three-story concrete hut with intricate moldings and took a wide berth around the kidney-shaped, dark-blue lagoon that hugged the edge of the property. After passing by a totem pole, a Mayan gazebo, and a two-story log cabin, they reached the back of Arielle's bungalow. There were two screened windows separated by a giant guava tree whose branches were bent down under the weight of its fruit.

Much to Plum's surprise, Juan Kevin quietly removed a screen and pulled up the window. It was low enough so he could nimbly dangle one leg over and then pull himself into the structure. He pushed aside the curtains, held out his hand for Plum, and helped ease her into the bungalow. She blinked several times, attempting to acclimate her eyes. At first everything was pitch black, but slowly shapes and shadows came into focus, and she could see that she was in a bedroom.

"My heart is pounding," whispered Plum. "Maybe we should have just asked if we could check it out?"

Juan Kevin, who still held on to her hand, shook his head. "No. I did ask. Dieter said the police had already been in here and there was no reason for me to further examine it. That piqued my interest."

"What if they find us here?" asked Plum, who at the end of the day was a rule follower.

"I'll tell them that I was trying to seduce you and stumbled into the nearest cabin."

Plum was grateful that it was dark so Juan Kevin couldn't see her face flaming with embarrassment. And desire. His statement hung in the air, and Plum wondered if she should suggest that they actually kiss, if only to not have to lie if exposed. But because she couldn't see his face, she didn't want to misread the situation.

"What are we looking for?" she whispered. Her voice was now squeaky and hoarse. Why did it suddenly sound unnatural?

"I'm not sure," said Juan Kevin.

He pulled his phone out of his pocket and turned on the flashlight. It provided a dim illumination but at least afforded a pinprick glimpse of the accommodations. Plum glanced around and was grateful that the decor was not similar to the Playboy Mansion but was actually quite mundane. A mahogany, four-poster bed with a pink floral duvet and lime-green pillows stood sentinel in the center of the room. Next to the bed was a side table with a wood accent lamp. There was a dresser, a white mirror, and a watercolor of the beach in a gold frame adorning the wall. It had the faint whiff of mildew.

Juan Kevin directed his flashlight on every surface and corner of the bedroom, but nothing stood out to Plum. He even bent down and looked under the bed. He opened a door and walked into the bathroom, with Plum closely following. The floor was comprised of small Spanish tiles, and the grouting was dirty and in dire need of replacement. The chrome sink and bathtub fixtures were old and could have used an update. There was a dark-blue shower curtain with a map of Paraiso on it that bordered the tub. The toilet was the only dramatic piece that Plum had espied so far: it was hot pink and had a four-inch, squishy, pink seat.

"I have the exact same toilet seat!" enthused Juan Kevin.

"You do?" asked Plum, surprised. But then she realized he must be kidding. "Ha, ha, very funny."

"I thought we could use some levity at the moment."

They retraced their steps through the bathroom into the bedroom, pausing to open the walk-in closet. A few green plastic hangers hung idly from a rod, and there were drawers and cabinets that were revealed to be empty except for a waxy lining when Juan Kevin opened them. In the living room, the seating area had a blue tiled floor with a few striped dhurrie rugs sprinkled on top. There was a white sofa with Indian throw pillows; two cane chairs; a low, walnut coffee table, and some botanical prints on the wall. It was all very generic, thought Plum, and resembled almost every guest accommodation that she had seen in villas on the island. The only anomaly was a large, sixty-inch flat-screen television mounted on the wall, below which was an old gaming console as well as a DVD player and a VHS machine. Stacks of DVDs and video games were jumbled in piles on shelves below. On the floor next to it was a surge protector with six tangled cords plugged into the outlets, including one attached to a large, brass floor lamp.

Juan Kevin once again swept the room with the tiny light on his phone. If they had hoped to discover any obvious remnant from Arielle or the fact that she had stayed in the room for a night (or less) before her demise, there was none.

"I guess the police took everything they needed," said Plum, eyes darting around for a final look.

Juan Kevin nodded. "Let's go."

Suddenly they heard a man's voice. They whipped their heads toward the front door and could see that someone was turning the handle back and forth.

"It's locked," a male voice said from the other side of the door. "No problem."

Juan Kevin grabbed Plum's hand and pulled her into the bedroom. They heard the front door open and two low voices. With a quickening feeling of dread, Plum rushed through the bedroom. Juan Kevin stepped into the bathroom, and Plum followed suit. He pulled the shower curtain around to envelop them, and they crouched down and huddled together in the tub. Plum's heart was thumping so loudly, she thought it would leap out of her chest and perform a little dance routine on the floor.

Plum gasped quietly. "Your phone," she whispered.

Juan Kevin's phone flashlight was still on in his pocket. He quickly fumbled and turned it off, plunging them into darkness. He was placing it back in his pocket when it slipped out of his hand with a thump and slid down the edge of the bathtub until it circled the drain. They both froze and squatted motionless.

They heard loud footsteps then a male voice in the distance. "Hey, is someone in there?"

The man's footsteps moved closer. Plum realized he had probably walked into the bedroom from the living room. Fear hung in the air, and Plum found herself holding her breath.

"Hello?" said the man.

Plum and Juan Kevin waited. She fully expected someone to come storming into the bathroom, rip aside the shower curtain, and...well, she wasn't sure what. Actually, it wouldn't really be the end of the world, would it? But why was she feeling so scared?

After a minute Plum heard the front door close. She and Juan Kevin waited with bated breath for an additional three minutes. She finally emitted all the air that had gathered inside her.

"That was close," she whispered.

"Yes," said Juan Kevin. "But I think we're in the clear. Maybe... you can stop impaling me."

To her embarrassment, she had been clinging to Juan Kevin's hand and digging her nails into his palm. "Sorry," she said, withdrawing her arm.

"Let's wait a minute more."

He kept his strong arm around her in the tub as they waited. Their bodies were so entwined that she could feel his heart beating. If she hadn't just been so terrified of exposure, this would be the most romantic and intimate moment she had ever experienced. His musky cologne was so inviting, and the firmness with which he held her made Plum feel safe and protected. But the fact that they were in the room of a woman who was recently murdered and whose murderer was still at large made the situation dangerous and forbidding.

They waited until the coast was fully clear then scrabbled out of the tub and scurried out of the bathroom. "Shall we go out the same window?" asked Plum.

"Let me check on one thing," Juan Kevin said.

He turned his flashlight back on and grabbed her hand. She followed him as he led her back into the seating area. A quick sweep of the room revealed that nothing had been disturbed. Juan Kevin walked over to the surge outlet and pulled at the cords. He held one up, revealing that although it was plugged in, it wasn't charging anything.

"What's that?" whispered Plum.

"It's a computer charger. For a Dell."

"Is it significant?" she asked, moving closer.

"I'm not sure," said Juan Kevin. He pulled it out of the outlet and pocketed it. "But it gave me an idea. Let's go."

They waited until they were far away from the bungalow, past the lagoon, before speaking. They paused by a statue of a lion that had floodlights shining on his teeth, which upon closer inspection appeared to be made of ivory.

Suddenly they heard voices again. They became louder and louder. Plum's heart began to race. This time there was nowhere for them to hide. Two figures were approaching out of the shadows.

It was Michael the bartender and Gary Grigorian. They were surprised to run into Juan Kevin and Plum.

"Oh, hi," said Michael. "Are you, er, lost?"

"Just getting fresh air," said Juan Kevin smoothly.

"Are you done dancing for the night, Gary?" asked Plum.

Gary shifted nervously then gave her a phony smile. "I wanted to have one of Michael's fruit punches—no one here makes them better than him—but the pool bar was closed."

"Yes, I'm heading home," said Michael. "Off duty now."

They both walked briskly away into the darkness.

"Do you think it was them that we heard in the bungalow?" asked Plum.

"Probably," said Juan Kevin.

Plum racked her brain. "I wonder what they were doing there. It sort of seemed like…"

"What?" asked Juan Kevin.

"That they weren't supposed to be there either and were up to no good. The way they didn't really investigate if we were there… If they were supposed to be there and thought they heard something, wouldn't they have walked all over the bungalow and opened the shower curtain?"

"Good point," said Juan Kevin.

"And why are they all buddy-buddy?" mused Plum. She looked in the direction they left, but they were no longer in view.

"And jumpy," added Juan Kevin.

Plum nodded. She motioned to Juan Kevin's pocket, where he had placed the extension cord. "Why do you think that's important?" whispered Plum.

"I know that the police collected a laptop and a cord from the bungalow when they did their search yesterday. It may not mean anything, a previous guest may have left a cord, but what if there was another laptop?" he asked.

"Interesting," said Plum, nodding her head. "Good idea. We need to find out."

"Yes."

"How do we do that?" asked Plum.

He shrugged. "I guess we need to just keep our ears out."

Plum wanted to continue talking but remembered Gerald. He was no doubt incapacitated by now. "I should get back," she said with a sigh.

"Right," said Juan Kevin.

When they returned to the disco, they found Gerald lying on the floor outside, half-asleep.

"He's not going to make it in your golf cart," said Juan Kevin, staring at the drunken man. "I'll give you a ride home."

"I need my cart," she said, wishing that they had taken a taxi to the party. "If you don't mind, bring him to my town house, and I'll meet you there."

"No problem."

They helped Gerald to Juan Kevin's car, and Plum gave the latter the keys to the condo, assuming he would be there way before she would as his car was a million times faster than her cart.

"You can just put Gerald inside my town house. You don't have to wait," she said, secretly hoping he would demur.

"No, it's okay, I'll wait for you," said Juan Kevin, and Plum's pulse quickened. With Gerald passed out, it would just be her and Juan Kevin.

Juan Kevin's phone rang. He pulled it out of his pocket and glanced at the number. "Excuse me, I have to take this."

Plum heard a woman's voice on the other end of the phone, but Juan Kevin moved away to talk. He was speaking in Spanish, in a low tone. He finished the call quickly.

"I'm sorry, but I do have an early start tomorrow," Juan Kevin said. "If it's okay, I'll leave Gerald in the house and head home."

Plum deflated but quickly recovered. Who had called that made him change his plans? A girlfriend?

"Absolutely no problem," she said matter-of-factly. "You have a lot of responsibilities. We will be perfectly fine."

Although she couldn't help but think she would be perfectly fine if he ended up in her bed beside her. And for the rest of the night, she wondered if he was in anyone else's bed.

11

PLUM AWOKE TO THE SUNLIGHT streaming in her window and the palmchats singing their little hearts out in the trees outside her window. How such small animals could make such noise was a mystery to Plum. She was still getting used to the sounds emanating from the creatures she shared the island with, and although she generally enjoyed it, there were times that she would have preferred hearing a car honk or a bus's screech of brakes instead of a frog shrieking its mating call. But that urge was becoming less frequent.

After doing her morning routine, which besides brushing, washing, and putting makeup on, now required the application of a vat's worth of sunscreen, Plum donned a seafoam green, sleeveless dress and a light, white blazer and went to get a cup of coffee. Lucia was already at her desk, having let herself in and also having brought her delicious guava cream pastries.

She frowned at Lucia. "I thought you were going to stop bringing sweets."

"And I thought you were going to stop fooling yourself that you don't want them," she retorted. She looked up and down at Plum over the edge of her glasses and then shook her head with reproach.

Plum selected a smaller pastry and took a bite. She had no willpower anymore. There was once a time in her life when she really hadn't cared about food, but Paraiso had unleashed all of her sensual cravings.

"Gerald is here," said Plum.

"I heard him," said Lucia. "He snores as loudly as a leaf blower."

Plum laughed. "True."

"I ended up going to the disco last night," confessed Plum.

"I knew you would," said Lucia.

Plum sat down at her desk, which was directly across from Lucia's. "How did you know I would? *I* didn't even know I would."

"Because now that you solved one murder, you will try to insert yourself into this investigation," she said confidently.

Plum bristled. "That's completely untrue. I have absolutely no desire to get mixed up in that again."

Lucia's eyebrows rose to the ceiling. "It would mean spending time with Juan Kevin again," she muttered under her breath.

"Excuse me?" asked Plum.

Lucia gave her a blank look. "What? I didn't say anything."

"You said I wanted to spend time with Juan Kevin," said Plum accusingly.

"I can't imagine I did," said Lucia. "But sometimes things pop out of my mouth that I have no control over. It's age. I'm an old lady."

"I think you knew exactly what you were saying," said Plum, eyeing her shrewdly.

They had a staring contest until finally Plum glanced away. This was childish. She didn't have to convince Lucia that she was not interested in Juan Kevin. She might have had a glimmer of hope for romance last night, but now that he was running off to see other women, there was no doubt that she had to forget about him. Although she didn't have proof that he ran off to see another woman. But in any event, it was useless. Plum decided to make sure he knew their relationship going forward would be strictly professional.

Plum turned her attention to her computer. She scanned her emails, dumping spam into the trash and postponing opening missives that she knew would be grievances from annoying clients complaining about water pressure in their shower and silly stuff like that. *I mean, really,* she thought, *don't they know they're in the Caribbean? On an island? And not everything works perfectly?* People were so impatient and demanding, it drove Plum mad. As she scrolled down, she saw that there was an email from Giorgio Lombardi. She clicked it open and read it quickly.

"Alexandra Rijo wants to meet with me at five o'clock today at her house," enthused Plum.

"That's wonderful news," said Lucia. "Have you prepared your pitch?"

"Of course," said Plum. "I put together a PowerPoint presentation yesterday."

"That won't work with her."

"Why not?"

Lucia rose to fetch herself more coffee. After pouring a large cup and dousing it with heavy cream, she returned to her desk. "She is a businesswoman. And the truth is, Jonathan Mayhew does well for her."

Plum was about to protest and say what she thought of Jonathan Mayhew and where he could go, but Lucia put her hand up to stop her. "I know very well what you think about Jonathan. But it's true. You need to appeal to the other side of Alexandra."

"What other side?"

"Alexandra is very smart. She is aware when someone is, as you would say in America, kissing her ass. She is wary of phonies."

"That's excellent, because I was never good at being phony," said Plum. "Sucking up to people was the hardest and least natural part of my previous job."

"I can see that," said Lucia matter-of-factly. "But you'll need to turn the tables on her. Make her the one who suggests working with you. She built Las Frutas with Emilio and was crucial to his success, yet she never received the credit for it. She likes recognition. But she is no one's fool."

Plum nodded. This was good intel. "I think I have an idea how to approach it."

"Remember it will take time," warned Lucia. "Patience is a virtue. It is a cliché, but there is truth."

Gerald made a dramatic appearance several hours later. He had a sleep mask hanging off one ear and wore a short, dark-blue bathrobe that hung open, revealing leopard-print silk boxers. His eyes were bloodshot, and his meager hair was sticking out in little greasy clumps.

"Coffee," he rasped. He collapsed onto the sofa with his hand flung over his eyes.

"You had a little too much fun last night," chided Plum. "I thought we were supposed to be there for work!"

"Have mercy," he whispered.

Plum poured him a coffee and brought him one of Lucia's guava pastries. "Eat and drink," she commanded.

After slowly eating and drinking, while moaning and groaning, Gerald slightly revived. He was ultimately able to sit up and request water, Advil, and more coffee.

"I don't know if I'll be able to work on solving the murder today," he said. "I may have to lie by the pool at the hotel."

Plum rolled her eyes. "I think that was your plan all along."

There was a loud knock at the door, and Lucia and Plum exchanged glances. "Are you expecting anyone?" Plum asked.

"No," said Lucia.

Plum inwardly groaned when she found Captain Diaz standing on her doorstep. The short, squat policeman had a malicious twinkle in his eye, and Plum knew that it meant trouble for her.

"What do you want?" she asked ungraciously.

They had a fraught history, and each regarded the other warily and with light contempt.

"I'm going to need you to come with me to police headquarters," said Captain Diaz.

"What for?" demanded Plum. She knew it was not below Captain Diaz to waste her time on some inane pretext.

"Your business card was found among the belongings of the deceased, Arielle Waldron. I have learned that you are one of the few people who met with her during her short tenure on our island. Therefore, I require your presence to debrief me on your interaction," he said, staring up at her.

Plum sighed and kept her hand on the doorknob, as if primed to slam it in his face at any minute.

"I can save your time and myself a trip. My friend Gerald asked me to intervene on her behalf at the hotel. She was having problems with Juan Kevin Muñoz. I showed up, straightened everything out, handed her my card, and was off. All I did was fix the situation," said Plum, inflating her role.

He nodded. "I would still like you to come. I need to learn more about the victim."

"I don't know anything about the victim!" protested Plum. She opened the door wider so he could see into the living room. "If you want to talk to anyone, it's Arielle's boss, Gerald Hand. He has flown down here to assist the police and solve the crime."

From his sick perch on the sofa, Gerald threw her a contemptuous look.

"Splendid," said Captain Diaz. "That will also be helpful. I request you both accompany me now."

Out of nowhere a deputy materialized behind the captain, and Plum knew she could not resist.

"I blame you!" she snapped at Gerald when she went to the table to retrieve her handbag and cell phone.

"Stop yelling, my head hurts!" moaned Gerald.

The police headquarters was an ugly, stubby structure located between Las Frutas and Estrella, the neighboring town where Plum did all her grocery shopping and errands. The dusty stucco building was so unremarkable that it would be unnoticeable to those passing through except for the large flagpole in the front of the lot, bearing both the Paraison flag and the national Paraison police flag.

The first time that Plum had visited, a month prior, the interior had been oppressively hot and the lack of air-conditioning was offensive. This time was no different, and the smell of sweat hung thickly in the air. That, coupled with Gerald's hangover stench, made Plum nauseous. Not to mention that Captain Diaz had them squished together in the corner on two collapsible chairs with nary a window or fan in reach.

The discomfort felt strategic.

"Let's go through this again," commanded Captain Diaz.

"We've been over it three times," whined Gerald. "Can't you record me? I don't understand why I need to repeat myself." He turned to Plum. "Am I missing something? This is all a waste of time."

"What you consider a waste of time, we consider being thorough," announced Captain Diaz.

Plum had already delineated her measly connection to the deceased four times, so now it was Gerald's fourth turn. In a flat, bored tone, he reiterated how he knew the victim and why he had come down to Paraiso. Only this time, in his utter and complete exasperation, he spat out at the end of his statement that the reason he came from New York to assist the family of the deceased was because the police were so useless!

Anger flickered across Captain Diaz's face, and Plum threw her head back in disappointment. Now they would be there forever.

"Captain Diaz," said Plum, with all the politeness she could muster. "Perhaps if you told us what was among Arielle's possessions, we could be more helpful. Something might jog Gerald's memory, or he might make a connection?"

Plum held out little hope that he would acquiesce, but to her astonishment he agreed. "That might be beneficial. Come with me."

They followed Captain Diaz across the room and past his colleagues, who were lackadaisically chatting on the phone and with each other. Plum noticed that no one seemed rattled by the latest murder to hit their island. Although what did she expect? That they would wail and scream and cry? Round up villains? How could she really know what a working police office was like when she had only ever seen one on television? Real life seemed much more mundane.

They walked into a back room with a long, scarred wooden table in its center. Along the walls were racks of miscellaneous items that each bore a large, yellow tag with a case number scribbled on it. Plum immediately spotted Arielle's Chanel bag on the bottom rack; to be fair, it was the lone fancy item on its shelf—competing for space with a beaten-up violin case and a brown grocery bag. Captain Diaz picked it up and gingerly removed all the items that were inside, placing them carefully on the wooden table.

Plum felt as if she were watching an episode of *Let's Make a Deal*. Never had she been so intrigued with the banal contents of someone else's purse. It reminded her of that standard column format in a magazine, where editors have a celebrity dump out their pocketbook and reveal what they "always" carry around with them. She knew from the magazine world that it was all staged and complete baloney; the contents were curated and coordinated with the advertising department to market certain brands, and in all probability, the celebrity had never even seen some of the featured items before.

"As you will see, the deceased had one hairbrush," began Captain Diaz, pointing to each object as he identified them. "One MacBook Air laptop computer with a charger; one gold bangle bracelet in the shape of a snake; one Polaroid of the victim embracing a naked man; one diamond hair clip; one Maxima makeup bag containing lipstick, mascara, eyeliner, and eye shadow; three elastic bands; one business card for Plum Lockhart Luxury Retreats; one Target credit card or possible gift card; and one wallet containing an American Express Black Card; a Visa Platinum Card; a New York State driver's license; as well as two thousand U.S. dollars in one-hundred-dollar bills."

He ended on a crescendo, marking his last item with a dramatic flourish.

Plum's mind was flooded. Her interaction with Arielle and their exchanges came jolting back and hit her brain like a tsunami hits a coast. Sorting through Arielle's belongings made her fully comprehend the reality and sadness of the young woman's death, and she felt nauseous.

"Are you okay?" Gerald asked, concerned.

"Huh?" said Plum, glancing up.

"Senorita Lockhart, you do not appear well. Do you need to sit down?" asked Captain Diaz.

For the first time since she had known him, Captain Diaz spoke to her with genuine warmth and chivalry.

"I'm fine," whispered Plum.

But she wasn't. Her head felt dizzy, and her heart was pounding. In fact, she *did* need to sit down.

"Please bring her a chair," Gerald asked Captain Diaz, before adding, "and one for me also."

The captain left the room and returned with two folding chairs. She slumped into hers, and Gerald sank into his as well. Plum put her head in her hands and took deep breaths. She felt feverish. She knew it wasn't from the heat but rather from something deeper.

Being in such close proximity to a murder and a murder victim was chilling. Finally, she sat up and stared at Captain Diaz. She was grateful to note that somehow in the past few minutes he had also brought her a glass of iced water, which she drank greedily. Her thought process was so knocked out of line that all she could wonder about was how he had managed to find ice. (Ice being something of a "hot" commodity on the island.)

"Okay, I'm better," she said, finally.

"What's going on?" asked Gerald, his voice full of worry. "You had us scared to death."

"I don't know what came over me. I'm sorry," she said meekly. "I think it all just hit me, that Arielle is dead and there is a murderer out there."

"That's it, we need to take her home," said Gerald with authority. "I will not have my friend suffer another minute in this dreary police station."

Plum waved him away. "It's okay, I'll be fine. I want to help. I think I can."

Captain Diaz scrutinized her. "Was there something in her belongings that gave you a sense of unease?"

Plum nodded and pulled herself together. "Although my interaction with Arielle was very brief, she did make an impression, and I know her opinion on certain things." Plum motioned toward the makeup bag. "Arielle told me that Maxima was one of the tackiest brands, and she basically wouldn't be caught dead owning anything produced by the label."

"She's right," conceded Gerald.

Plum bristled. "I have a Maxima cardholder and bag."

"I rest my case," murmured Gerald.

Captain Diaz ignored him. "You believe that this might not be her makeup case?"

"We know she had a history of kleptomania. She must have stolen it from someone."

Captain Diaz's face became excited. "That's very good information. Anything else?"

"She probably snatched the Target gift card from someone on the beach. I doubt she would shop there," said Plum.

"Never," agreed Gerald.

"Good, what else?" asked Captain Diaz.

"Yes," said Plum, pointing to the wallet. "You said there are two thousand dollars in the wallet. Arielle pointedly told me that she never carries cash."

"She could have taken it out from the hotel," said Captain Diaz. "We must check."

"That's possible," said Plum. "But maybe someone gave it to her."

"You think she was a call girl?" asked Gerald, brightening and sitting up.

"No, well, actually, that didn't occur to me," said Plum. "I thought maybe she was blackmailing someone."

A glint of respect came into Captain Diaz's eyes. "That is possible," he said. "Very possible."

"Can we see the naked Polaroid?" asked Gerald.

Captain Diaz seemed about to demur but then reconsidered and handed it to them. The photo was blurry, as if the camera had been moving when the picture was taken. Arielle's long, blond hair was flying and covered her face, and it appeared as if she were wearing a lacy bra with matching underwear. A man was embracing her, his head turned away from the camera, and his only identifying feature was that he had a red arrow tattoo on his butt.

"He's fit," cooed Gerald mischievously.

"I wish I could recognize him, but you can't even see his face," said Plum.

"Yes, he is difficult to identify, except for the tattoo," remarked Captain Diaz.

Plum studied it. Had she seen anyone with that tattoo? She

didn't think so, but then again tattoos were so ubiquitous these days that she hardly even noticed them. She returned the Polaroid to the table and flitted her eyes across the remaining items. The snake-shaped bracelet could also have been pilfered. She didn't know anyone who was missing one, but she would be on the lookout. Ditto with the hair clip. She suddenly realized that she shouldn't only look for what was there, but for what wasn't.

"Where's her phone?" asked Plum suddenly.

"Ah, you noticed that it is missing," said Captain Diaz. "We have been unable to locate it at all. Her service provider says it is either off or destroyed, because they have no signal for her."

"I remember it had a purple case. She seemed quite attached to it, so I doubt she would go far without it," said Plum.

"I can confirm that," said Gerald. "It was another limb for her. I had to peel her off it in order to do her actual job."

"We will keep looking for it," said Captain Diaz.

They went through every item again, but nothing else stood out to either Plum or Gerald. Captain Diaz finally took mercy on them and drove them back to Plum's town house.

"Stay in touch," he said when Plum exited the car. "And," he hesitated. "Let me know if you hear anything."

"I will," she promised.

It dawned on her that it was much more pleasant to be working in tandem with the police than parallel to them. She would try to remember that.

12

"I'M STARVING," GERALD ANNOUNCED WHEN they were back in the town house. "And I absolutely do not want one of your homemade sandwiches. Let's go to Coconuts and get a decent lunch."

"You weren't complaining about my sandwich yesterday," said Plum. She was at her desk checking her messages on the computer.

"I wasn't hungover yesterday," said Gerald. "And besides, you need a break. You were completely rattled at the police station."

"True."

"It'll be my treat. And I'm going to put on my swim trunks, so after we eat, I can dunk myself. I think submerging in the water will help my headache."

"I can't hang at the beach. I have an important business meeting this evening," said Plum.

"That's fine, you can pick me up after. I'll segue from swimming to tanning time to cocktail time."

While he was changing, Plum opened an email from Juan Kevin. It was brief, which Plum knew meant that he was irritated.

> Went to inform Jessica Morse of her friend's death, but she said she had already been notified by a Plum Lockhart.

Plum did not like the tone of his email. *Juan Kevin had no reason to be mad,* steamed Plum. Jessica was going to learn sooner or later, and why not sooner? It wasn't her fault, and actually, he should be grateful that Plum had delivered the horrific news.

But there came a prick in her defensive shield, and she did feel a slight twinge of guilt. There was the small possibility that he had the right to be irked, she conceded to herself. Plum decided she would be the bigger person and extend an olive branch. She wrote him back that she and Gerald were heading down to Coconuts now for a late lunch and did he want to join them? She offered to update him on her visit to the police station if he came.

Juan Kevin hadn't answered before she left. He was probably carousing with the lady on the phone, who was no doubt a bombshell, Plum fumed. But then remembering that she had shifted into an exclusively professional relationship (in her mind) with Juan Kevin, she pushed the thoughts away and remained unaffected.

Coconuts, situated on Playa del Sol, consisted of a thatched-roof bar connected to an airy and spacious whitewashed restaurant. After parking the cart, she and Gerald ambled down the pebbled path that meandered through the powdery-white sand toward the restaurant perched on the edge of the sea. Paraison music played softly on the speakers, and the beach was cluttered with sunbathers sipping fruity cocktails. The afternoon sun was fierce and high in the sky, and Plum was grateful to slip into a wicker chair under the shaded double-height ceiling at the restaurant.

"Gorgeous," Gerald announced as he slid across from her. "There is nothing better than lunch with a view of the sea."

"I agree," said Plum, her eyes sweeping the coastline. Waves lapped at the craggy coral rocks beneath the edge of the restaurant.

A young girl was collecting seashells on the sand and carefully dropping them in her pink plastic bucket. There were older children squealing with delight on a raft floating in the shallow surf. Plum watched as a woman held up her ponytail and turned her back to a man, who rubbed sunscreen onto her shoulders. Her mind drifted, and she imagined what it would be like to have Juan Kevin massage sunblock onto her shoulders.

"Here you are," said the waiter, placing a basket of herbed flatbreads and a dish of plump kalamata olives on the bleached white table. Plum was immediately brought back to reality.

"Don't go away," warned Gerald, holding his finger up to the waiter and scanning the menu quickly. "I'm famished and need to order as soon as possible."

The waiter, whose name tag said *Franco*, smiled warmly. "Of course, sir, what can I bring you?"

"I'm extremely hungover, so I am going for grease. Let's see, I will have an all-American burger with cheddar cheese and bacon, cooked rare. Extra buffalo sauce, please. Definitely fries. And onion rings. And some fried yucca. And a Corona," said Gerald.

"That's a lot of food," remarked Plum.

"I'm on vacation!" sniffed Gerald. "I starve myself in New York. I have the right to let loose here."

"No judgment," said Plum.

"And for the lady?" asked the waiter.

Plum gave Gerald a snarky look. "Yes, so much for ladies first, Gerald."

"Oh, please, you're a feminist!" he sneered.

She rolled her eyes at him and returned her attention to the waiter. "May I please have the prawn and avocado salad with passion fruit dressing? And an iced tea."

"Of course," said the waiter.

"I'll have an iced tea also," said Juan Kevin, who materialized behind the waiter and sank into the chair next to Plum.

"Anything to eat, Senor Muñoz?" asked the waiter.

"No, thank you, Franco, I have already eaten," said Juan Kevin.

"I didn't expect you to come," said Plum. She was annoyed with the blooming pleasure she experienced.

She gave him the once-over. He was wearing his work uniform—blue blazer, well-pressed khakis, checked button-down shirt. As always, he appeared crisp, clean, and despite the humidity, unwrinkled. She glanced down with dismay at her own linen skirt, which was a mass of zigzagging creases. How could some people appear so pulled together in the tropics and others such a mess? And why was she in the latter camp and he in the former?

"Before you lecture me on Jessica Morse, I will say that I am sorry that I informed her of Arielle's death," began Plum. "It was brutal."

"See? It's not pleasant," said Juan Kevin.

Plum filled him in and answered his questions. When she was finished, he spoke.

"I heard you visited my friend Captain Diaz," said Juan Kevin. He leaned back in his seat.

"Yes," said Plum.

"She almost fainted," said Gerald mirthfully. He cracked off a large piece of flatbread and took a bite.

"Really?" asked Juan Kevin, with concern.

"Absolutely not," she said, staring daggers at Gerald.

"Oh, honey, there's no crime in being squeamish," he retorted.

Plum was about to explode; she did not appreciate Gerald outing her weaknesses, but Juan Kevin said gently, "I was disturbed when we saw her body. I thought I might faint then."

Plum relented. "I was really shaken into reality when I saw her belongings. It's strange, it had more of an effect on me to see what was in her handbag than to see her lying dead on the beach. I can't figure out why."

"Maybe something struck you that gave you a clue into who killed her," offered Juan Kevin.

"It's possible," said Plum.

As the waiter brought their drinks and later their food, Plum recounted the items that had been recovered from Arielle's purse. Plum mentioned that the two thousand dollars in cash and the Maxima makeup bag were particular red flags for her. She also declared that she thought the bracelets and hair clip might be contraband.

"And there was the laptop and charger," she said, pointedly. "Which means the charger we found in her bungalow remains a question mark."

Juan Kevin nodded. "Yes, I am still thinking about that."

Plum speared a chunk of avocado and a piece of shrimp and took a nibble. "Have you discovered anything on your end?" she asked.

"Unfortunately, yes," he said. "And it's mostly setbacks. The security cameras that are situated on Dieter Friedrich's beach and all the access points, including the dock and the staircase, were disabled. Therefore, we have no video footage of the crime."

"That's odd. Doesn't that mean it's an inside job?" asked Plum.

"Sure sounds like one," added Gerald, his mouth full of cheeseburger.

Juan Kevin shook his head. "Not necessarily. Of course, we looked at that angle first, but it seems that there was an electrical outage on the coast of the peninsula that evening. Charles Nettles's house also lost power along their beachfront."

"That could be connected," said Plum.

"It could be, but there is such bad blood between Dieter and Charles that I sincerely doubt they were in collusion," said Juan Kevin.

"It doesn't mean someone else wasn't in collusion with one of them," said Plum. She glanced down to take another bite of her salad and was astonished to discover that she had finished it.

"Come on, Juan Kev, tell me, do we have any suspects?" said Gerald, before devouring another chunk of burger. "I need to produce some intel for Arielle's father so he doesn't think I'm just down here partying and eating."

Plum arched her eyebrow and looked at him askance.

"I don't think we have a prime suspect yet," confessed Juan Kevin. "Everyone remains under the cloud of suspicion."

"You need to find out who was in the Polaroid with Arielle," said Plum. "Can you ask the men who were there the night of the murder to reveal if they have tattoos?"

"Not a bad idea," said Juan Kevin. "But we can only ask them, we can't demand they reveal their, ahem, buttocks."

"Then the one who refuses is guilty!" shrilled Gerald. "Oh, I love this, solving crime. So easy!"

"I wouldn't put the cart before the cheetah," said Juan Kevin.

"You mean before the horse," corrected Plum.

"The horse? Why the horse?"

"That's the phrase," she said. "Don't put the cart before the horse."

"Oh, in Paraiso the phrase is the cart before the cheetah," Juan Kevin replied.

Plum shook her head. There were so many random but subtle differences between Paraiso and the United States that she would never comprehend.

"Look who's here," said Gerald, a wicked glimmer in his eyes. "Maybe we can ask him to drop his pants and get it over with."

Plum and Juan Kevin turned and followed the direction of Gerald's gaze. They watched as Gary Grigorian and Hallie Corona were seated in a corner table. The busboy filled their water glasses and scurried off, and the couple was left staring at each other. Plum noticed that neither appeared happy. They both picked up their menus and gazed at them in silence. Then Gary looked at his phone and tapped an email. Plum swiveled back around and returned her attention to Juan Kevin and Gerald.

"Not their usual euphoric selves," she mused.

"No," agreed Juan Kevin.

"I thought they were supposed to be on Johnny Wisebrook's yacht today?" said Gerald. "Weren't they bragging about that?"

"You're right," said Plum. "Hallie did say that."

"Johnny had to depart for Miami unexpectedly today," said Juan Kevin. He brushed away the trail of breadcrumbs Gerald had scattered on the tablecloth. "I know because the police had wanted to interview him about the evening before Arielle's death, but he had some sort of emergency to attend to."

"Is that suspicious?" asked Plum.

"I don't think so," said Juan Kevin. "He often travels back and forth. I believe he has a child who resides there with her mother. And anyway, Johnny Wisebrook is not a serious suspect. He is a wonderful man."

"Oh, you're showing your bias!" said Plum.

"Yeah, rock stars can be murderers," said Gerald. "Tons of them have killed someone. Although I can't think of one at the moment…"

"I'm going to go and say hello to Hallie and Gary," said Plum, standing up. "Maybe I can get some information."

Hallie's miserable facial expression quickly morphed into one of ecstasy as soon as she saw Plum, and the latter couldn't help but think that perhaps Hallie was a much better actress than she had given her credit for. The closer Plum moved toward their table, the closer Hallie inched over toward her reluctant husband. She began stroking his hairy arm, an adoring gaze now firmly entrenched on her saggy face.

"Plum!" squealed Hallie. "How fun. Gary and I snuck away from the villa to have a romantic lunch alone, as we always love to do, but it is so wonderful to run into you. What are you up to?"

Gary stood and grazed both of her cheeks with a European-style kiss, which always annoyed Plum on so many levels, the first being that they had just seen each other the day before. Not only did she hate the social kiss, but the double whammy of the Euro one left her doubly bent out of shape. Now she had saliva on both of her cheeks. She wondered how she could subtly wipe off his spit without appearing offensive. Ah, the trappings of polite society!

"Wonderful to see you, Plum. Would you like to join us?" asked Gary, courteously.

"Thank you, but I'm just wrapping up lunch with Gerald and Juan Kevin. It's such a beautiful day, I thought you would be on Johnny's yacht?" asked Plum.

Gary and Hallie both spoke at once.

"He had to leave town," said Gary, while at the same time Hallie said, "We decided to have a romantic day together."

They gave each other aggravated glares. But then, as if realizing she had an audience, Hallie reached over and clutched Gary's hand. "We were so relieved to be able to slip away."

"I imagine the mood at Dieter's must be morose, with Arielle's death," said Plum.

"Not really," said Hallie, before quickly adding, "although it is tragic."

"Yes, we are so sorry for that tragedy," remarked Gary.

"I've heard they have made some progress," said Plum.

"Oh?" asked Hallie. She took a casual sip of water.

"Yes, apparently Arielle was having an affair with someone that she called 'Mr. Big.' And there is a photograph of him that was found in her possession, in which he is naked."

Plum watched Gary and Hallie carefully. She wanted to see if they were nervous or revealed anything that would suggest that Gary had been Arielle's lover. But unfortunately, neither seemed fazed.

"That's interesting," said Gary, breezily. "I hope they find him."

"Obviously it doesn't mean that Mr. Big killed her," said Hallie. "But maybe he can provide some information."

"Do you have any idea who it was?" asked Plum.

"How would we know?" asked Hallie, her eyes narrowing into slits.

"I just mean because you were with her on the last night of her life. Maybe you saw her with a man?"

"Honestly, we really didn't pay attention to her," said Gary. And this time it was he who initiated physical contact with his wife. He picked up her hand and kissed it. "My wife and I only have eyes for each other."

"Right," said Plum.

The waiter brought their drinks, and Plum knew that she shouldn't linger any longer. She said her goodbyes and returned to her table.

"They're not giving anything up," she told Juan Kevin and Gerald, as she sank back into her chair.

"What do you expect?" asked Gerald. "They're actors."

"He's a game show host," Plum corrected.

"Even worse," said Juan Kevin.

13

PLUM KNEW WHERE THE GATE to Alexandra Rijo's house was located—everyone at Las Frutas did—but when she pulled into the driveway, she thought there must be some mistake. Considering Alexandra's immense wealth and the fact that she owned Las Frutas, Plum had expected a giant mansion with all the bells and whistles lurking behind the thick hedge. Instead, she found an understated, Balinese-style beachfront cottage connected to two casitas by open walkways. Luxuriant green foliage hugged the exterior walls.

A uniformed maid showed her into the great room, which featured blood-mahogany floors, sumptuous, sink-in white sofas, teak chairs, and a dizzying array of rainbow-colored tropical plants. She had expected to find Picassos and Matisses, but the only artworks were framed family photographs, and, perhaps equally as beautiful as masterpieces, ocean views from every window.

Plum sunk down into the sofa, as instructed by the maid, and awaited her hostess. She heard children playing in a pool in the distance, and the soft hum of the birds outside. It was a relaxing retreat.

"Miss Lockhart," said an accented voice.

Plum shot up from her slumped position. "Yes, I'm Plum Lockhart."

Alexandra Rijo was in her early sixties but looked younger. Her dark hair was swept back into a chignon; her green eyes were lined but clever. She was immaculately put together. Plum took in the subtle gold jewelry that adorned her neck and wrists, including small gold hoops in her ears. She wore a tan shift dress and had excellent legs, with slim ankles and narrow feet shod in beige mules. She was the picture of elegance.

After brief introductions, which included Plum's enthusiastic compliments of the house and Alexandra's calm, patrician acceptance of her praise, they broached the topic of business.

"Some may call you greedy," said Alexandra, who sat across from Plum. A small, white Maltese had immediately joined his mistress in her chair and nestled into her lap. She stroked his soft, white hair.

"Greedy?" asked Plum with confusion.

"Yes. You already represent one Mrs. Rijo's rental property, and now you would like to represent the original Mrs. Rijo's property," Alexandra responded, referring to herself in the third person.

"I don't think I'm greedy," said Plum. "I'm ambitious."

"Ambitious. Yes, a masculine word. Very sexy when applied to men, harsh and demeaning when applied to women," said Alexandra.

"I couldn't agree more," said Plum truthfully. "When I worked in publishing, a number of times people said to me, 'You're so ambitious.' And I would reply, 'Thank you,' and they would say, 'It's not a compliment,' to which I would respond, 'Then why would you say it'?"

Alexandra laughed, and Plum felt as if she had broken the ice. "I don't doubt it," said Alexandra.

The maid came in and placed a tray with a china tea service on the table. There was a plate of small dulce de leche sponge cakes as well. The maid deftly poured the steaming tea and handed Plum a saucer and plate.

"Milk or sugar?" she asked.

"Milk, please," said Plum.

The maid placed a slice of lemon in Alexandra's tea and handed it to her. Alexandra took a dainty sip.

"Plum," said Alexandra when she had blotted her lips with a napkin. "Why do you think I should take my business away from Jonathan Mayhew and allow you to represent my villas? He has always done a good job for me. Reliable, steady."

"Thank you," Plum said to the maid, while accepting a napkin. She then turned to Alexandra. "That's not why I'm here."

"No?" asked Alexandra with surprise.

"No," said Plum.

Alexandra scrutinized her. Although she was all politeness and formality, there was something steely underneath her demeanor that made Plum feel uneasy. It wasn't that she was rude or appeared ruthless—it was life experience that exuded from Alexandra, as if she knew where the bodies were buried, as the saying goes. And it was evident that she was shrewd and sharp.

"Well, initially it was an idea of mine, I confess. I had planned on pitching you," said Plum. "But I realized that was stupid. I don't want to waste your time. I am a newcomer here. Jonathan Mayhew has done a good job for you, and I don't want to tussle with him."

"That's true," agreed Alexandra. "And I firmly believe in not fixing what isn't broken."

Plum nodded. "I wanted to meet you because now that I'm here to stay, and I have established my business, I would like to be more involved in philanthropic endeavors. I know you have done more than anyone on this island on behalf of charity. And I am aware that you are the founder and chairman of the Paraiso Animal Rescue Shelter. I thought perhaps I could offer my humble services."

Alexandra's eyes swept over Plum before she responded. It was only a few seconds before she spoke, but it was enough to make Plum second-guess herself. Had she laid it on too thick with the flattery and using the word *humble*? she wondered.

"That's a wonderful idea," said Alexandra finally. "We are always looking for people to help with our fundraising efforts."

"Great," said Plum. She took a sip of her tea. "I know that you just had your benefit, so I am sure there is downtime before the next one. You probably regroup in the fall?"

"Oh, no," said Alexandra. She placed her teacup in the saucer. "We start planning the day after the benefit. In fact, we have a meeting tomorrow. I would like for you to come."

Plum thought of her giant workload, the renovations that needed to be made to Villa Tomate, as well as her side project investigating Arielle Waldron's murder. She really didn't have time to toil on a benefit. What was she thinking? She loved being charitable but more in a theoretical check-writing capacity than getting her hands dirty. But perhaps it was all tea sandwiches and fake participation like many benefit committees. Surely Alexandra was not very hands-on.

"I would love to come," said Plum.

"Wonderful. The meeting tomorrow is two o'clock at Casa la Manzana. Wendy Nettles's villa," said Alexandra.

Before Plum could even process how fortuitous it was that she would get a chance to meet Mrs. Nettles, Martin Rijo strode into the room like a dark cloud appearing over a blue sky. He wore shiny athletic clothing over a white tank top, and a thick, gold chain hung around his bulky neck.

"Mamá, where are the keys to the Mercedes?" he asked, addressing Alexandra. He stopped dead when he saw Plum sitting across from his mother. His pugnacious eyes narrowed into hostile slits. "What's *she* doing here?"

Alexandra turned and faced her son. "Martin, that's very rude."

"You know she's friends with the whore?" he said.

Plum felt her face redden.

"Martin!" admonished Alexandra. She turned to Plum. "I'm sorry, Martin doesn't think before he speaks."

"Yes, I do," he growled.

"It's okay," said Plum, unsure what to say. She couldn't protest that she wasn't really *friends* with his stepmother, Carmen, that it was more of a work relationship. But either way it would not be good to go on record.

"She's in business with her," said Martin.

Alexandra spoke in a patient tone, the same that one might use with a toddler. "Martin, I am well aware that Miss Lockhart represents Number Two's rental property. She is here to talk about becoming involved in the animal shelter. As you know, it is a cause close to my heart."

He sneered and flexed his muscles. Plum's eyes were immediately drawn to the ropes of veins that bubbled under the skin of his arms.

"I don't trust her."

"Please leave, Martin," said Alexandra. "The keys are in the dish in the front hall."

Martin stood in place long enough to give Plum a dangerous stare. He made her feel shaky and disconcerted. He finally stomped out of the room.

"I'm sorry about that," said Alexandra. She smoothed her skirt and then picked up her teacup and took a sip.

"It's okay," said Plum.

"Martin is very protective of me. When his father left me for Number Two, he took it personally. He wants to make sure I am okay."

"I understand," said Plum. "If I may be so bold, Martin seems very different from you."

"Oh, he is," said Alexandra. "He's not our biological child. We adopted him when he was five."

Plum nodded sympathetically while Alexandra continued.

"Unfortunately, he had a terrible early childhood."

"That's too bad," said Plum. She thought of her own childhood. Her parents were punitive and neglectful, and worst of all, completely apathetic toward her. But she had made her own way, changed her name (from the hideous Vicki Lee to Plum), moved to New York, and worked tirelessly to ascend the corporate ladder.

Alexandra motioned to a picture on the table next to her chair. It was of a handsome man with a blond woman, holding a baby.

"That's my other son Julian with his wife, Susan, and my first grandchild, a girl named Lillian. I adore her. Susan is wonderful as well, and Julian runs our family foundation."

"I hope to meet him," said Plum.

Alexandra looked pensive. "Yes, he is settled now. Always bumpy with boys, but Julian is thriving. I hope that Martin will soon be too. He was very angry when Emilio left the family for Number Two."

When she said the last part, Alexandra's face darkened.

"That's tough," said Plum.

Alexandra waved her hand in the air. "Enough of that. We will meet again tomorrow at the Nettleses'. We will discuss your participation in the animal shelter. You will not be at a loss for things to do! We need active participants."

Plum groaned inwardly. "Can't wait!" She beamed.

When Plum walked out to her golf cart, she found Martin Rijo leaning against his Mercedes, arms folded, glowering at her. She could tell he was waiting for her and that made her nervous. She tried to casually walk to her cart, but he stepped in front of her, blocking her route.

"Excuse me," she said, feigning a relaxed tone, but her voice quavered.

"I won't," he said.

She stared at his beefy arms and clenched fists and prayed to God that Alexandra had a high-tech security system where there were armed guards watching the driveway, ready to swoop in and save her.

"Look, I think we got off on the wrong foot," she began.

"You bet we did," he growled.

"It is true that I represent some of Carmen's properties..."

As soon as she said the name *Carmen,* Martin spat on the ground. *This is not going well,* thought Plum.

"Okay, well it's business. Surely you understand business?" she asked.

Martin sucked in his breath. "I understand business. But there are ways to do things on Paraiso. And more especially, ways to do things at Las Frutas. And I am giving you a warning: you're on the wrong track. You'll not last long here if you align yourself with Number Two. She was sent from the devil, and she will return to the devil. Make sure you're not riding on her back when she heads back down to hell."

Martin's eyes remained locked on hers. She finally glanced down at the ground. He obviously took that as a concession and strode past her and got into his mother's Mercedes convertible. He gunned the engine then took off. Plum felt as if her knees were knocking.

14

"GUESS WHO I MET AND am going out to dinner with tonight?" shrieked Gerald gleefully.

Despite the late hour, Plum had found him still reclining in a lounge chair at the beach, sipping a daiquiri and listening to music with his earbuds.

"No idea," said Plum. She was still too shaken by Martin to humor Gerald with a conjecture.

"Cornelia Nettles!" he said, sitting up and swinging his legs around the edge of the chaise.

"Cornelia Nettles?" asked Plum.

"She's Charles and Wendy Nettles's daughter," he explained. "Dieter Friedrich's neighbors. She's so chic and fun."

"I'm supposed to meet her mother tomorrow," said Plum. "At a meeting for a charity event."

"Snooze," said Gerald. "I mean, have you really sunk so low? You may as well say you're meeting her mom for a colonoscopy."

"It could be a good lead! She might enlighten me on the feud between Dieter and her husband," said Plum defensively. She sank into the lounge across from Gerald.

"Forget the mother!" yelped Gerald. "Cornelia could be a good lead for you! She knows everything."

"Really?" asked Plum. She slipped off her shoes.

"Yes, Cornelia's like a search engine. I was throwing out names, and she could rattle off all sorts of tidbits."

"Right up your alley," said Plum.

"Totally," agreed Gerald. "And the bonus is that Cornelia is a blast. Just like a surge of energy. She totally sought me out. I was in the water, trying to swim my hangover away, and Corn and her friends were on a raft discussing favorite bands, and we were so in sync! She suggested we go out tonight, and we are meeting them at the sushi place at the marina."

"Gerald, it's a workday for me," said Plum, wiggling her toes in the sand. "You have to remember I'm not on vacation."

"Um, I mean, hello? I'm *technically* not on vacation either," said Gerald, who then took a giant sip of his daiquiri. He removed the umbrella from the frosted glass and placed it behind his ear.

"I thought you said you were on vacation?" asked Plum.

"Did I?" mused Gerald. He shrugged. "I'm on a workation."

"Not sure I know the difference."

"It doesn't matter. Just don't be a buzzkill. Consider this a workation for you as well. Remember, you find out who murdered Arielle, and her father—who owns an entire publishing empire that can make or break your career comeback—will owe you big time. We are basically doing this for your future!"

"Sounds devious."

"It is what it is. So buckle up honey, put on your fancy shoes and your lacy underwear, because we are going out on the town!"

The marina was buzzing. Situated where the La Cereza River meets the Caribbean Sea, the marina accommodated up to three hundred and fifty yachts and was designed by an Italian architect inspired by the seaside villages in the Mediterranean. Within the marina complex were villas, town houses, and a wide variety of restaurants and shops. Most of the restaurants were centered around a piazza (reminiscent of St. Mark's Place or other famed squares in Italian cities), and tables from each restaurant spilled into one another. There was a Paraison restaurant, an Italian restaurant, a tapas restaurant, and a sushi restaurant, where Cornelia Nettles and her friends Amber and Maia were holding court.

The evening was warm, with nary a breeze despite the proximity of the water. Unfortunately, that allowed for a slight, pungent smell from the nearby stagnant salt water and the fish that resided in it. The moon was high, and the dark sky was clotted with stars overlapping one another. Plum and Gerald were ushered to their table by a perky waiter. Plum wore a light-pink dress with spaghetti straps and sandals and had a light-violet shawl draped around her arm in case the weather turned cool. She hadn't bothered with her hair tonight and had instead allowed her curls to cascade around her shoulders, much to Gerald's disdain. He'd begged her to use her straightening iron, but she hadn't had the time or energy to primp, which resulted in him branding it a cop-out.

"Oh my god, you came!" squealed Cornelia.

She stood to embrace Gerald as if he were her long-lost brother before turning to Plum.

"So nice to meet you!" she enthused as she shook Plum's hand.

Cornelia was striking. She had an angular face with a strong nose, wide mouth, and perfect teeth. Her hair was a dirty blond, and she wore it in a loose knot. Her outfit was unmemorable—a light-colored tunic over a skirt or pants, Plum couldn't decipher, that covered her ample curves. She smiled warmly, and Plum liked her at once.

Amber and Maia were equally bubbly but more forgettable. Honestly, after the night was done, if Plum had had to pick them out of a lineup, she wasn't sure she could have. But they were relaxing dinner companions.

"Gerald has told me all about you," remarked Cornelia when introductions were over.

The way she said it made Plum feel as if Cornelia and Gerald had been life-long friends and she had only now entered the equation.

"Oh, really? Like what?" asked Plum.

Before Cornelia could answer, the waiter arrived, and Cornelia and Gerald embarked on ordering epic amounts of sushi. Plum stared at the menu and listened as they ticked off items, reciting each sushi roll and special roll and chef's suggestion. She mentally calculated the prices, noting that, for some reason, raw fish cost more than cooked fish and that copious amounts were required to fill you up. The tally in her mind ran to the several hundreds of dollars, and Plum fervently hoped that Gerald planned to expense it. She thought about Lucia chiding her for spending too much money in restaurants.

"I was telling you what Gerald had said about you," Cornelia reminded Plum when the waiter was gone. Plum was grateful that she didn't have to repeat the question and that Cornelia had remembered. Plum attributed that to good manners.

"Yes, what *did* our Gerald say?" asked Plum. She picked up an edamame out of the dish that the waiter had placed down on the table and began sucking the beans out of the pod.

"He said that you are very smart. That you are on Paraiso to regroup, but he thinks you are spinning your wheels and wasting your time and you need to get back to New York and save the publishing world," said Cornelia. She smiled.

"That's very flattering," said Plum. She turned toward Gerald and eyed him skeptically. "But I know Gerald very well, and I have an extremely hard time believing that he really said that."

"Obviously," confessed Gerald before quickly adding, "I don't want to refute my new BFF Corn, but that's not exactly what I said."

"Oh, it was the sentiment!" said Cornelia.

"You are too nice," said Gerald. He turned to Plum. "I told you, she is such a doll!"

Plum ignored him and stared at Cornelia. "I'm more interested in you, Cornelia. What do you do? Do you live here full time?"

"I'm very boring, not like you guys with your brilliant careers," she said modestly. "I'm kind of a trust-fund baby. Oh, I went to Brown and got my masters in art history from Bard, but I basically just buy paintings for my father's museum—I'm the director of Nettles Art Foundation, a glorified title. My father decided that he owed it to the world to allow everyone to visit his collection, and he put me in charge."

"That's interesting," said Plum genuinely. "I'm sure you meet a lot of fascinating people."

"Not really," said Cornelia. She leaned back in her seat as the waiter placed trays of dumplings and rock shrimp tempura in front of her. "I meet a lot of people who kiss my ass. Pardon my French. But they all want our foundation to buy their art and put it in our museum. I used to think art was judged by merit, but now I realize it's just a game. Whoever schmoozes the biggest art buyers wins."

"Sweetie!" exclaimed Gerald. "Don't be so down on yourself! I know for a fact your foundation makes a huge difference."

Cornelia shrugged. "Maybe. It was very exciting in the beginning, when I thought it was all about craft and skill. I'm less enamored now that I know it's a popularity contest."

Gerald shrugged. "Who cares? You're young and pretty. I'm sure you're totally distracted by all the men banging down your door."

"I wish," said Cornelia.

"Come on," said Gerald.

"There are very few. And the ones I like are always deemed unsuitable by my parents. I guess my problem is I like a 'little bit of rough,' as my British nanny used to say. I'm tired of the generic, entitled guys I grew up with. Here's our food!" she exclaimed.

The waiter began to bring tray after tray of Japanese delicacies. There was every variation of sushi and sashimi, as fresh as if the fish had just been caught five minutes prior. After several rounds of sake, Gerald challenged Cornelia and her friends to go head-to-head with him on shots. Plum pretended to imbibe but discreetly sipped her drinks. She wanted to remain sober to continue to glean any information she could from Cornelia. When she could tell that Cornelia seemed significantly buzzed, she decided to raise the hard-hitting questions.

"May I ask about your neighbor? Dieter Friedrich?" Plum inquired.

She braced herself for Cornelia's face to darken and for her to ultimately spew a venomous response. She could not have been more surprised by Cornelia's reaction.

"Dieter is a riot," said Cornelia with a laugh. "He is so much fun. His parties are epic!"

"But," said Plum, confused, "isn't he feuding with your father?"

Cornelia shrugged. "I guess. But you know, neighbors always get on each other's nerves. They fight, they're friends, it's fluid."

"But I thought they hated each other?" Plum pressed.

"Don't believe what you read in the news," said Cornelia. She popped a spicy tuna roll in her mouth. "They want to sell papers. You should know that, right?"

She was right. Plum should know that. How many times had she written travel stories inflating dramas or exaggerating details? But those were travel stores, and this was real. "But didn't they try to kill each other?" she asked.

"Plum!" scolded Gerald. He gave her a look of disdain as if to warn her she had gone too far. But it was too late, she couldn't back down.

"Sorry if I'm being too blunt," added Plum. "Occupational hazard."

"No worries," said Cornelia breezily. "Yes, apparently they each said they wanted to kill the other. But they weren't serious. It was a silly noise dispute. We're all friends now."

"Plum is being ridiculous," announced Gerald. He glared at Plum. "Of course, we know your dad and Dieter were not homicidal. She's watched too many television shows."

"Well, there was a murder at Dieter's house," conceded Cornelia.

"We'd heard that too," said Plum coyly. "Do you know anything about it?"

"No," said Cornelia quickly. "I mean..."

"What?" asked Plum.

Cornelia paused. "I did meet Arielle. It's a strange coincidence, but I was at the pool with Amber and Maia..."

When she said their names, both of her friends turned and nodded. They smiled eagerly.

"And what happened when you met her?" prompted Plum.

"I don't know," said Cornelia. "The girls and I went to the spa, and afterward we went in the hotel pool to get all that icky body oil off of us, and she was in the pool, standing by the edge, yelling at her friend, who then left. Then she turned to us and said, 'Oh, my friend is such a bitch. She ran off with the guy I like. She's only after him because I liked him.'"

Jessica, thought Plum. *And Max*. "Did she seem really angry?"

"Not sure, I didn't know her," said Cornelia.

"Was that your only interaction?" asked Plum.

"Yes," said Cornelia.

"Did she introduce herself?" asked Plum.

"No," said Cornelia.

"That was the extent of your conversation?" asked Plum.

"Yes," said Cornelia, giving her a wary look.

"Jeez, Plum," said Gerald. "Back off. You are like the Grand Inquisitor. She said that was it."

"Right, I just thought maybe you talked with her more," said Plum.

"Nope," said Cornelia. She then turned and began chatting with her friends.

Plum hesitated but then asked, "How did you make the connection that it was Arielle who died?"

"Excuse me?" asked Cornelia.

"Well, how did you know it was Arielle who was in the pool, complaining about her friend, if she didn't even introduce herself?"

Cornelia stared at her blankly. Finally, she said, unconvincingly, "I guess she did introduce herself."

But for the first time, Cornelia's words didn't ring true to Plum. There was something that Cornelia wasn't telling her. She would have to get to the bottom of it.

At that moment a giant, one-hundred-and-fifty-foot yacht slowly navigated its way to the marina. It was a beauty, mused Plum. The boat was called *Moving Target*, in reference to Johnny Wisebrook's iconic band. A huge crew was at the helm, pulling it into moor.

"That must be Johnny Wisebrook's boat," said Gerald. "I love it, so big and fancy. I hope he'll give me a ride on it one day."

Cornelia turned around and looked at it before turning back to Gerald and Plum. Her face was angry. "I'm no fan of that scumbag."

Plum's ears pricked. "Really? Why?"

"He's a predator," said Cornelia firmly. "A manipulative jerk. The people on Paraiso and at Las Frutas think he's so wonderful because he says hi to everyone and signs all these autographs and does these charity events. But let me tell you, he is a monster. No friend to women."

"How do you know?" asked Plum.

"Trust me," Cornelia said with certainty. "You don't want to be anywhere near him. He hits on everyone."

15

DESPITE GERALD AND PLUM'S HALF-HEARTED insistence on paying the check, Cornelia put down her black American Express card and treated everyone. Her friends Amber and Maia didn't even make an attempt to chip in. The way they acted, it was normal for Cornelia to pay. Plum supposed when your father is a billionaire, a few plates of sushi don't make much of a dent.

When they returned home, Gerald was tipsy and exhausted and decided to retire for the night. It wasn't even a solid ten minutes before Plum heard his snores drifting through the town house. She made herself a cup of hibiscus tea and sat down at her desk and clicked on her computer. Plum began an internet search on Johnny Wisebrook. Because he had been a famous rock star, there were tons of links that appeared in the search engine, requiring her to narrow her quest. She typed in *Johnny Wisebrook, women, predator*. Several items popped up.

Now, Plum knew enough to take everything with a grain of salt. Being a celebrity meant you were an open target, and people came out of the woodwork to accuse celebrities of different things. There were always long-lost relatives, shunned classmates, and begrudged waiters who cashed in their fifteen minutes of fame by charging a famous person with some bad deed. But after weeding through the obvious crazies, Plum found an article in a respectable newspaper from two years prior that did a roundup of all the legitimate-sounding women who had accused Johnny of being sleazy.

There were two women who piqued Plum's interest. Both described Johnny as heavily pursuing them on a beach, and one of them called him a "gross, old man," while the other one called him a "letch." He didn't assault or attack either of them, so nothing ever came of their accusations, but Plum wondered what if perhaps Johnny was provoked by being rebuffed and decided to kill someone.

Plum sat back in her chair and stretched her arms over her head. She was tired, but this was an interesting lead. Could Johnny have tried to have his way with Arielle and, when she fought back, killed her? It was possible. Arielle was a known celebrity stalker, but maybe he pushed her too far? Plum copied the link and put it in an email then sent it to Juan Kevin. She wrote a question mark in the subject line.

She looked through some of the other articles, but none appeared to be as damning as the one she sent to Juan Kevin. Lots of unsubstantiated claims by spurned lovers looking for a payout. She started to get up from her desk when her email pinged. It was Juan Kevin. He asked if she could talk. Plum dialed his number.

"What made you decide to look into Johnny?" Juan Kevin asked by way of greeting when he answered the phone.

"I met Cornelia Nettles tonight, and she is definitely not a fan of his. She called him a monster."

Juan Kevin was quiet on the other end of the phone. Plum strained her ears to hear if someone was with him at his house, but it was silent. She felt relieved and glad that he was alone then mad at herself for caring.

"You know...I have heard buzz about Johnny before," said Juan Kevin, finally. "I always brushed it off, because you know..."

"Because you think he's so wonderful? Because he's famous?"

"Maybe," Juan Kevin admitted. "But maybe there was something to the rumors."

"Definitely worth checking out," said Plum.

"I'll get on that tomorrow," he said. "Thanks for alerting me to the article."

"Do you know if the police have any leads?" she asked.

"If they do, they're not saying," said Juan Kevin. "And I'm busy doing damage control. It is not good for Las Frutas to have another murder. I'm trying to contain it."

"That will be difficult," said Plum.

"Yes and no," said Juan Kevin. "The fact that Arielle was the daughter of a media baron helps. He has forbidden his magazines and newspapers from reporting on it as he and his family grieve."

"Good luck with that," said Plum. "It's going to get out, and the press will be crawling around soon enough. They're vermin," she added, ignoring the fact that she'd been one of those vermin herself not too long ago.

"Yes," agreed Juan Kevin. "We're being extremely careful about who we let into the resort. We are not letting anyone make new reservations, only those with standing ones are allowed in. That way we know they are legitimate vacationers."

"Smart."

There was a pregnant pause where Plum wanted to ask him what he was doing and suggest getting together, but she didn't have the nerve. Finally, he spoke.

"Well, get some sleep. I'll probably talk to you tomorrow," he said.

"Okay, good night."

She went to bed angry at herself for the missed opportunity. She could have asked him over for a casual drink to discuss business. That and nothing else. There was nothing untoward suggested. Why had they suddenly become strangers? They'd been on the brink of a real friendship (and possibly more) a month ago. Had she driven him away with her own insecurity? She put her pillow over her head, ignored the buzzing mosquito, and forced herself to sleep.

Lucia was able to tap into her network of friends at the resort and learn that Shakira Perez, Dieter's girlfriend, took a dance-based cardio fitness class every morning at the hotel gym. Plum decided it would be a good time to ask her a few questions, especially since Dieter would not be around. *Isolate the subject* was a command that Plum had learned on an interrogation website.

Although she hadn't exercised in months (maybe years), Plum was undaunted by attending the class. She put on a pair of Tory Burch sweatpants (more of a fashion statement than actual athletic wear) and the only T-shirt that she owned, which had been part of a promotional package she had received during her editorial days. It was from a now-defunct hotel that had targeted wealthy, single millennials. It had pictures of famous couples emblazoned on the purple shirt, and the inscription said, "Find eternal love like they did." Sadly, all of the couples featured had split up.

The hotel gym was located near the spa. It had the requisite sports equipment—treadmills, StairMasters, elliptical machines, weights, as well as a smoothie bar. Upon check-in at the reception, Plum was offered a small towel the size of a cocktail napkin, which had clearly spent many turns in the dryer judging by its hard surface and lack of fuzz, as well as a bottle of water. She glanced around at the other women who were checking in but did not see Shakira.

They were ushered into a studio where a perky and petite Paraison woman with an enviable figure identified herself as Coco and immediately warned them that they would be sweating like never before. The other participants were obviously familiar with the program and instantly cheered then merged into two rows, like a chorus line. Plum somehow ended up front and center just a few feet from Coco. When the teacher went to turn on the music, Plum glanced around the room one more time and was relieved to see Shakira in the corner. Even in workout clothes, she looked very glamorous, and the tight spandex leggings and tank top that she wore accentuated her curves.

Then suddenly the room descended into darkness and a disco ball dropped. Strobe lights began to highlight individuals in the studio as the music blared at a level that Plum thought probably carried to the Nettleses' villa. Coco began dancing at a frenzied pace, clapping her hands, moving left and right, and to Plum's horror and consternation, everyone else did the same. After thirty seconds Plum was panting as if she had run up Mount Everest as fast as she possibly could. *How were these women able to clap and keep the beat?* she wondered.

There was a strong chance that she might be sick.

Coco noticed Plum was struggling and moved over to her. A strobe light immediately focused on Plum, and she could not have felt more exposed.

"What's your name?" Coco bellowed.

Plum was so out of breath, she could barely talk. "Plum," she whispered between gasps.

"Okay, Plum, let's get going. Ladies! Let's give it up for Plum! She needs all your encouragement!"

While Coco clapped, the ladies immediately began cheering and yelling, "Go, Plum! You can do it!" They didn't even break their routine as they did so.

Plum smiled weakly. Everyone had their eyes on her, especially Coco, who kept nodding along and staring at Plum flailing under the glare of the spotlight. Plum thought of people escaping prison and the light from the towers tracking them in the courtyard and considered this situation not dissimilar.

Despite Coco's encouragement and the ladies "giving it up for her," after the first song ended, Plum excused herself to go to the bathroom and never returned.

It didn't matter that the rest of the class was thirty more minutes, because Plum took that time to sit on the bench outside and recover. At first she had to put her head between her legs so she wouldn't throw up, but after she guzzled three of the water bottles that the kind receptionist bestowed upon her, she began to feel less dizzy. She could not imagine that people did this every day. And by choice.

When the class ended, people began filtering out. Plum was amazed to notice that some of the women didn't even appear to have broken a sweat. Their makeup (who wears makeup to work out?) was still perfectly in place, and only a few dabbed themselves with a towel. Meanwhile, Plum had lasted five minutes and had sweat stains all over her clothing.

She saw Shakira dart out and begin to head to the locker room. Plum quickly followed.

"Shakira!" she said.

Shakira turned around and looked at her blankly.

"It's Plum Lockhart. We met at Dieter's the other day."

"Oh, right," said Shakira. She didn't look convinced that she had met Plum, which the latter found offensive.

"I wanted to ask you about Arielle Waldron," began Plum.

"What about her?" asked Shakira.

"I'm a friend of the family," lied Plum, "and we are trying to find answers. I wonder if you have any idea of what happened. Or who might have killed her."

"That is for the police to decide, no?" she asked. She began to walk toward a locker, and Plum followed suit.

"Yes, of course, but maybe you had some ideas."

"No," said Shakira. She picked up a towel from the clean stack by the wall. "I did not know the girl."

"But I heard that you whispered something about the Nettleses and Dieter saying to get rid of the girl," said Plum.

Shakira took a moment to dab herself with her towel before she responded. "I do not remember that."

"Even after she was killed, you didn't remember that you didn't want her there?"

"Many people come to the villa."

Shakira typed in a combination, and the locker door swung open. She pulled out a giant Maxima bag and placed it on the bench in front of her. She reached in and retrieved her cell phone and scanned the messages, and then, as if deciding there was nothing important, dumped the phone back inside. She then pulled out a Lucite cosmetic bag, the cheap kind that one might pick up at a pharmacy. It had a brush, some lip gloss, blush, foundation, eyeliner, mascara, and eye shadow in it.

"That's very organized to bring your makeup to the gym," said Plum, attempting to continue the conversation and lead it on a friendlier path.

"I do not shower here, too dirty. But I need my makeup to refresh before I leave," she said. "Didn't you bring yours?"

"No," confessed Plum. It hadn't even occurred to her.

"You're single," said Shakira, more as a statement than a question.

"Yes," Plum confirmed.

Shakira took her bag and walked to the mirror. "I always carry it with me wherever I go. But I keep an eye on it now. My makeup kit was stolen the other day. I am very angry. It had my favorite skin cream in it."

A light bulb went off in Plum's head. "What kind of makeup kit was it?"

Shakira was staring at herself in the mirror as she meticulously applied eyeliner. "What do you mean?"

"I mean, what label was the bag?"

"It was Maxima. Such a pity. Went with my gym bag. I had the set," Shakira said. "I hope the little bitch who stole it has an allergic reaction to my makeup."

After the gym Plum headed over to Villa Tomate to do a walk-about and assess the progress. She also wanted to make sure the handymen, painters, and landscapers had shown up for work on time, which unfortunately was sometimes considered optional in Paraiso. Plum was on a tight schedule if she wanted to be able to rent it quickly.

Plum thought about her conversation at the gym. It had to have been Shakira's makeup kit that Arielle stole, but the question was, did Shakira know that? Did she love that makeup kit so much, she would kill Arielle for it? Probably not. But it could be one reason she wanted to banish her from the house.

Plum was pleased with the progress of the villa. The walls had been painted, and the artisans were grouting the broken tiles. After leaving the villa in the hands of the workmen, she was heading back to her office when she saw Gary Grigorian in a golf cart, turning into the hotel. He was alone, which appeared to be an anomaly for him, what with his desperate wife always hanging all over him, and Plum couldn't resist the opportunity to chat with him without her pesky interference. Perhaps he would be more candid.

Gary was already inside the hotel lobby when she entered, and she saw that he veered into the gift shop. Plum followed suit. It was an elegant little boutique that sold the requisite candy bars, magazines, and paperback novels but also offered a wide variety of shirts, baseball caps, fleeces, and other paraphernalia emblazoned with the Las Frutas logo. Additionally, there was an entire wall with racks of expensive bathing suits, tunics, and cover-ups, marked up to extremely high prices to take advantage of those poor souls who had forgotten their beach outfits. Plum found Gary at the counter, chatting with a pretty saleswoman helping him select a cigar from the giant humidor.

"I'd like a big one," said Gary.

The woman eyed him flirtatiously. "I think I know what you mean."

Gary put the cigar in his fingers. "Yes, this will do."

"Hi, Gary," said Plum.

Gary quickly swung around gave her a look as if he had been caught in a scandalous act. "Plum, I'm buying a cigar."

"So I see," she said.

"Hallie doesn't like me to smoke. I have to sneak around. That's why you scared me," he explained.

Is that why you nearly jumped out of your skin? Plum wanted to ask. *Or is it because you were flirting with the saleswoman? No wonder Hallie keeps you on a tight leash.*

"I don't blame her," said Plum. "I can't stand the smell of cigar smoke. Or any smoke for that matter."

Gary gave her a charming smile, the kind she had seen him use on old lady contestants who got the wrong answer on his stupid game show.

"I'll make sure not to smoke anywhere near you," he said. He pulled out his wallet and handed the saleswoman his credit card.

"How are things going at Dieter's?" asked Plum.

"Fine," Gary replied blandly.

"Are the police swarming all over? Is everyone being interviewed?" asked Plum.

Gary gave her neutral stare. "No. They questioned us, but it's pretty obvious none of us had anything to do with the murder, so they're looking elsewhere."

"Huh," said Plum. "No one is a suspect?"

Gary cocked his head to the side. "You really think one of us would have killed her? We didn't even know her."

"You never met her before?" Plum pressed.

"Where would I have met her?"

"I don't know, but I was curious," said Plum.

Gary gave her a haughty look. "It's possible I met her. I'm a celebrity, and people come up to me all the time and want an autograph or to take my picture. I cannot one hundred percent deny that I may have met her."

The saleswoman returned and handed Gary back his credit card, as well as his cigar in a little pouch. He thanked her, and she gave him a coquettish wink. Plum was repulsed. Gary wasn't even handsome but because he was a minor celebrity some women threw themselves at him?

"Nice seeing you," said Gary, who then left the store before Plum could fire any more questions at him.

She lingered for a bit, as if to emphasize that she was not following him, then exited the store.

When Plum exited the hotel, she approached her golf cart and was about to pull out her key when she saw Gary emerge from a side door of the hotel and walk out to the veranda in the company of a pretty, redheaded woman. She was wearing a dark-blue dress that was a bit formal, and high-heel pumps. Gary craned his neck around, as if making sure no one could see them, and Plum quickly darted behind a truck that was parked next to her. When she peeked out, she saw that Gary and the woman were talking in the corner of the veranda. Gary's back was to her, so Plum was obscured from his view. She was able to study the woman, who was listening intently.

Plum slunk her way around the truck and kept her body low to the ground. She crept toward the edge of the veranda and crouched down in front of the neatly clipped bushes that lined the hotel. Plum felt fairly hidden from their view; that is, unless Gary and his companion craned their necks searching for someone below, which was unlikely. From this location, she was able to hear their conversation as long as she ignored the quizzical looks from departing guests who undoubtedly wondered why she was lurking in the grass.

"We can't be seen together," Gary said.

"I know, I know," said the woman.

"No one can know you're here," Gary insisted.

"Don't worry, I was super careful. And I'm sorry that I made you come to the hotel, but I had to talk to you about…her."

"We don't have to worry about her," said Gary. "I told you."

"Are you sure?" asked the woman, her voice uncertain. "I'm scared for you. It just seems like you might be exposed. I think you're vulnerable."

"No one saw, no one knows," insisted Gary.

"Well, except…"

"He's not a problem," said Gary.

"But what about the evidence…"

"It's taken care of. No one will ever see it," said Gary.

"How can you be so sure?" asked the redhead.

"Money talks," said Gary with certainty. "And now I really have to go, Hallie is waiting for me. I don't want her to come looking, she'll get everyone involved, and then you will be discovered."

"Okay, okay."

"I'm going to see you soon enough," said Gary. "Don't worry, we won't need to hide much longer."

"Yes," sighed the redhead. "It's all this sneaking around that puts me on edge. I'm not used to it."

"Me neither. I'm counting down the minutes. I'll catch you later."

Plum heard Gary move and quickly scampered around the edge of the hotel, practically diving into a bush. She pressed her entire body into it, the spiky branches stabbing her in the back, and wished she could camouflage herself. Fortunately, Gary was in too much of a rush to glance her way, and she only saw the back of him thundering down the stairs. She waited until he had tucked himself into his car and then unfurled herself from the bush. After brushing herself off, she glanced up and realized with horror that she was face-to-face with the redhead. The woman appeared disconcerted to see Plum emerging from the foliage.

"Oh, sorry," said Plum. She instantly improvised. "I was playing hide-and-seek with my son. You didn't see a small boy, about two years old, wearing a sailor suit?"

The redhead gave her a concerned look. "No, do you need help searching for him?"

"That's okay, I'm sure he'll turn up," said Plum lightly.

"Yes, but he's only two years old? There's lots of water around here. What if he's gone missing?" she said urgently.

"I'm not worried. He's a good swimmer," said Plum. "And if he doesn't turn up, que será, será."

"You can't be serious," said the redhead.

"Of course I am," said Plum, but she decided she had to make a break for it. "Anyway, thanks, I'll check the beach."

She darted away and left the red-haired woman shaking her head.

16

THAT LITTLE SNEAK IS DEFINITELY *having an affair*, Plum decided. Should she feel guilty that she was secretly pleased? Hallie was so smug and braggy; it was irritating that she tried to project the image of domestic bliss when her husband was cheating on her. But it wasn't nice for Plum to take pleasure in someone else's pain, so she decided to feel very sorry for Hallie. She would be extra sympathetic the next time she saw her.

Plum wondered how long the affair had been going on. And obviously he had stashed the redhead at the hotel because he couldn't bear to be away from her. They must have been seen by someone, a man, and Plum wondered who it was that could possibly expose them.

Plum was waiting at the stop sign for a large tractor to do a three-point turn (which it was doing at a snail's pace) when a Jaguar with tinted windows pulled up next to her. Suddenly, the window in the back slid down, revealing the fully made-up face of Carmen Rijo, aka Number Two, aka the Second Mrs. Emilio Rijo.

"I thought that was you, Plum," said Carmen.

Carmen Rijo was undeniably breathtaking. While her predecessor, Alexandra, was a subtle and classic beauty, Carmen was a bombshell. She had long, glossy, dark hair, plump lips, feline eyes fringed with thick eyelashes, and creamy, caramel skin. Carmen exuded sexiness and femininity, and it was easy to see why men fell to their knees for her. She was smart but cunning, her only weakness her belief in black magic.

"Hello, Carmen, how are you?"

"I'm very well. I have been meaning to talk with you."

"Oh, about what?"

Plum noticed the tractor trailer had gone and there was a car behind her, but she didn't want to blow off Carmen.

"I have heard you were planning on doing business with my beloved late husband's ex-wife. I hope that is not true."

Plum gulped. "It's not," said Plum. She was grateful she had not pitched Alexandra so she could answer honestly.

Carmen raised an eyebrow. "Are you telling me the truth?"

"Of course, I'm telling you the truth," said Plum smoothly. "I cannot believe you would even deign to ask me that. Who do you think I am? Do we not have a very successful business arrangement? Why would I jeopardize that?"

A car behind Carmen's honked, but she appeared nonplussed. "That's good to know, Plum. Because I do not want the person who represents my properties to work with that woman. Do you understand?"

"Absolutely," said Plum, nodding.

Carmen gazed at her for another few seconds before motioning to her driver to continue. The car behind Plum honked, and she turned to leave as well. *This island is too small,* she thought. News traveled at record speed. She would have to be more careful.

Gerald was in a tizzy when Plum returned to the town house. He had risen early to complete the graphics for the magazine's latest issue, which had made him completely irritable due to the island's snail-paced Wi-Fi. Then, Arielle's father, Gerald's boss, had called and was apoplectic. He accused Gerald of not doing anything to help find his daughter's killer and said he was just squandering his money, exploiting the Waldron family's grief, pretending to help, and enjoying a Caribbean vacation at his boss's financial and emotional expense.

"I mean, can you believe that?" asked Gerald, shaken. He flopped down on the sofa and began kneading his temples. "He has the nerve to imply that I am not spending every waking hour investigating Arielle's murder."

From behind her desk, Lucia raised an eyebrow but said nothing.

Plum flipped through the stack of paperwork that Lucia had left for her. "Maybe you should return to New York and let the police finish up the investigation."

"No, I can't do that. I need to solve this crime. I *will* solve this crime," he said.

"Okay, then," said Plum, sitting down on the armchair across from him. "What's the plan?"

Gerald's eyes flitted between Lucia and Plum. "Well," he said. He shifted in his seat, crossing then recrossing his legs. "I'm thinking about it."

"So no plan?" asked Plum.

"It's not like there's a guidebook that tells you how to solve these things," whined Gerald.

"There probably is," said Plum.

"Yes, it's called a detective's manual," agreed Lucia. "That's why the people who solve crimes, otherwise known as the police, attend the police academy."

"Fair enough," said Gerald. "But look, Plum, you are a master at solving things. Pretty please with sugar on top help me?"

Plum sighed. "I know when someone is brownnosing me."

"And I am shameless about it!" Gerald boasted. "I was about to tell you how fabulous you look today and that your skin is positively glowing..."

"You are incorrigible," said Plum. "But okay, I'll tell you what I learned today. Maybe it will help you."

After filling him in on Gary and the mysterious redhead, as well as the internet search on Johnny Wisebrook, Gerald's mood significantly improved. He decided to call his music business contacts back in New York and see if they had any information on Johnny.

"You could also ask Charlie Mendoza," offered Lucia.

"Who's that?" asked Gerald.

"He's in charge of events at Las Frutas. You remember, he's the one who arranged for Leonard's dance troupe to perform here last month," said Plum. "He was very helpful."

"Oh, right," said Gerald. "But judging by the way Juan Kevin kowtows to Johnny, I'm sure another hotel employee will be no different."

"Suit yourself," said Lucia.

"Unfortunately, I have to leave. I need to go meet with Alexandra about the animals," said Plum.

"Do you really need to do something for charity now? Can't it wait?" begged Gerald.

"It's important to give back to society," Plum pronounced. Although she did think the whole thing was an annoying blot on her busy schedule, she felt smugly cleansed by the idea of being charitable.

The cool, minimalist Nettles mansion was the antithesis of Dieter Friedrich's elaborate and over-the-top compound. From the front, it had an industrial facade, concrete accents, and large glass walls. It lacked personality and was absent of all the exaggerated theatrical nuances that were so blatant at Dieter's.

Unlike most of the properties that Plum had been to at Las

Frutas, the landscaping was stark and monotone: all greens and whites. There was no blooming bougainvillea or the kaleidoscope of colorful flowers that could be found everywhere else. The bushes were clipped in a uniformly round shape, the flower boxes encased in slate boxes, the trees perfectly manicured.

Plum was met by a housekeeper who led her through the front hall, where light from the skylight above bounced off the black resin floors. There was a matte-black indoor lap pool to her right, and then she was led into a large living area with an entire wall of windows that faced the Caribbean Sea. It had a spectacular view, just like all the views from the houses of rich people at Las Frutas.

Several seating areas were clustered around the great room. It was mostly modern Swedish furniture, with an emphasis on straight lines and functionality. The decor was mostly black, white, and gray. Stark, modern paintings hung on the wall. It was beautiful but impersonal, Plum thought, more like a hotel than a private residence. It didn't match Cornelia's personality at all. Cornelia was as warm and ebullient as the house was cold. As they continued out to the patio, Plum did see a few framed pictures on a console against the wall. There was a picture of Cornelia and another girl (her sister?) on a boat. Plum stopped abruptly and squinted. Cornelia was wearing a gold snake bracelet around her upper arm. Could that be the same one found in Arielle's Chanel bag?

"This way," said the housekeeper briskly. She opened the screen door, and Plum stepped out onto the shaded patio, which hung over the edge of the ocean.

"Ah, this is Miss Lockhart," said Alexandra when Plum was escorted to the table where she sat. Alexandra was wearing a dove-gray sleeveless shift dress and, despite the humidity, had a leopard scarf knotted around her neck. "This is Wendy Nettles."

Plum greeted the cool, thin blond seated next to Alexandra. Her hair was chin-length, and she wore it swept back from her face. Her eyes were set wide apart, and she had a narrow nose and a wide mouth with thin lips. Plum guessed she was in her late fifties, but she was well maintained. Cornelia looked like a more vivid version of her mother, which gave her a warmth her mother didn't seem to possess.

After they exchanged pleasantries and there were offers of coffee and snacks, they settled down to business. Plum was dismayed to realize that this would be an actual work meeting. Both Alexandra and Wendy had laptops in front of them that they began tapping away at, and there were spreadsheets covering the table. The two ladies bantered about new locations and themes for the next animal rescue benefit. Every time Plum opened her mouth and offered up a suggestion that she thought was revolutionary and cutting-edge, they informed her that it had been done before. Plum had been confident she would add value to the committee, but as of yet, she had contributed nothing. And Plum did not like to be considered dead weight.

Alexandra's phone rang, and she excused herself to walk across the lawn to take the call. She had been apologetic but implied it was a time-sensitive issue. Plum was glad to have a few minutes alone with Wendy so she could get a sense of her hostess and possibly find out more about her relationship with her neighbor. She decided it would be best if she eased into the questioning.

"I met Cornelia yesterday. She is lovely," said Plum.

Wendy raised her eyes and gave her a strained look. "Where did you meet Cornelia?"

"My friend Gerald had met her then we had dinner at the marina," said Plum. "She seems to get along with everyone easily. She even had kind words to say about Dieter Friedrich, who I understand has been a challenging neighbor."

"Cornelia is very active when she is down here," Wendy remarked. "We choose to live more of a quiet existence."

"Then the noise from next door must have really been

exasperating," Plum lamented. She was like a dog with a bone, needing to elicit information from her hostess.

"The noise, yes. Also, the low-quality people that go in and out of that villa day in and day out," Wendy snarked. "It's like a revolving door of unsavory and trashy people. I tell Cornelia to stay away from that villa. It's no wonder someone was murdered there. It was only a matter of time."

"You think?" asked Plum, intrigued.

"Yes. Dieter is rumored to be in bed with the Mafia—they back his garment company, and I have heard they even own Villa la Grosella Negra. He is their front man, laundering their money. I mean, really, could you make that much from acid-washed jeans? Those have been out of style for three decades."

"I didn't think of that, but it makes sense," agreed Plum.

"And there are lots of young women coming in and out, and all sorts of thuggish men. It's why we have the armed guards."

Plum saw Alexandra in the distance, and she appeared to be wrapping up her call, so Plum had to make her move. "It seems so odd, but someone suggested that you had a romantic relationship with Dieter back in the day?"

Wendy stared at her, emotionless. Plum expected a rebuttal, but her response was surprising. "When I was young and naive and I first came to Paraiso thirty years ago, we had a brief fling," she admitted. "But I quickly realized what a trashy man he is. And I was lucky that on the same vacation, I met Charles, and we have been together ever since."

Alexandra took that moment to return, and they went back to the business of rescuing dogs and cats. Plum snuck surreptitious glances at Wendy and tried to conjure up the image of the elegant blond with the cheesy Dieter. It was hard to imagine. Maybe they both had drastically changed since then.

"Hello, ladies, apologies for my tardiness, but you will love the reason why!"

Plum turned around, and her face darkened. Her nemesis and former business associate, villa broker Damián Rodriguez, was strutting toward the table with his customary misogynistic swagger. Plum glanced back at Wendy and Alexandra and was astonished to see both women redden and sit up straight in their seats. Damián was handsome, but not enough to set these two society doyennes all aflutter. But it was clear when Damián greeted both women with a kiss on each cheek that they were admirers of the man Plum equated with the devil himself. How irritating!

"Hello, Plum," said Damián, as he sat down. He didn't offer her a kiss or even a handshake. She didn't care. He was a swine.

"I know you both worked together and it ended badly, but I trust you will put aside your professional differences as we labor together for this good cause," said Alexandra.

Before Plum could speak, Damián cooed, "Of course, Alexandra. There is no bad blood on my part. And I am so thrilled to have Plum on board to help out with the small details that we don't have time to oversee."

He placed a hand on top of Alexandra's, and Plum could swear the woman swooned.

"I am sure that with my background, press contacts, and professional know-how, I can add more value than small details," said Plum tersely. It took only a smidgen of competition for the entrenched New Yorker in her to overpower the nascent Paraison.

Damián gave her a patronizing look. "Wendy and Alexandra are champion fundraisers, and I have learned from the best. They taught me to start small, and then the world opens up. You should learn from them."

"Oh, Damián, you really listened to everything we said," laughed Wendy.

It was the first time she had smiled since Plum had been there. Could she really think this lizard was charming?

"Of course, I listen to everything you ladies say," Damián cooed. "You have softened all of my rough edges."

"Rough edges?" laughed Alexandra. "Please."

Plum felt like she was in an alternate universe. She was wholeheartedly regretting her offer to volunteer for this charity. She'd end up a work mule, doing all the grunt work and gaining nothing. There was a tiny voice inside of her yelling, *Abort! Abort!* She stood.

"If you'll excuse me, I need to use the restroom," said Plum.

"It's down the hall to the left," said Wendy, who remained fixated on Damián.

Plum walked down the corridor, where several charcoal doors were shut. It was difficult to decipher which one was the bathroom. She heard voices at the end of the hall and continued, hoping to obtain directions. When she entered the room, she was surprised to see Captain Diaz sitting with a man in a book-lined study.

"Miss Lockhart!" said Captain Diaz with surprise.

"I'm sorry to interrupt. I was looking for the bathroom," she said, eying the other man with curiosity.

He was in his early sixties with gray hair slicked back and wire-rimmed glasses. His features were pointy, but he was attractive and fit, with sinewy muscles and a lean physique. He wore a fitted polo shirt with the crest of a country club above the pocket and khaki chinos. He stood to greet her.

"I'm Charles Nettles," he said, giving her a firm handshake.

"Plum Lockhart," she said.

His eyes were electric blue, the type that characters in science-fiction movies had, and Plum wondered if they were real or contacts. Either way, the effect they had was as if they could see straight through her.

"Nice to meet you," said Charles. "I heard from my wife that you will be joining her committee. She is very pleased. Animals are her passion."

"I love animals too," said Plum. "Do you have many pets?"

He shook his head. "We have a Havanese, and we keep birds in Connecticut. And, of course, I have horses. I play polo. Do you have many pets?"

"No," said Plum. She realized that her supposed interest in animals now seemed hollow. "Such a busy schedule," she added pathetically.

"Nonetheless, it's good to preserve different species," said Charles.

"Indeed," said Plum.

She glanced around the room and noted that all the books on the shelf were antique, leather-bound tomes. She wondered if they were ever opened or if they were props.

Captain Diaz stood. "I think I have enough from you, Mr. Nettles. Thank you for your time."

"Of course," said Charles. "I'm sorry I couldn't be of more help, but as I reiterated, I heard nothing that night. I was home asleep, and now that Dieter has soundproofed his disco, there are fewer disturbances."

"Yes," said Captain Diaz.

"I'm sure you need to look carefully at his guests. He attracts very unsavory sorts," added Charles.

That's what Wendy said, Plum thought.

"We are checking everyone thoroughly," said Captain Diaz.

"Wonderful," said Charles.

Captain Diaz stared to leave the room and then stopped on the threshold. "One thing."

"Yes?" asked Charles briskly.

Captain Diaz shifted in his stance, as if bracing himself. It wasn't a defensive move, Plum thought, but more like a bull getting ready to take on a lesser foe. "We found on your beach—the part that abuts Dieter Friedrich's property—shards of purple plastic scattered along the shore. You don't know what that was, do you?"

"Of course not," said Charles. "It could be anything. Someone dropped a bottle, or the tide brought in roughage. Why do you ask?"

"It's probably not important," said Captain Diaz, stroking his chin.

Then he turned and locked eyes with Plum. She knew what it was about. She had told Captain Diaz that Arielle had a purple plastic cover on her cell phone. The cell phone that had not been found. The missing cell phone. Plum started doing enthusiastic cartwheels in her mind. She had been proven right!

"Thank you for your time," said Captain Diaz.

When Captain Diaz left, Plum realized she was standing in the study with no good reason. "Sorry, I guess I should find the restroom," she said.

"Yes," said Charles distractedly. He stared at the ground before meeting her eye. "What do you think about all this? My wife told me you were a journalist."

"Former journalist," Plum corrected. "Editor of a travel magazine. Now a villa broker."

"Ah yes," said Charles. "Well, it won't be good for your business now that someone was murdered."

"No, it won't," agreed Plum.

He shook his head ruefully. "Dieter always surrounds himself with danger. It's why I so despise having him as a neighbor. It's always something. Some sort of scandal. He thrives on it."

"You think he manufactured this one?" asked Plum.

"For the record, I will say no," exclaimed Charles. "We have had many years of courtroom battles, and I will be very careful what I utter about him. I can only maintain that there is always drama."

"It appears to be so," Plum said.

Charles looked about to dismiss her, so Plum quickly added, "I met your daughter Cornelia last night. She's great."

He looked befuddled. "Cornelia? Oh, yes."

"She was telling us about what a monster Johnny Wisebrook is," said Plum brazenly.

If Charles had an opinion on the rock star, he didn't reveal it. "I don't know him. We prefer to keep to ourselves when we are here."

"It seems like most people who live down here have had some interaction with him."

"Not me. I have enough interface with people in New York and Connecticut. This is my resting place."

"It is very peaceful here," assented Plum. "Although must be annoying when Dieter has those parties."

"They are over now," said Charles. "I won that court battle. Now we live in total harmony."

"That must be nice," offered Plum.

"It is," said Charles unconvincingly.

CHAPTER 17

PLUM SUFFERED THROUGH THE REST of the meeting with Damián, Wendy, and Alexandra. He behaved like a favored pet and preened and basked in the praise of the two older women. Plum wanted to vomit. His ambition was so transparent; how could they not see through him? Their cluelessness reduced them in Plum's book, and she swore that when she became a woman of a certain age, a handsome man would never relegate her to a blithering idiot.

Plum excused herself after an hour and a half and was frustrated that Damián also took his leave when she did. That forced them to walk outside together and maintain the facade that they would be able to work together amiably. When they arrived at the driveway, Plum was only too eager to take leave of him, but Damián stopped her.

"Plum, let's not fight," he said. He extended a hand as if to offer peace. Plum ignored it.

"Let's cut the crap," she said truculently. "We're not friends, we're competitors. You're a liar and a cheat, you tried to ruin me, I hate you, and that's all."

"You hate me?" he repeated, in a mockingly wounded tone.

"Yes, actually, I do," she said. Plum wasn't sure she actually hated him; did she really care enough to hate him? But she despised him. Was that the same thing?

Damián gave her one of his dazzling smiles, the kind that she was certain launched heart palpations in every single woman that he encountered in Paraiso. It wouldn't work on her.

"I think we are too much alike. I think we are both ambitious and hungry. We want things more than most people. We have a need for them...an urge. And that makes us one and the same. For now, it makes us enemies. But one day, it will be different."

"It will never be different, Damián," scoffed Plum. "We are not the same. I couldn't be any more different than you if I tried."

A spark flared in his eyes, and he kept his gaze on her. "Not true. Just wait. We are under each other's skin. In Paraiso, whether it be through war or peace, once you are under someone's skin, your destiny is intertwined."

"Dear God, I hope not," said Plum. She turned on her heel and made her way to her golf cart, checking her emails while she awaited Damián's departure. She didn't want to be in front of him and have his speedy car idling behind her pokey golf cart, and she also wanted to make sure there was a big distance between them before she set out.

Despite herself, his words nagged at her. And that made her even more annoyed. Yes, he was under her skin. Like a disease—eczema or psoriasis. Something itchy and uncomfortable that caused red scales. Maybe she would need to talk to Carmen and find out some sort of black magic cure to get rid of him. Either that or bathe herself in Clorox. She had very little patience for the likes of womanizer Damián Rodriguez.

She was glad that she checked her phone before she set off because Gerald had sent her a discombobulated, somewhat frantic text. He informed her that he had connected with Hallie Corona and was at Dieter's and she should join them as soon as she was finished at the Nettleses'. Seeing as it was right next door and she had nothing else pressing, she acquiesced.

A "French" maid directed her to the pool area. Plum shared the path today with several pheasants. She still had the daylights scared out of her when she passed a cauldron and it started spewing large flames, as if she had stepped on a sensor to set it off. Was it really relaxing to live in this carnival atmosphere? She found Gerald seated on a gold chaise engaged in a cozy tête-a-tête with Hallie Corona. They were both wrapped in towels, their hair wet as if they had been swimming, and sipping cocktails. Gerald was thrilled by her arrival.

"Plummy!" he said. "You have to hear this!"

Plum walked toward them warily. She knew from experience that Gerald could be a little loose-lipped when he had been drinking, and she didn't trust him to keep all of their sleuthing information to himself. And Hallie was of course an actress, and fake as all can be, not to mention pushy and aggressive.

"What's up?" asked Plum.

"Hallie has been telling me the most dramatic story ever," said Gerald solemnly. "Hallie, please tell Plum. It's so major."

Hallie took a deep breath as if she were a priest about to deliver the last rights to a war hero. "Yes, I'll tell her," she conceded.

Plum sat down on a chaise across from them. Hallie pulled her elastic out of her messy ponytail then gathered her hair together again in a bun and tied it tightly.

"I was telling Gerald about my interaction with Johnny Wisebrook," said Hallie gravely. "It's…very upsetting. Not just to me, but to my husband Gary, who is very offended and devastated by the incident."

"Oh no," said Plum with concern she didn't feel. "What happened?"

"Go on, tell her," prompted Gerald. He took a sip of his cocktail and leaned back in the chaise.

"Well, the night we were all playing poker, I was very tired. I had been so busy the entire week, shooting this new pilot and dealing with my agent. She wants me to do this new series, but it's shooting in Canada, and I'm not sure I want to be away from Gary for that long. You know, we are basically inseparable, so it's like removing a limb when we are apart."

She paused after she spoke, waiting for Plum to interject with the requisite "of course" and "you're awesome" or whatever obsequious and sycophantic platitudes she was used to. After Plum merely nodded, Hallie continued.

"Anyway, I was done with the game. It was obvious Gary was going to win, of course, so I folded. Johnny folded also. And I said my goodbyes and started walking to my bungalow. The next thing you know, Johnny is next to me. I thought he was being a gentleman and escorting me to my room, but he starts in on how amazing I am, how beautiful I am. He also, it turns out, is a huge fan of mine and watched my entire web series, 'The World According to Hallie.' I'm sure you've seen it."

Plum had not. And she didn't want to pretend she had. "I'm sure," was all she said, feeling that it was enough of a noncommittal answer to placate Hallie's thriving ego.

But Hallie took that as encouragement. "I mean, I know on my series I played a woman who was always looking to hook up with any guy, but in real life—as anyone not living under a rock knows—I'm married to one of the most successful men in show business. Gary Grigorian is world famous. And we are madly in love. So I'm not quite sure why Johnny got the wrong impression."

"What impression was that?" asked Plum.

"He started hitting on me. Telling me how beautiful I was, that he wanted to, you know...be intimate with me. I told him I was flattered but obviously married."

"And how did he respond to that?" asked Plum.

Gerald sat up in his chaise and poked Hallie. "Go on, tell her what he did. This is where it gets crazy, Plum."

Hallie sat up straighter and thrust her shoulders back. "Yes. Johnny didn't want no as an answer. I'm sorry to say, he really had developed a massive crush on me. I guess through my show and then meeting me. But he was very persistent. He wanted to take me home."

"And then what happened?" asked Plum.

"What do you mean?" Hallie said.

"I mean, did he take it badly?" Plum queried.

Hallie gave her a quizzical look. "No, he didn't do anything outrageous...but he was very crushed."

Plum sank back in her stance. "Oh."

Responding to Plum's level response, Hallie became animated. "But it was obvious he was upset."

"I get it," said Plum.

"I'm not sure you do," pushed Hallie. "He was very sad I didn't go for him."

"Right," said Plum. "But he wasn't violent."

"No, but that doesn't mean that I didn't destroy his ego. I mean, this rock star is world famous, and no one ever says no to him. I was probably the first to turn him down," Hallie pressed.

It wasn't worth it for Plum to argue. Hallie had such an inflated sense of self that she would always believe that men worshiped her. Plum couldn't waste her time refuting that.

"Good for you for saying no" was all Plum said.

Hallie appeared bereft that Plum was disinterested in her unique saga.

"Plum, this is major," insisted Gerald. "It shows that Johnny pursues women."

"Was that ever a question?" asked Plum. "Of course, he pursues women. He's a rock star. But all this shows us is that he backs off when a woman tells him no. End of story."

"I'm not just any woman," snapped Hallie. "I'm a famous actress who has worked her way to the top. Without nepotism. I never had anyone help me get to where I am. I've dealt with extreme adversity because of my family. I'm not like that little pathetic Arielle Waldron whose daddy gave her all her money and who thought she could do whatever she wanted. Who thought she could hit on anyone and they would come running to her. That tart."

Plum waited for Hallie's outburst to hang in the air before she spoke. "I thought you hadn't spoken to Arielle."

Hallie waved her hand in the air dismissively. She breathed in and out carefully and rhythmically before she responded. "I didn't. Just for a second. Arielle was arrogant. She thought everyone wanted her. She was just a groupie."

"Did she hit on your husband?" asked Plum.

Hallie's nostrils flared, but no emotion crossed her face. "Yes. But he didn't bite. Gary is very loyal. He would never cheat. Not even with a trashy girl like her."

"Vat is zis, vat is zis?" boomed Dieter, who came strolling out to the pool area. He was wearing an open shiny-silk bathrobe over his tanned chest and European-style leopard-print bathing suit. Two attractive young women in bikinis walked alongside him, and he was holding onto a leash. At the other end of the leash was a lion.

"Hi, Dieter!" said Hallie brightly. Her offended demeanor transformed into that of a gregarious and friendly guest.

"Are you having fun? Ve need to have fun. I have the most beautiful villa in the world; my guests need to be happy. If zey are not happy here, zere is no hope for zem. It is chemical," he said.

"I'm having the best time," gloated Hallie. "It's just what the doctor ordered."

"Very good, excellent," muttered Dieter. "I am going now to the beach, to do my exercises."

"Does the lion participate?" asked Plum.

Both Dieter and the lion gave her serious looks. "He is my

inspiration," said Dieter. "Lions are zee most majestic creatures. Ve should learn from them. I may lead him on a leash, but he leads me zrough life."

He rubbed the lion on the chin.

"He's fabulous!" crowed Gerald. "I need to get a lion."

"Everyone should get a lion," agreed Dieter. "Life would be better."

Plum didn't even want to ponder what a ridiculous statement that was. Instead, she changed the topic. "Dieter, are you allowed to work out on your beach?" asked Plum.

"Vy not?" he asked.

"Because isn't it a crime scene?" she said.

Dieter shook his head. "It is my beach. The crime has now been washed away. It is over."

"But the case isn't solved," pressed Plum. "Do you have any more thoughts as to who did it?"

Dieter chuckled. He turned to each of the two women escorting him and guffawed, and they followed suit. Soon, resounding laughter filled the air.

"It was a stranger who came up from zee beach," insisted Dieter. "Perhaps a pirate."

"I see," said Plum. Dieter remained uninterested in aiding the investigation.

"The police are back down there, you know," said Hallie. "That captain and his deputy came by a little while ago to comb through the beach again. Jeremy's down with them."

"How inconvenient!" said Dieter. He turned to the two women. "Let us go back to zee gym. I vill vork on my muscles there. Zen ve have a sauna."

The women wordlessly followed him, as did the lion.

"You know, I do want to have a word with Captain Diaz," said Plum. She stood from her seat.

"Fine, I'll hang here with Hallie while you do," said Gerald. He gave Plum a surreptitious wink. "And Hallie, darling, you are so astute, I would love to hear your theory on Arielle's murder."

Plum walked to the edge of the cliff and stood on top of the narrow metal staircase that led down to the beach below. It was a straight shot, and if someone had vertigo, it would not be a pleasant journey down. She saw Captain Diaz pointing out things for his deputy to bag. Jeremy Silver stood on the side, a clipboard in his hand, taking notes. Plum slowly walked down, feeling as if she were a prisoner walking a plank to her death. She wondered if Arielle had felt like that.

The policeman on guard at the bottom of the stairs listened to Plum's request to speak with Captain Diaz because she had something she thought might be relevant to the murder. He went and conferred with Captain Diaz, who came over, looking curious.

"I didn't have a chance to tell you earlier about the conversation I overheard between Gary Grigorian and a redheaded woman," she said.

"What's that?" he asked. He appeared surprised that she had something to share.

She debriefed him on Gary's secret rendezvous and advised the captain to have someone find the woman at the hotel and question her.

"I really think Gary could be the man in the picture with Arielle," insisted Plum.

Captain Diaz nodded. "Perhaps," he said.

Jeremy Silver trudged through the sand in Gucci loafers and approached the captain. He was talking into a cell phone and put it down when he stood in front of Captain Diaz.

"Excuse me, but Mr. Friedrich wants to know when you will be finished. He would like to use the beach," said Jeremy, his tone impatient.

"We will be done shortly," replied the captain.

Jeremy was ruffled. "You said that an hour ago. We have been very cooperative with you, and we would like to finish this up. It would be preferable to do that peacefully, without involving legal action."

Captain Diaz's upside-down, V-shaped eyebrows shot up. "But, Mr. Silver, why would you do that?" He clucked his tongue. "No, no, no. So unnecessary. If you involve the lawyers, it would only draw out the investigation and make Mr. Friedrich appear as if he has something to hide. Something very dangerous. Perhaps his guilt. No, let's continue to work together, and then we will have a conclusion at last."

A deputy called to Captain Diaz. He pointed to something in the water. Captain Diaz hustled over to the man, and they bowed their heads in discussion. They stared at the filmy waves lapping the shore. Plum remained with Jeremy, watching from several yards away.

"You still think it was Johnny Wisebrook who killed her?" Plum asked Jeremy.

He chose his words carefully. "I don't want to be quoted, but it's a strong possibility."

"I have heard some bad things about Johnny since we last talked," confessed Plum.

"His reputation was bound to come out."

"But as Dieter's gatekeeper, didn't you try to warn him not to have Johnny around?" asked Plum.

"Mr. Friedrich is very independent. I can advise, but he decides what to do. And he is friends with Johnny."

Plum watched a pair of seagulls swoop down and land on the jagged rocks by the edge of the beach. The day was still, no zephyr, no air, just heat. It was also quiet, the only sound the waves and the birds.

"It seems like the war between Charles Nettles and Dieter Friedrich has concluded," said Plum, breaking the silence.

"That was all overblown," said Jeremy disdainfully. "Someone wanted to sell papers."

"It made for good copy," said Plum.

"Scandal always does," agreed Jeremy.

Plum and Jeremy walked back up the steep staircase together. Plum paused for a minute to look down and felt a wave of nausea. She wasn't afraid of heights, but it was very steep. She clutched the banister tightly.

They parted at the pool area. Jeremy went on his way, and she went to retrieve Gerald. He was still lying in the same position on the chaise, gossiping with Hallie Corona.

"Plum, Gerald was telling me that you are conducting your own investigation into Arielle's murder?" asked Hallie.

"Not really," Plum said with a shade of vexation. "Gerald is merely assisting her father with making sure the police are doing everything they can."

"Good!" snorted Hallie. "Because it's better if you stay out of this. It will only ruin your reputation. I mean, I assume you ultimately want to get off this island and back into the real world, working in magazines. Dabbling in all these side projects like renting villas and looking into murders is really not on brand. You might want to remember that."

Plum felt herself flush with anger. "I really don't have to take career advice from you, thank you very much. I've been able to do quite all right on my own."

Hallie scowled. "I am only trying to help you. I don't want to sound condescending, but you have really hit bottom. Gerald and I were just talking about it."

"Ladies," said Gerald. "Let's talk about fun stuff again."

Plum turned and stared at Gerald crossly. She felt betrayed. "You were talking about me hitting bottom?"

"It was all done with love," retorted Gerald.

"Don't shoot the messenger," advised Hallie. She took off her sunglasses and stared directly at Plum. "We want you to get your life together."

Plum bristled. “Maybe you should start with your own life and your own marriage.”

Hallie appeared confused. “What’s that supposed to mean?”

“I happened to witness your husband having a clandestine meeting with a very attractive woman today. He’s got a lot of secrets. I’d be careful,” Plum snapped.

Before Hallie could respond, Plum barked at Gerald, “It’s time to go. I’ll meet you in the driveway.”

She walked to the exit, leaving him to gather his belongings. She was halfway down the path between the large temple and the entrance when she heard Dieter’s unmistakable voice seething with rage. She stopped to listen, grateful that she was concealed by the thick vegetation.

“Zis is an outrage!” Dieter fumed. “Ve need to get zem off the beach as soon as possible. What if zey find out?”

Jeremy’s voice responded calmly. “I’m doing my best. I don’t know why they came back.”

“Vy did this girl have to come here? I don’t need zis trouble.”

“There’s nothing we can do about that now,” said Jeremy placatingly.

“If they discover anything on the beach, I’m ruined. I could be arrested. You realize that, don’t you?” steamed Dieter.

“Of course,” said Jeremy. “But I don’t think you need to worry. It’s very well concealed, and it would take more than a few policemen staring into the water to find incriminating evidence.”

“You better be right! Zis is a disaster!”

Plum was stunned. Had Dieter killed Arielle? And did Jeremy help him? And what was buried on the beach? She thought it might be a murder weapon, but Arielle was strangled. It didn’t make sense. Plum couldn’t hear them talking any more, so she craned her neck to listen. At that moment Dieter appeared in front of her.

“Vat are you doing?” he snarled. “Ver you eavesdropping on me? Very rude.”

"I didn't hear anything," lied Plum.

Dieter glowered at her and moved closer. So close that his strong aftershave curled up into her nostrils. "You better keep vat you heard to yourself, or else."

"Or else what?" she blurted.

His eyes narrowed. "Or else I ruin you."

Plum took a step back. "Ruin me? How?"

"I know people who can make your life very difficult. Painful. Zen maybe no more life."

Plum quickly thought of how Wendy Nettles suggested that Dieter was in the Mafia. She gulped, but then felt a surge of bravery. "I can tell the police."

Dieter cackled. "I have been here a long time; I have many friends. You have been warned."

Plum stood straighter and pushed her shoulders back. "I'm not afraid."

"You should be. Now get off my property."

18

PLUM WAS FURIOUS AT GERALD for trash-talking her to Hallie Corona, which made her unwilling to share with him the harrowing threats that Dieter had leveled at her on their ride home.

"How dare you talk about me with her behind my back? I'm feeding and sheltering you and helping you find out everything about Arielle, and you're backstabbing me?" Plum fumed as she made a very sharp right turn in her golf cart.

"Can you please slow down?" wailed Gerald, clinging to the armrest. "It's not worth us dying over."

"You're a traitor," Plum seethed. She zipped past a biker, narrowly missing an oncoming car.

"Plum, I was trying to ingratiate myself to Hallie so I could pump her for information."

"You didn't have to throw me under the bus!"

"I wasn't trying to. I was trying to help you!"

"You were trying to help *you*!" snapped Plum.

Both Plum and Gerald were equally stubborn, which meant that it took a while for them to back down from their positions and admit any wrongdoing. Instead of offering up an apology, Gerald folded his arms and pouted until they arrived at the town house.

Plum flicked on the lights once they were inside and went upstairs to shower. She turned on the water and set it to a temperature that was hot but bearable. The water pressure on the island left a lot to be desired. The water usually only trickled out, so it felt like ages before the small bathroom steamed up. She undressed and stepped in the shower.

Plum found that bathing helped clear her head, and she needed that more than ever. She had to figure out a plan. Should she take Dieter's threats seriously? Was he really in bed with gangsters? And was there truth to what he said about the police? Did he own them?

She thought of Captain Diaz. Their relationship was fraught, and she did not consider him the sharpest tool in the shed, but was he dishonest? If he were, then why would he be down on Dieter's beach searching for clues? And yet, what if that was all a front? What if he had to make it look as if he were investigating but he was really just using it to get payoffs from Dieter?

Then there was the possibility that it was not Captain Diaz on the take but maybe his boss. She didn't know who the police commissioner was. Maybe he was Dieter's buddy also. It could be very dangerous for her to mess around with these people on Paraiso. It was not, as Dieter said, the United States. Things were different, there were different rules and different laws. She had to remember to take a look at their constitution, because the reality was she knew very little about the government or legal system, which probably wasn't wise considering she was now involved in her second murder case.

After showering, she put on her bathrobe and went into her bedroom. Her window had flown open, and her curtains were fluttering in the breeze. She closed the window and returned to the bathroom to apply lotion and fix her hair. She plugged in her hair dryer and began blowing her curls dry and was irritated to hear Gerald stomping around his room next door. He could really be such a turncoat.

When she left the bathroom, her window was open again, and she shut it. The town house was in poor condition, and the windows were faulty. There was never enough cold air from the ancient air-conditioning units installed in the ceilings. Often, on very hot days, she would stand under the wimpy airstream and try to cool down, to no avail. It was a pity that nights were never cool enough to open the windows. She sighed and put on a striped T-shirt dress.

When she went downstairs, she walked over to the kitchen and poured herself a large glass of white wine. She scanned the contents of the refrigerator and decided a trip to the grocery store in Estrella was in order. She was low on produce and all of the basic culinary staples and needed to stock up so that she could eat more meals at home. Dining out all the time was expensive, and she needed to be careful about her budget. She had learned that it was not ideal to eat at the resort, as all the prices were inflated. She had to live and eat like a local.

She brought her wineglass out to the balcony. Gerald had knocked over a chair (probably when he was drunk), so she picked it up and set it straight. It was dusk, and sunbathers were fleeing the beach, heading home for a siesta before they hit the nightlife.

Gerald came out to the balcony, his hair wet from a shower. He wore a short-sleeved button-down tucked into green pants with an Hermès belt.

"What are we going to do tonight?" grumbled Gerald.

"I don't want to do anything with you tonight," said Plum. "You're on your own."

"It's childish to threaten me," he wailed. "You need to stop holding a grudge!"

"You're the childish one. And you need to stop banging around the house and knocking over things," she chided.

"What are you talking about? I don't knock over things. You're the Amazonian woman; I feel like I'm living with Thunderfoot."

"You're very rude," she snapped. "And you don't have to live with me. Go stay in the hotel. I would like my privacy."

"I would love my privacy also," he snapped. "You shouldn't go marauding in my room, leaving me stupid signals that you're mad at me. It's very immature, not to mention it's bad manners."

"What are you talking about?"

There was a loud knocking on the front door, and the doorbell began buzzing simultaneously, pressed over and over again with urgency.

The pounding and buzzing continued. Plum and Gerald exchanged surprised looks. She stood and rushed through the living area to the front door and opened it.

"I'm coming!" she yelled. "Stop buzzing."

"Plum!" came Juan Kevin's anxious voice from outside. "Are you there? Are you okay?"

Plum swung open the door. Juan Kevin stood on the threshold, out of breath and distraught.

"Thank God," he said when he saw her. His face was full of alarm, and he was perspiring.

"What in the world is going on?" she asked.

"Are you okay?" asked Juan Kevin. He strode into the town house. "Who's here?"

"Just me and Gerald."

As if on cue, Gerald entered from the balcony. "Where's the fire, Juan Kev?" he demanded.

Juan Kevin seized the handle of the coat closet and quickly opened it. A few rarely used umbrellas leaned against the back wall, in front of which was a lone windbreaker hanging on a wooden hanger. He swiftly examined every inch of the closet before closing it. He walked into the living room and looked carefully under the skirted table in the corner. Dust motes floated into the air when the skirt dropped down. He rose and craned his neck around the room, eyes scanning.

"What's this about?" Plum asked, worry in her voice.

"I received an ominous call from a man who said that you were in grave danger and if I knew what was good for you, I would make sure to let you know to back off," said Juan Kevin.

He eyed her warily, and her heart began to thump. Plum sank down onto the arm of the chair. "Oh no," she said.

He gave her a curious look. "Do you have an idea who would say that?"

Plum nodded, too distressed to speak.

"What's going on?" he asked.

"I'm being threatened," murmured Plum in shock.

"Who do you believe is behind this?"

"Dieter Friedrich," she whispered.

Juan Kevin sighed deeply and groaned.

"Dieter?" squawked Gerald. "That's ridiculous! That man is as mild as a lamb. And we were just at his house!"

Plum kept her eyes on Juan Kevin. "He threatened me there, and—" Plum remembered the window opening and closing during her visits to the bathroom and the banging she heard when she was blow-drying her hair. She had assumed it was Gerald. "I think someone might have been in my room while I was taking a shower," Plum said. She turned to Gerald. "And didn't you say you thought I was in your room? Why did you think that?"

"Because of the knife you put on my bed," he said.

"What knife?" asked Plum, her voice trembling.

"The one on my bed," repeated Gerald, but slowly, as if the reality that Plum didn't leave it was dawning on him. "You didn't leave me a knife? I thought you were trying to show me how angry you were with me."

"I didn't leave you a knife," said Plum.

"Stay here, I'm going upstairs," warned Juan Kevin. He made a move toward the stairs.

"Do you have a gun?" asked Gerald.

"No," said Juan Kevin.

"How are you going to shoot a possible intruder?" Gerald yelped.

"I have an idea," said Plum.

She ran to the kitchen and pulled a knife out of the butcher's block on the counter. She noticed that the largest knife was missing. That must be the one that was left on Gerald's bed. She began shaking.

She handed Juan Kevin the knife at the same time he went on his walkie-talkie and asked his deputies for backup.

"Jairo and Bryan will be here in a minute," he said. "You know them, Plum. Don't let anyone else in."

Plum and Gerald nodded. They immediately collapsed together on the sofa.

"If we die, I just want to say you were my best friend," whispered Gerald.

"Thank you," Plum murmured.

Gerald detached from her and gave her a wounded look. "Aren't you going to say I'm your best friend also?" asked Gerald.

"Let's take things one minute at a time," she said.

There was a noise upstairs, and they both glanced up at the ceiling, as if they could see through it. They huddled even closer.

"Okay, maybe I'll say it," she whispered.

"I knew it!" said Gerald.

They heard footsteps above, and the opening and closing of doors.

"Should we go help him?" asked Plum. She felt guilty to leave Juan Kevin without backup.

"I want to live, so no," said Gerald.

"It's all clear," Juan Kevin yelled downstairs. "But I'd like you to come upstairs, please. I want you to identify if anything has been disturbed."

Clutching hands, Plum and Gerald ascended the staircase, both feeling terribly brave. Juan Kevin was in the guest room, standing in front of Gerald's bed. It smelled faintly of cigarettes, and Plum was momentarily distracted by her annoyance that Gerald would smoke in her house. But then Plum looked down at the immaculately made bed (she was impressed at the hotel quality that Gerald had attained) and shuddered when she saw the knife neatly perched on his pillow.

"Oh no," said Plum.

"Don't touch anything, I want to have the police fingerprint it," Juan Kevin warned.

His walkie-talkie crackled, and he spoke into it. "Yes, come inside," he commanded his deputies. "I'll just run down and let them in."

Plum and Gerald clung to each other. "Are you sure it's safe for us to wait here?"

Juan Kevin looked at Plum intensely. "There's no way I will let anything happen to you. Don't worry, I checked everywhere."

Plum felt like it was hours before he returned with his deputies, but it was probably not more than thirty seconds. She glanced around the room, tension flooding her body.

"It freaks me out that someone was up here when we were," she told Gerald.

"It was obviously a very large man, judging from the stomping."

"Hey, you thought it was me stomping."

"Yes, you stomp like a man," said Gerald. "And I wish it *had* been you. But it was...a possible killer."

Juan Kevin and his deputies Jairo and Bryan followed Gerald and Plum through the upstairs to check and see what was amiss. Plum was mortified to find her bra and underwear thrown on the armchair in the corner of her room where she had recklessly discarded them when she flung off her clothes to bathe. She discreetly picked them up and dumped them in the hamper.

She told them about the window, and Juan Kevin and his men

spent time examining it, musing about why the intruder opened and closed it. Using it as an exit would not have been ideal as the intruder would have had to leap into a thicket of prickly bushes below.

"Maybe they wanted to scare you?" Juan Kevin wondered.

They did a thorough sweep to ensure that no recording devices had been placed inside the room, and Plum was relieved when they came up empty. After leaving no stone unturned in their search, they regrouped in the living room. Jairo and Bryan left, but one promised to remain outside for the remainder of the evening, and the other to be on the lookout as he made his rounds at the resort.

"I need to call the police and report this," said Juan Kevin.

"Um, is that a good idea?" asked Plum.

"Why don't you start from the beginning and fill me in," commanded Juan Kevin. "Then we can decide."

They all sat down. After Plum debriefed Juan Kevin about what she had overheard Dieter saying and how he then threatened her (all the while ignoring Gerald's interjections about how insulted he was that she didn't inform him), Plum went and poured them all stiff drinks. Juan Kevin refused his, but after gulping down his own, Gerald drank Juan Kevin's. He remained rattled, although his mood mellowed a bit after the cocktails.

"I have to figure out what to do about this," said Juan Kevin. He sat on the sofa.

"Do you think Captain Diaz could be on his payroll?" she asked.

"I don't think so. But I don't know. There is corruption here," he admitted. "There is a very small dark underbelly in Paraiso. It's disappointing but a reality."

"Maybe we should go to the press!" enthused Gerald. "A preemptive strike. Tell the world that you were threatened so if anything happens to you, or me, now that you dragged me into it, they know who did it."

"And have him sue me for slander?" asked Plum. "No, it can't be proven."

"And I would hypothesize it was not Dieter himself who placed the call," added Juan Kevin. "The man had no German accent."

"It was probably one of his associates," lamented Plum. "He may have called in the artillery. And that's who came to give us the warning as well."

"I suppose. But this is all on the supposition that the person who called me and came in here worked for Dieter," said Juan Kevin.

"Who else could it be?" asked Plum with alarm.

"I don't know," said Juan Kevin. "I don't want to rule anyone out."

Plum thought about how she had gotten in deep and perhaps it was time to back off this investigation entirely. She should send Gerald home and be done with all of it. Although quite frankly, she was relieved to have a man staying with her.

"You think we're safe to remain here?" she asked Juan Kevin.

"I'll have a guard outside twenty-four seven."

"Sounds like fun," said Gerald, who was now tipsy.

"I think maybe we shouldn't report this to the police," said Plum. "Maybe that will just aggravate Dieter or whomever."

She expected Juan Kevin to protest, but to her surprise, he nodded his assent. "I agree. Let's keep a lid on this until we explore further."

"Then how are you going to get the fingerprints checked?" Gerald demanded.

"I'll take some pictures myself and then bring the knife to my cousin Patrick. He works in a lab, and I can have him run the prints for me," said Juan Kevin.

"Your cousin's name is Patrick?" asked Gerald. "I thought you were Paraison. What's up with the Irish names?"

"My mother is Irish," said Juan Kevin.

"Weird. Does she live on the island?" asked Gerald.

"Yes. I see her often. In fact, that's why I couldn't wait for you after the disco, Plum. She needed me to fix her cable," said Juan Kevin.

Plum felt a rush of joy. Juan Kevin hadn't abandoned her for a hot lady; he had gone to help his mother. Could he be any more endearing? She wanted to hug him.

"What is it with old people and cable?" asked Gerald. "But in the meantime, what are we going to do about dinner?"

Plum was in a benevolent mood. "I guess I'll make something," said Plum. "I'm not sure I have the energy to go out."

"Boo," said Gerald. "You're a lousy cook."

"I've gotten better," insisted Plum.

"You know what, you have been through a lot in the past hour. Allow me to make dinner," said Juan Kevin.

"Is he a good cook?" asked Gerald suspiciously.

"Excellent," said Plum, who remembered the delicious meal that Juan Kevin had made for her at her previous town house.

19

IT WAS INTERESTING TO PLUM that she could look in her kitchen and think there was absolutely nothing to cook or eat, but then along came someone like Juan Kevin who could riffle around in her freezer and refrigerator, defrost various foods, and whip up a masterful meal. Even Gerald, who considered himself a discerning culinary critic, was impressed. All the while Juan Kevin made it appear effortless.

"We need you to move in with us, Juan Kevin," said Gerald after taking yet another bite of his dinner.

Juan Kevin had prepared braised chicken thighs with roasted red peppers, creamy rice with stewed beans, and jicama salad. Plum had bought the jicama on a whim, not certain she would ever know what to do with it. And the truth was, she still didn't know what to do with it.

They sat on the balcony, listening to the coquis, a very musical breed of frogs that entertained the island at night. The evening was still warm, and the stars were out. Plum and Gerald had finally started to relax, and they had purposely talked about things other than the intruder during dinner to avoid the proverbial elephant in the room.

There was a pinging sound, and Gerald pulled his phone out of his pocket and glanced at the screen. He read the text then looked up at Juan Kevin and Plum.

"I just received a Google alert that Gary Grigorian is about to be interviewed about Arielle's murder on Channel Seven," he said.

Plum sat upright. "What?"

"I set a notification to let me know if any press arose about Arielle," explained Gerald. "And now the chickens have come home to roost."

"Inevitable, but not good news," said Juan Kevin. "What time is the interview?"

"It says ten o'clock Eastern Standard Time," he read.

Juan Kevin glanced at his watch. "That's now."

"No, it's nine," Gerald corrected.

"Nine in Paraiso, but ten o'clock in New York," said Plum.

"Then turn on the TV!" barked Gerald, his eyes flitting around the room to locate a television.

"I don't have a TV," said Plum.

"What?" roared Gerald. "Are you a barbarian?"

"All of the programs are in Spanish," she explained.

"I thought you said you spoke fluent Spanish?" asked Gerald, an amused look on his face.

She scowled. "It's a work in progress. Let's look on the computer."

Plum brought her laptop over from her desk, and the trio squeezed together on the sofa and crowded around the computer. They located the channel and caught the beginning of the broadcast. The camera started on a redheaded woman opening the show.

"That's the woman I saw with Gary!" squealed Plum. She pointed at the screen.

"The one you thought was his lover?" asked Gerald.

"Yes," said Plum. She quickly realized the possibility that she had been wrong in her conjecture that it was his lover but did not want to declare that self-awareness out loud.

"Let's listen," said Juan Kevin.

"Good evening, I'm Lucinda Waters, broadcasting live from Las Frutas Resort on the Caribbean island of Paraiso. This world-famous, exclusive resort has been rocked by the murder of beautiful publishing heiress, Arielle Waldron, the daughter of Glen Waldron," explained Lucinda. "Tonight, we have an exclusive interview with renowned television personality Gary Grigorian. Gary and his wife, comedienne Hallie Corona, not only knew the victim but have been vacationing at the same mansion where she was killed."

"This is not good," muttered Juan Kevin.

They watched as the pretty redhead outlined the events of Arielle's murder. That she was a billionaire. That she was at billionaire Dieter Friedrich's mansion. That he is at war with his neighbor, billionaire Charles Nettles. (Plum wondered how in the world there could be so many billionaires. And was the term used loosely, or did these people really have all that money?)

As Lucinda Waters continued her narration, the camera cut away to a montage of pictures of Arielle, Dieter, and Charles Nettles. There were pictures of their properties taken by a drone. There were also pictures of Emilio Rijo with his first wife, Alexandra, greeting dignitaries such as Queen Elizabeth and Henry Kissinger and actors like George Clooney at the resort. Interestingly, there were no pictures of Emilio and his second wife, Carmen, and Plum was sure that would please Alexandra and annoy Number Two.

Finally, the camera returned to Lucinda and pulled back. She was sitting in a cornflower-blue armchair across from Gary. She wore a sleeveless green blouse, white capris, and gold sandals. There was a notebook propped on her lap. Gary's hair was combed neatly, and he donned a checkered shirt and a light-blue blazer. He sat in a wicker chair in front of a painting of a golf course.

"They're filming this in the study at the hotel," said Juan Kevin.

"Hush," Gerald reprimanded. "I want to hear this."

"Gary, we are so grateful to have you here with us," said Lucinda, her voice oozing obsequiousness. "All of your television colleagues as well as your friends are so relieved that you and your wife were not victims of this heinous crime."

"Thank you," said Gary, his tone humble.

"And I would like to extend my deepest sympathies on the death of your friend Arielle," cooed Lucinda.

"Friend?" squawked Plum. "He barely knew her."

"Celebrities are such fakers," agreed Gerald, forgetting that he had just admonished Juan Kevin for talking.

Lucinda leaned in toward her interviewee, adopting a conspiratorial pose. "Tell us, Gary, what exactly happened?"

Gary cleared his throat. "Lucinda, this is a horrible tragedy. You know, as journalists, we report on things like this, but we never want to be part of the story. Sadly, that's what happened this week. My wife and I were down here on Paraiso for a much-needed vacation. We have been working intensely, and this was our romantic getaway, staying at our friend Dieter Friedrich's house with several other friends. Arielle Waldron, a vibrant young woman, was also at the villa. We only met her briefly, but she made an impact. Hours later, she was dead."

"Horrible," gushed Lucinda. "Someone so young, with such potential, to have her life extinguished like that..."

Gary nodded. "It's horrific. And not to mention the fact that my wife and I were sleeping only fifty yards away from the beach where she was found murdered. What if my wife had been out that morning? Hallie has jogged on the beach and around the cliffs of the island alone every single morning we've been here. I shudder to think of the possibility that the same thing could have happened to her."

"How horrible," said Lucinda.

Plum and Juan Kevin exchanged skeptical looks.

"Hallie jogging? If that's true, she needs to fire her trainer," attested Gerald.

"To think that it could have been my beloved wife..." Gary was saying on-screen. His voice was choking with emotion.

"Gary," said Lucinda, after pausing the right amount of TV time for the impact of his emotional reveal to move the audience. "Who do you think killed Arielle? And why?"

Gary sucked in his breath and then pursed his lips.

"It's an ongoing investigation, so I cannot comment," he said. "But I've been working with police, as has Hallie. In fact, Arielle had a candid conversation the night before her death and told Hallie some pretty incriminating things about someone who was harassing her. If the police do their work correctly, and this person ends up being the killer, Hallie will be a very damning witness."

Lucinda nodded. "And we all know Hallie is a force to be reckoned with."

"Yes," agreed Gary. "My wife always does the right thing and never backs down."

The rest of the interview was basically salacious attempts to rephrase the same sentiment over and over again. There were the identical shots of the villas and pictures of Arielle. Gary said a few vaguer things about Dieter and what a great host he was but was actually pretty reticent about the murder.

"I wonder about his motivation," said Juan Kevin when the broadcast had concluded.

Juan Kevin rose from the sofa and went to sit on the armchair. Plum could still feel the warmth on her leg where his leg had touched her as they crowded around the computer and wished he had remained. She had to extricate herself from Gerald, scooting over on the sofa, as he didn't appear to be in any rush to move.

"He wants to make sure he is part of the story, and this is the only way he can ensure it," said Plum.

"I suppose," said Juan Kevin. "But if we are going with the

theory that it is Dieter, then why would Gary say that while he is staying at Dieter's house?"

"Maybe he doesn't think it's Dieter," said Gerald. "Maybe they think that whomever it was that Arielle said was harassing her is the killer."

"Johnny Wisebrook?" asked Plum. She tucked her legs underneath her on the sofa.

"Could be," said Juan Kevin. "But then what evidence is on the beach that Dieter was so worried about?"

"Maybe he is covering for his friend," said Gerald.

"It's true, Jeremy Silver said Johnny is an old friend of Dieter's. Maybe he saw what happened," Plum offered.

"Could be," said Juan Kevin. He stood. "I should go."

Plum felt a pang. She didn't want Juan Kevin to leave for many reasons. If Gerald weren't there, would he offer to stay the night? Even just to offer protection? She suddenly despised Gerald and wanted to throw him out of the town house. She turned and glared at him, but he was staring at Juan Kevin.

"Why did someone call you to warn you about Plum?" Gerald asked Juan Kevin. "How would they know that you were friends with her?"

"I'm not sure," said Juan Kevin. "Maybe they saw us dancing at the disco together."

Gerald nodded. "Right. And they knew that you had to be a good friend to subject yourself to dancing with such a crappy dancer!"

Plum's face turned crimson. *Yes*, she thought. Definitely time for Gerald to go.

"She's a wonderful dance partner," insisted Juan Kevin. "I would take her over anyone else any day of the week."

He looked directly at Plum when he spoke, and she felt as if they were the only two people in the room. After he had left, she floated to bed.

CHAPTER 20

THE FOLLOWING MORNING, GERALD AND Plum woke to the breaking news that Hallie Corona was dead. The media was flooded with stories about the famous "comedienne" who had tragically fallen off a cliff on her morning jog on Paraiso. A spokesman for Gary Grigorian had already released a statement that the "famous television personality was devastated at the loss of his beloved wife, a true talent in every sense of the word."

"Gary has blood on his hands," said Plum as she stared at the headlines on her computer.

"Another tragedy," Lucia clucked. She had arrived at the usual time and made coffee, and now she began dispensing steaming mugs to Gerald and Plum. She also passed around a tray of mango tartlets, a culinary delight that Plum hadn't known existed until recently.

Gerald, who was curled up on the sofa under a blanket, still bleary-eyed and resentful that Plum had awoken him with the news, tore off a large chunk of the pastry and stuffed it in his mouth.

"Why do you think Gary is guilty?" asked Gerald, crumbs spraying across the blanket.

Plum winced at Gerald's atrocious manners. "I'm not sure he's guilty in the sense that he physically pushed her off the cliff. But he outed her on international television last night. He told everyone that Hallie knew incriminating evidence and would testify against Arielle's killer, and then he added that she walked alone every morning. He basically handed a loaded gun to the killer."

"But they say it was an accident," Lucia reminded them. She returned to her desk, sat down, and blew on her coffee to cool it down.

"I'm sure it was made to appear to be an accident, but she was pushed," Plum insisted. "There's someone mad as hell out there, who wants this all to go away. I'm getting scared."

"Why?" asked Lucia.

Plum and Gerald filled Lucia in on the intruder, and the latter listened with astonishment. "You know, when I left here yesterday, I did notice that there was a car idling across the street. I thought maybe someone was getting picked up. But perhaps it was someone casing the town house."

"What kind of car?" asked Plum.

"It was silver. I'm not sure what kind. A sedan. Maybe Toyota?" Lucia said, straining to remember.

"I'll need to tell Juan Kevin," said Plum.

"You'll need to be careful is what you need to do," warned Lucia. "I told you nothing good ever stems from Villa la Grosella Negra. The place has been cursed since it was built. Innocent people have been killed. There is something evil there."

"Angels," murmured Gerald. "Led to an early slaughter."

"Let's not engage in revisionist history," warned Plum.

"What do you mean?" asked Gerald. He greedily licked his fingers after inhaling the last bite of his pastry.

"Well, come on, Arielle and Hallie were not angels."

Gerald looked at her blankly. "But they're dead."

"Just because they're dead doesn't mean they were nice," said Plum. "Let's be honest, these women were horrible."

Lucia appeared stunned and quickly made the sign of the cross. "Let's not talk ill of them, dead or alive," she reprimanded.

They were interrupted by the telephone. It was Juan Kevin calling Plum, asking if she had heard the news about Hallie. After a quick exchange, he told her that Captain Diaz was coming to his office at noon, and he thought Plum and maybe even Gerald should be there to fill him in.

"But can we trust him?" asked Plum.

"We need to take a chance," said Juan Kevin. "This is getting bigger than we can handle."

When Plum hung up, Lucia held up a copy of *Chisme* from behind her desk.

"This is the gossip newspaper I was telling you about," she said.

"Let me see," said Plum, extending her hand.

"It's in Spanish," said Lucia.

"I know Spanish," insisted Plum.

Lucia gave her skeptical look but wordlessly handed over the newspaper. It was a xeroxed printout with little effort in the way of art direction. Gerald leaned over and gaped at it.

"I shudder to think what kind of creative director would allow that to be released into the world. I would call for their immediate termination," he said, before heading to the kitchen.

"It's more about the content than design," said Lucia.

Plum stared at the newspaper. She squinted, but she could only make out a few words. She handed it back to Lucia.

"Thanks for letting me read it," she said nonchalantly, as if she had understood it.

Lucia smiled. "On the other side is an article about Charles Nettles and Dieter Friedrich. I thought you might be interested. And if you will indulge me, I will read it to you."

"That would be lovely," said Plum.

"I want to hear this also," said Gerald, who had wandered out from the kitchen where he had procured another tartlet.

Lucia put on her reading glasses, cleared her throat and held the newspaper up in her hand.

"The fire and rage between Charles N. and Dieter F. is alive and well. It is not true that they have made amends. Our excellent sources have told us they got into a big fight two days ago. There was a very dramatic moment when Charles N. shoved Dieter F. Our excellent source is not the most fluent English speaker, but he is one hundred percent certain it is about a woman. Stayed tuned to this ongoing fight between these two macho men."

"Juicy!" squealed Gerald.

"This means they both lied to us," said Plum. "Their battle is alive and well. Why wouldn't they want anyone to know?"

"Maybe the woman in question is the reason," offered Lucia.

"Could be," said Plum. "And there's no way of finding out who their 'excellent sources' are?"

Lucia shook her head. "We don't even know who produces the newspaper. As I said, it's all very secretive. But it always ends up being accurate."

"Good to know," said Plum.

Even when paradise was under a dark cloud, it still looked and felt like paradise, Plum thought as she and Gerald made their way to Juan Kevin's office later that day in her golf cart. The pristine air, the palm trees swaying, the sun blazing, the birds chirping. There was nary a piece of litter on the immaculate streets, and the gardens were beautifully manicured with tamed thickets of brightly colored flowers exploding all over the resort. It didn't feel like a gritty crime scene or the place where you would be dodging homicidal maniacs. It was almost antiseptic in its criminal deficiency.

Gerald chattered about Hallie while checking his phone for the latest updates on her demise. Plum listened half-heartedly and knew she should be more horrified or at least distraught over Hallie's death, but all she could focus on were her thoughts of Juan Kevin. He was such a gentleman! It was so sweet of him to say that he enjoyed dancing with her. She was not used to compliments. Her dating life in New York City had been a series of one-time meetups with various men that she found online. They often told her she was too high-maintenance, which she found incredibly insulting.

"Are you listening to me?" asked Gerald.

"What? Yes," she blustered.

He looked at her askance. "Then what did I say?"

Irritation flooded her. "Oh, I don't know, probably something inane and celebrity-related. You can really have a one-track mind."

"That's not true," squabbled Gerald. "It's relevant because a celebrity was murdered,"

"She wasn't a celebrity," snapped Plum.

"She was a well-known comedienne."

"I don't understand why she was called a comedienne. She was in *one* funny sketch show fifteen years ago, and she's forever a comedienne. I went to college fifteen years ago, can I refer to myself as a college student?"

"If it's your truth," said Gerald.

Plum waved her hand in the air. "I didn't like Hallie. I'm not happy she was murdered, but I am no fan and don't want to hear people gushing about what a wonderful person she was, because she wasn't."

"Fair enough," said Gerald. "I thought you were enjoying the conversation because you had a dreamy look on your face… Wait a second!"

"What?"

Gerald craned his body so he could fully face Plum and studied her from head to toe. He giggled. "You have a crush on Juan Kevin."

"What?" exclaimed Plum, but unfortunately, her translucent skin failed her, and she blushed as red as a tomato. "That's not true."

"You finally made an effort with your hair; you put your false eyelashes back on; you're all dressed up fancy. It's the first time since I've been here that you shed that I've-given-up spinster attitude. You're in love," he teased.

"Don't be insane."

"Honey, there's nothing wrong with being in love."

"I'm not in love," insisted Plum. "That's ridiculous."

Of course I'm not in love, she thought. *What's that fluttery feeling?* her inner voice challenged. *It's a crush,* she told herself. Just a crush. Which was possibly very fleeting. Or not.

Juan Kevin's office was a small stucco building with a Spanish-tiled roof near the main entrance of the resort. She had been there before and knew that it boasted a sterile atmosphere but an enviable air-conditioning unit.

Patricia Martinez, the office manager, was seated at her desk by the entrance. She was an attractive brunette with intelligent brown eyes, smooth skin and no appearance of wrinkles. Plum's jealous side did not lay dormant at the thought of this pretty, young woman sitting a stone's throw from Juan Kevin on a daily basis, although there had been nothing untoward or suggestive in their interactions.

After greeting one another warmly, Patricia asked Plum and Gerald to have a seat in the reception area for a moment. Through the glass partition that separated his office from the general pool, Plum could see Juan Kevin and Captain Diaz engaging in a heated discussion. The normally unflappable Juan Kevin appeared flustered, and Captain Diaz was using his index finger to poke invisible holes in the air, directed at Juan Kevin.

"This will be fun," giggled Gerald as they sat down on the bench. "They look pissed."

"Murder doesn't make anyone happy," said Plum. She smoothed her skirt and made sure it hadn't hitched up her legs.

"That's not true at all," protested Gerald. "I think murder makes *you* very happy."

"Don't be ridiculous," Plum snapped at Gerald for the second time that hour.

As soon as they entered the office, Captain Diaz attacked Plum.

"You're meddling, Miss Lockhart, and people are dying," he said accusatorily.

Plum was immediately put on the defensive, and she lashed out, as she usually did when she felt threatened. "This investigation would be at a standstill if not for me."

"You have been described as antagonizing Miss Corona and snooping around Dieter Friedrich's house," insisted Captain Diaz.

"That is not true at all," said Plum, though it was actually quite true.

Captain Diaz was agitated and accusatory, and Plum felt as if all the progress they had made at establishing a rapport flew out the window. He berated her with a litany of recriminations, blaming her for interfering in his investigation by alerting witnesses of Arielle's death (Jessica and Max) and insinuating herself into the Nettles house, no doubt to ask questions about the murder, which Plum hotly denied.

Plum knew Captain Diaz was undoubtedly under pressure, but that still didn't mean he was competent. Not to mention that there was the underlying question of whether or not he was on Dieter's payroll. However, the manner with which he spoke of the German acid wash king made her reluctantly doubt it.

"If Mr. Friedrich had allowed my detectives to perform a proper search of his premises and evacuated his guests, this would not have happened," seethed Captain Diaz. "But instead that stubborn and foolish man thinks he knows best, and now another one of his friends has died. This would have been avoided if he did not have such an ego."

"Maybe it would have been avoided if you had caught Arielle's killer," said Plum.

This made Captain Diaz explode. Gerald watched the bickering saucer-eyed until Juan Kevin put out his hands to stop the fighting.

"This is not helping at all," said Juan Kevin. "We need to work together, as I do believe we all want the same thing. To stop these murders and to find the killer, or killers."

"Miss Corona's death is still not officially a murder," said Captain Diaz.

Plum rolled her eyes. "That's what you said the last time, when I insisted that you look into a mysterious death that ended up being a murder. Which I single-handedly solved."

The vein in Captain Diaz's forehead throbbed. Plum stared at it, waiting for it to pop.

"Let's all take a deep breath and sit down," commanded Juan Kevin.

"I'm glad I have a front-row seat to this," said Gerald, pulling up a chair and sitting down. "I only wish I had popcorn."

"We've gotten off on the wrong foot today," said Juan Kevin. "Let's all take a moment."

Patricia, as if sensing the acrimony (and no doubt hearing it), entered with cold bottles of water she dispersed to the grateful combatants. Something about her presence in general was soothing, and the tension in the room depleted when she softly closed the door behind her.

"As you can imagine, I'm now having a challenging time detaining the press from entering Las Frutas," said Juan Kevin. "The investigation will be compromised by all the amateur detectives trying to assist in finding out what happened."

"Are you implying something?" asked Plum defensively.

"No," said Juan Kevin wearily. "I actually appreciate your help. And I think Captain Diaz should as well. I have made him aware of the latest information that we have learned."

"You should have told me about the break-in at your town house," he snarled.

"I couldn't be sure you're not a dirty cop," she spat at him.

Tempers flared again, and Juan Kevin had to stand up and silence the room. "Captain Diaz, we are here, and we can be helpful. It is unwise not to ask us to assist you."

"The police are doing just fine," he said, shifting in his seat.

"I know you are," soothed Juan Kevin. "But there must be some capacity in which the police are denied access that we have."

Captain Diaz appeared to be about to deny that suggestion and tell them to get lost, but he obviously thought better of it. With extreme reticence, he spoke. "I will concede that yes, there is one person we have trouble accessing."

"Who's that?" asked Juan Kevin.

"Johnny Wisebrook," said Captain Diaz. "He met with us briefly, but his lawyer will not allow us to follow up or ask any official questions. He won't tell us where he was the morning Arielle was killed."

"Are you sure he wasn't home?" asked Juan Kevin.

"Before our interview with Johnny, we asked the security guard who controls the grounds of his property if he had seen him the morning of Arielle's death. He told us that Johnny had gone out at eight a.m. that day. I'm sure that guard lost his job, because when we confronted Johnny with this information, he was furious and would not reveal where he went."

"Doesn't he have to?" asked Plum.

"Not under Paraison law," said Captain Diaz. "He's not really an official suspect, so he has the laws of privacy on his side."

"Why wouldn't he say where he had gone, unless he had gone to kill Arielle?" said Plum.

"Not necessarily," said Juan Kevin. "I'm sure he has many things going on that he doesn't want anyone to know about."

"That's what we need to find out so that we can eliminate him as a suspect or arrest him," said Captain Diaz.

"I'd love to help you with Johnny Wisebrook," Gerald said in a perky tone. "I'm totally on the same page as him."

Plum gave Gerald a disdainful look. "What are you talking about?"

"I love his music," insisted Gerald. "It's so my jam."

"I've always had a good relationship with Johnny," said Juan Kevin. "I think he would meet with us, and we could gather some information."

Captain Diaz nodded. "I don't hold much faith, but it is worth a try. He is currently impenetrable and what we would call a hostile witness."

"We'll do our best to soften him," said Juan Kevin.

Captain Diaz's eyes slid to Plum and narrowed. "If she's involved, make sure she doesn't screw it up."

Plum frowned. "I will take that as a challenge," she said.

CHAPTER 21

CASA GUAVA, WHERE JOHNNY WISEBROOK resided, was a glamorous, Moorish villa perched on a cliff high above the sultry greenery of Paraiso. Cooled by tropical breezes coming off the quicksilver sea, the sprawling Moroccan-style palace was built around an infinity pool that appeared to drop off into the edge of the ocean.

A butler greeted Plum, Juan Kevin, and Gerald and told them they were expected (Juan Kevin had called ahead). He led the trio across the tiled floor in the columned entrance, through an open pavilion with a crenellated rooftop and toward the patio. Hibiscus and jasmine bushes hugged the surrounding enclosures, in front of which were rows of established guava trees swaying in the gentle wind. The views were stunning, the variety of blues from the sky, the sea, and the pool popping against the whitewashed walls.

Johnny was lounging on a chaise, wearing a bathing suit and a short-sleeved patterned button-down in a soft, coral cotton. He had on his sunglasses and was reading a book, which he promptly put down when his guests were announced. He rose and motioned them to join him in the seating area, which was a cluster of teak furniture upholstered in vibrant Turkish fabrics. There was an abundance of throw pillows in varying shapes and sizes, including several on the floor for seating.

A maid appeared, and a formal tea service swiftly materialized, which included scones with guava jam, *coconetes,* and delicate egg salad along with cucumber and salmon sandwiches on thinly sliced white bread. They all received a cup and saucer as well as a small plate to put selected snacks. No time was wasted in offering guests food or drink; the assumption was that everyone would partake.

Johnny was the only one who received a special order. In lieu of a teacup, a large thermos with a foamy green concoction was placed in front of him by his butler. He took a large swig of the murky liquid and grimaced.

"I despise this, but they say it's good for the libido," he said with a wink.

Johnny had been famous for most of his life, so he possessed that insouciant and arrogant air that was a second skin for celebrities. The overwhelming impression to those that came into contact with him was that he could do whatever he wanted. *And it was probably true,* thought Plum. As a rock star, he had been performing for crowds of adoring fans for decades. It made him otherworldly.

In his early years, Johnny had been a rebel, a renowned lothario, and a bad boy. He had long hair and was known for a prodigious drug habit. But as the decades wore on, his social conscience emerged, and he began to campaign for the environment and clusters of war-ravaged refugees from various countries. This allowed him a modicum of respectability, which he capitalized on. He ultimately was awarded an OBE by her Majesty the Queen of England and shed most of his vices to transform himself into a well-respected superstar. The word *legend* was often attached to his name, and he had settled into life as someone perceived as possessing maximum talent and respectability. *The latter of which was about to be debated,* Plum thought.

She studied him with curiosity, excited despite herself to be this close to him. Johnny was not traditionally handsome, with dark, sunken blue eyes and a physique that was too slight for Plum's taste. But she did concede that he had plump, sexy lips, and incredible bone structure—razor-sharp cheeks and an aquiline nose—that rendered him striking.

As with every celebrity-to-civilian interaction, Johnny led the conversation and the others found themselves nervously laughing at unfunny quips and musing how friendly and "normal" he was. The conversation was mundane, thought Plum, although laced with excitement that it was this legend speaking. He made brief chitchat about his latest fishing expedition before he appeared suddenly bored and spoke bluntly.

"What's this all about, mate?" he asked Juan Kevin. "I've told the police everything. I only agreed to meet with you to discuss this out of goodwill. And because you were bringing a sexy lady with you."

He winked at Plum as he said this, and she was secretly thrilled, in spite of her best efforts at self-preservation. How fun to have a rock star flirt with her! Then she realized he must do that to everyone, and she tried to quell her excitement. Not to mention, she had to remember those women who had accused him of becoming aggressive. He was a possible predator. Or killer.

"I appreciate you meeting with us, Johnny. I know how busy you are and how important your time is, and I consider this a huge favor," began Juan Kevin in an obsequious tone that made Plum stare at him quizzically. She knew that he was there in a professional capacity, but did he really need to be so sycophantic? It seemed to work, though, because Johnny nodded and sat back in his seat.

"I'll tell you what I told the police guy," he said. "I was playing cards at Dieter's, and this young woman—the now-dead one—comes in, and it's the usual, she loves me, etc. She's a nice piece, and I'm pleasant, but I'm in the middle of a big-stakes game. I don't get distracted when I play the big stakes."

"How big?" asked Juan Kevin.

"Big," said Johnny. He paused for effect before continuing. "Then Dieter tries to shake her, and she does not want to go. Been through this story before. She wanted in on the action, in every sense of the word. She stalls and then begins ad-libbing. Claims that she and I had some sort of thing recently. Finally, they get rid of her, and that was the end of it."

Plum had so many questions, but Juan Kevin had instructed her and Gerald to remain quiet and allow him to lead the conversation as much as possible. Juan Kevin believed because he had a previous relationship with Johnny, it would make the "inquisition" more informal. Plum felt the task to remain silent difficult and unnatural.

"Of course, I am certain that is all there is to it, but if you will indulge me for a minute, I just wanted to ask, why do you think Arielle claimed to have a relationship with you?" asked Juan Kevin.

Johnny rolled his eyes and gave Juan Kevin a look as if he thought he was daft. "I'm famous. Unfortunately, I have people claiming things from all angles."

"Therefore, you are quite certain you never met her?" asked Juan Kevin.

"No, I'm not at all certain," said Johnny. "It's entirely possible. I meet thousands of people. Most of them women. And most of them have fantasies about me. They want me to notice them."

He smiled at Plum when he said the last part. She wanted to say, *But do they want you to strangle them?* just to zing him. But she bit her tongue.

"I can imagine!" squealed Gerald.

Juan Kevin gave him a disapproving look to shush him, and Gerald stuck out his tongue.

"I have a system," Johnny said, taking another swig of his drink.

"There is some vetting, of course, when it comes to women I am interested in."

"What's the system?" asked Juan Kevin.

Johnny's eyes gleamed. "A man never reveals his moves."

"But can you be certain that Arielle didn't pass your vetting?" asked Juan Kevin with curiosity.

For a fraction of a second, Johnny paused, about to say something. But then he said offhandedly, "I don't remember hooking up with that dead girl. I can smell crazy a mile away, and she was crazy."

"How so?" asked Juan Kevin.

"It's the eyes," Johnny explained. "There's this sort of frantic look that some of these women have. Desperate but panicky. Easy to sniff out, and I steer clear."

"That's a little misogynistic," Plum blurted. She had been asked not to interject, but she could not allow this sort of conversation to transpire without an editorial comment from her.

"No, no, you're not getting it, love," said Johnny. He shook his head and leaned closely across the table. Plum could smell his breath, which had the whiff of broccoli. He kept his eyes locked on hers. "I love women. But I have to be careful, because I'm famous."

"So true!" said Gerald.

Johnny took a sip of his green juice then licked his lips before he spoke. "These girls that throw themselves at me don't know me, but they think they do. And if I give a little, they want romance right away, and I can't give that to them. That's when they come after me."

"How do they come after you?" Juan Kevin asked.

He gave a sneaky smile. "They try and get this." And with a flourish, he pulled out his wallet, opening it to show he had several hundred dollars inside, and then threw it on the table. It was clearly an act that he had repeated several times, and they all laughed uncomfortably. Most of his credit cards slid out, which Plum was sure he did on purpose so that they saw that he had a black

American Express Card and a Dubai First Royale MasterCard mixed in with lower-end department store gift cards, including a Target card. How intentionally curated it was, aiming to show he was a man of incredible wealth who had two of the most exclusive credit cards on the planet but also a man of the people who shopped at Target, thought Plum.

"Thanks for coming by, Juan Kevin," said Johnny, patting the director of security on the back. "I'm glad I could help you out."

"Yes, thanks," agreed Juan Kevin. "It's great you are so forthcoming. But why won't you tell the police where you were the morning that Arielle was murdered? You could put this all to bed."

Johnny's smile fell, and then his face became hard. "I don't have to tell them anything."

"But this would be all over and done," said Juan Kevin.

"As far as I am concerned, this is over and done. I had nothing to do with that girl's death," said Johnny firmly.

Johnny abruptly stood as if to signal the meeting was over.

They all rose from the table. An enormous, six-foot-four bodyguard with a buzz cut and a thick neck appeared out of nowhere—he had possibly been lurking in the shadows for all they knew—and stood next to Johnny.

"It was brilliant to see you. Oliver will show you out now," said Johnny. He quickly slipped away into the house.

Oliver waited as they began to walk single file to the front door. On the way out, Gerald grabbed a scone off the table and popped it into his mouth.

"One for the road," he muttered to Plum and the bodyguard. The latter remained expressionless.

They strolled toward the exit, Juan Kevin and Oliver ahead, with Plum and Gerald trailing. She walked past the chaise Johnny had been lounging on and noted that the book he was reading was Dostoevsky's *Crime and Punishment*. *Guilty conscience or closet intellectual?* she wondered.

Plum was discouraged. She felt that it had been all for naught, that they really didn't ask Johnny any hard-hitting questions. Was it because he was famous that they were soft on him? Did famous people always get away with everything?

Oliver opened the front door and waited for them to exit. Plum thanked him, but Juan Kevin turned to ask him a question.

"Johnny was kind enough to tell us about his vetting process. I am sure you are instrumental in assisting him in that challenging endeavor."

Oliver grunted by way of agreement.

"He mentioned that he only had a hundred women on rotation at a time, or wait, did he say one hundred?" asked Juan Kevin.

Plum wondered what Juan Kevin was talking about and why he was acting suspiciously casual.

"Not a hundred, fifty," corrected Oliver, before snapping his jaw shut like an alligator that ingested a bird.

Juan Kevin nodded, "That's right. One hundred would be impossible."

"Anything is possible with Mr. Wisebrook, he's a legend," said Oliver. "But we have to be careful. Fifty is the limit. Everyone fully accounted for. You can't trust anyone."

"Got it," Juan Kevin replied.

They had decided earlier that they would not rehash their meeting in Johnny's driveway but instead regroup for an early dinner at Coconuts to compare notes, as Juan Kevin had a pressing appointment. He said a quick goodbye and set off as soon as he reached his car. Plum wondered if he had felt the same way as she did about the Wisebrook meeting, that it was a waste of time, and was it even worth meeting for dinner? There was not much to discuss.

"Please drop me at the beach," commanded Gerald. "I have been here forever and haven't even gotten a base tan."

"You really have your priorities in order, don't you?" she asked him.

"Absolutely," he said. "Man, that Johnny Wisebrook is dreamy."

"You think so?" she asked, turning down the winding road that his villa was perched at the end of.

"Totally," said Gerald. "And I'm glad he's innocent. I really would hate to have a rock star be a killer."

"Why are you sure he is innocent?" asked Plum.

"Oh, please, he wasn't hiding a thing. The man was an open book. And an open wallet."

Gerald immediately got on his cell phone and began calling every single frenemy in his life to rub in the fact that he had just been to tea at Johnny Wisebrook's mansion. Plum inwardly cringed as he embellished his relationship with the rock star, informing his friends that he would no doubt be front and center at the Moving Targets' next concert.

Plum dropped Gerald in the parking lot at the beach, and as she was navigating her car around the circle, she saw Max Stylo and Jessica Morse sitting in a parked golf cart in the shade. Max had his head in his hands, and Jessica was patting him on the back. Plum pulled her cart to the side and walked over to them.

"Everything okay?" she asked.

Jessica glanced up, the sun reflected in her glasses. "Oh, hi, it's you."

Max peeled his head away from his hands and stared at Plum. His beautiful face was awash with anguish, which did nothing to diminish his good looks and, in fact, made him appear more irresistible. There was a darkness emanating from his blue eyes, a fire that added substance, and his chiseled jaw was set in a clench that only accentuated his perfect bone structure. Plum's eyes slid over to Jessica's face and once again could not reconcile how these two were a couple. It was harsh, Plum knew, but Jessica was homely and plain.

"I'm sorry, I hope I'm not intruding—you're obviously upset, and I wanted to see if you needed any help," explained Plum.

"That's nice," said Jessica, her voice sweet. She smiled slightly and continued to rub Max's back. Plum could see the ripples of muscles through his tight, gray T-shirt. "We just learned the horrible news about Hallie Corona's death, and Max is stunned."

Plum was surprised. "Oh, did you know her?"

Max nodded, his face drawn. "Yes. I'd actually photographed her two days ago. I'd met her on the social circuit in New York, and we bumped into each other down here at Coconuts the other day, and she was like, can you take some pictures of me, and I said of course, and we had a great time. Now, she's dead, and I can't believe it."

"Yes, horrible," murmured Plum.

"First Arielle, and then Hallie," said Jessica, her voice quavering. "It's really devastating."

"It's creeping me out, is what it is," said Max. "We need to get off this island."

"Yes, I can understand that," said Plum. "And once again, you have my condolences."

"Thanks," said Max. He ran his hand through his wavy, blond hair, which immediately flopped down in front of his eyes, rendering him even more adorable.

"We were going to leave as soon as we heard about Arielle, but I knew she would want us to stay," said Jessica. "She always said, never leave a good time or a good party. So we felt that we were honoring her by staying. But now the party is not so fun with Hallie also dying. I mean, I know it was an accident, but it still feels awful."

"Alive one minute, posing for beautiful pictures on the cliffs, then dead the next day after falling off them," said Max. "The irony..."

"Right," said Plum. "What were the pictures for?"

"Her publicist was pitching a story about how one of her best friends was murdered. They wanted the photos to accompany it."

"Oh," said Plum. "Who was her best friend?"

He gave her a look of surprise. "Arielle."

"Arielle was her best friend?" asked Plum with astonishment. "I thought she barely knew her. I thought you were her best friend, Jessica."

"I am," said Jessica. "I mean, I was. But Hallie said they were close."

"But do you believe that?" asked Plum. She clearly remembered Hallie telling her that she had barely talked to Arielle. To even call them acquaintances would be an exaggeration.

Jessica shrugged. "Arielle had a lot of celebrity friends."

Plum nodded. Obviously, Hallie was trying to monetize her fleeting interaction with Arielle. It was a bit depressing that everyone was going along with it. She could picture the headline in *People* magazine. "Comedienne's Bestie Dies: Secrets She Took to the Grave." But now they were both dead. And those pictures that Max took would be worth a lot more money. Giving him a motive.

Plum stared at the young couple. "Were either of you able to think of anything or anyone who might have been responsible for Arielle's death since we last talked?"

"What do the police think?" asked Jessica.

"I'm not sure," said Plum. "Did they interview you?"

"Yes," she replied. "I told them everything I told you."

"Well, since then, have you thought of anything else?" Plum asked again.

Jessica looked at Max, and he shook his head.

"Something you're not telling me?" asked Plum.

"No," said Max quickly.

"Not really," conceded Jessica.

"It's crucial that you tell me," Plum pressed.

"Why?" asked Max. "Are you a detective?"

"No, but I am immersed in this quest for justice, and I'm a villa broker," Plum added, as if that would be a sufficient explanation.

Just then a security guard approached and told Max and Jessica that their golf cart was parked in an unloading zone and they would have to move it. Jessica popped out of the cart to stand with Plum while Max steered it over to the other end of the lot.

"What was it you wanted to tell me?" asked Plum. "It's obvious something is on your mind. If it could be helpful to finding Arielle's killer, you have to say something."

Jessica sighed, looking conflicted. She glanced over at Max, who was retrieving things from his cart.

In a low, confessional tone, Jessica whispered, "I was thinking more about Mr. Big."

"What?" asked Plum, moving closer. "Do you know who it is?"

"I think Gary Grigorian was Mr. Big!"

Aha! a tiny voice in Plum's head screamed. It was exactly the theory she wanted to hear. "Why do you say that?"

"I didn't know Gary was down here until we ran into him and Hallie after Arielle died. And I remembered that Arielle had told me she was at a party a month ago and Gary had hit on her. She said she thought it was random because he and Hallie were doing public displays of affection all over the place. But he said they had a business arrangement."

"Interesting," said Plum.

"Yes," continued Jessica. "Gary said that he and Hallie decided that famous people are more famous if they are in a couple."

"Makes sense," agreed Plum. "But was Arielle interested in Gary?"

"Yes, but only because he was famous," said Jessica.

"Why doesn't Max want me to know this?" asked Plum quickly. She could see Max approaching, and he was almost within earshot.

"He thinks Hallie was very genuine when he took her pictures. She talked about how in love with her husband she was. I said it could have been acting."

Probably, thought Plum. Although she never thought Hallie

was a very good actress when she guest starred on television programs. Maybe she reserved her acting ability for her life.

"Lovebug," she said overly enthusiastically when he returned. "Is my baby feeling better?"

He shrugged then smiled. "Now I am."

"Anything I can do to help?" Jessica asked.

"What did I do to get such a loving and supportive girlfriend?" he asked Plum.

Max leaned in and gave Jessica the most tender kiss. Plum may as well have been invisible. These two were really madly in love. At first it annoyed her, but then it actually gave her hope. Maybe there was something to be said for princesses and frogs, and vice versa. Plum wished them well, though they barely noticed her departure.

As she was walking back to her golf cart, she glanced back at the loving couple now heading to the beach. Max had his arm around Jessica, who was much shorter than he. She had her hand in his pants pocket, and because he was so much taller, she was pulling it down slightly. Plum couldn't believe her eyes. She saw the top of a tattoo peeking out of his pants that looked like it could be the one in the photograph in Arielle's purse. What did it mean? Had he been two-timing Jessica? Or was it an old photo?

22

IT WAS TIME FOR PLUM to check on the progress of Casa Tomate, and she had scheduled to meet with the contractor right before she headed back down to Coconuts to reconvene with Gerald and Juan Kevin. She was pleased to note as she plunged into the driveway that the exterior was much improved. The dead plants and shrubs had been cleared, the flower beds were alive with blossoms, and the front door and trim had been painted a nice cream color.

As she entered the villa and strolled through the rooms, she was excited that, under Lucia's guidance, the villa had already been transformed. The floor tile was no longer cracked and gritty; it even gleamed under the sunlight flooding in the clear windows. Plum sauntered through each room appraisingly and nodded to herself. This was a definite upgrade.

Plum had a brief conference with the contractor. He informed her the work would not be finished for another week, but Plum put all of her pressure on him and refused to accept that deadline. He protested and told her that certain items would not be available until *mañana*, but Plum wouldn't hear it. The contractor finally took off his cap, mopped his sweaty brow, and acquiesced. Plum could be very persuasive.

When she left the villa, she saw a car pull into the spacious courtyard in front of the house directly across the street. It was a large, stately, two-story villa, far superior to Casa Tomate, and the gardens were expensively maintained and lush. Plum was about to enter her golf cart when she saw that the two men exiting the car were none other than Damián Rodriguez and her former boss Jonathan Mayhew. Plum's eyes darted quickly to the entrance of Casa Tomate. She had no interest in interacting with her former colleagues, especially Jonathan, whom she had been able to avoid since her departure. Did she have time to escape undetected? Just as she was about to scurry back into the villa, she heard an approaching voice.

"Plum Lockhart," said Damián, strolling in her direction. He had on aviator sunglasses, a tight button-down shirt, and black pants. The smug look on his face instantly caused Plum's blood pressure to rise.

"Oh, hello, Damián," she replied in a contrived, nonchalant tone.

Jonathan Mayhew reluctantly followed his deputy Damián across the road to greet Plum. He was a slender, balding man in his midsixties, who wore the ubiquitous white suit he was renowned for. He had a clever face, discerning blue eyes, terrible teeth, and a deceptively courteous manner. Plum knew she should be somewhat grateful that he had recruited her to move to Paraiso and work for him, but the entire time (three months) that she worked for him, she had felt undermined and diminished. They left on bad terms (as to be expected, considering she launched a rival company) and had been evading each other ever since.

"Plum, lovely to see you," remarked Jonathan in his polished British accent.

Although Plum knew his words rang untrue, his delivery was impeccable, and an outsider would not gauge the wrath that lingered between them.

"How are you?" asked Plum brusquely. She leaned against her golf cart to appear casual and unflummoxed.

"Fabulous," said Jonathan. "We couldn't be better."

"Business is going very, very well," added Damián greedily. "We are working day and night. So many new clients. So many properties. We've just signed Casa la Toronja y Polmelo across the street."

"That's a mouthful," said Plum. "What an awkward name."

"But they're beautiful fruits," snapped Damián.

Jonathan's eyes slid over Casa Tomate. A look of distaste appeared on his face. He motioned toward the villa. "Is this your property?"

"This?" asked Plum. "Yes, it is, a small project that I took on for a friend."

She glanced back at the villa, and it no longer seemed improved to her. Despite the recent updates, it was still a dinky, one-story fixer-upper that had seen better days. A few coats of paint and a few plants thrust into the dank and squishy soil couldn't take away the years of wear and tear. It now appeared dejected in Plum's eyes.

Jonathan gave Damián a quizzical look. "Is this the one?"

Damián nodded. "Yes, this is it," he said, before turning to Plum. "The owners asked us—begged us—to represent it, but we said no."

"It was not up to the standards of Jonathan Mayhew Caribbean Retreats," said Jonathan snidely.

A surge of anger shot its way through Plum. "I enjoy a challenge. A renovation makes all the difference in the world."

"When are you going to renovate it?" asked Damián, a crocodile smile on his mouth.

Plum was certain that he knew she had renovated Casa Tomate since he last saw it. *That little petty cockroach*, she thought. "We are finishing it up now. I am so pleased with the progress. We already have lines of customers waiting to secure it for the season."

Jonathan gave the villa another disdainful inspection before shrugging. "Best of luck to you, Plum."

"Yes, you will need it," said Damián.

Plum hopped in her cart as they swaggered away. She allowed her anger to dissipate and refused to allow them to rile her. Success is the best revenge, she told herself. Her spirits began to rise as she set off to her town house to change before dinner.

The sun was still bright when Plum found herself at a stop sign behind a line of pickup trucks, buses full of staff leaving the resort for the day, and mopeds. She took the opportunity to reach into her glove compartment and fumble around for sunblock. Her pale skin required constant reapplication to refrain from a harsh sunburn. She poured a dab of the cream into her palm and pulled the rearview mirror down so she could rub all over her face. She could slowly inch her car up with the snaillike traffic and lather herself at the same time.

Suddenly her eyes caught something in the reflection. She saw a man in a helmet on a motorcycle stop on the side of the road in front of a woman. On closer inspection, Plum saw that the woman was Cornelia Nettles! He said something to her, she laughed and then got on the back of his motorbike. He handed her his extra helmet, which she donned. They started to slowly move in the opposite direction. Although she could only see his back, something about the man was familiar to Plum. It was his posture—erect and proper. She wasn't sure why, but she decided to make a U-turn to follow them.

It took several three-point turns for Plum to complete her mission, all the while accompanied by that horrific beeping sound that signaled the reverse gear. What would normally cause a cacophony of honking and infuriated outbursts in New York City was met here with equanimity. The Paraisons and tourists in the vehicles around her watched patiently. Waving in thanks, Plum realized once again something could be said for the slow pace of island life.

Cornelia and her motorcyclist had also been detained by traffic—in their case, a diesel truck in dire need of a new muffler was picking up the gardeners who had been leaf-blowing the road. Plum was one car behind them, but she could see how Cornelia's arms were tightly wrapped around the man who was driving her, and she had her head nuzzled against him in an affectionate manner.

The motorcycle cut right, with Plum in pursuit. As they continued on the sun-speckled route, Plum conjectured that they were probably headed to the taco trucks. And indeed, the motorcycle pulled up to the truck, and the driver turned off the ignition. Plum tucked her cart into the shade of a palm tree across the road, hidden from their view.

Cornelia took off her helmet, allowing her dirty-blond hair to cascade to her shoulders. Then her driver did the same. Plum's eyebrows shot up in surprise. It was Jeremy Silver! What was he doing with Cornelia? Jeremy Silver worked for Dieter Friedrich, who was the sworn enemy of Charles Nettles, Cornelia's father. She was consorting with the enemy?

He laughed at something Cornelia said before taking her hand and escorting her to the truck to place an order. They looked very much like a couple to Plum. She wondered what Charles Nettles would think of his daughter dating Jeremy. And she wondered who Jeremy's allegiance was to, Dieter or Cornelia?

Coconuts was busy with the early dinnertime tourist crowd, but fortunately Juan Kevin's position at the resort allowed him certain privileges, and one of them was a reserved corner table at a restaurant of his choosing, which he had taken advantage of today. The trio was flanked by families who had clearly come straight from the beach—they were still clad in cover-ups over damp bathing suits, their sandy feet hastily stuffed into flip-flops. Noisy children accompanied most of them, and Plum didn't hesitate to give reproving looks to the parents of the offenders in hope they would silence their offspring.

The hostess left them with menus, and the busboy immediately poured them water and placed the basket of flatbreads and olives on the table.

"That meeting with Johnny Wisebrook was totally unproductive," Plum announced. She thrust out her linen napkin with a flourish before placing it on her lap.

"I disagree," said Juan Kevin.

After settling his napkin on his lap, he extracted reading glasses from his blazer pocket and held them between his fingers.

"I also disagree," said Gerald. "I am now able to say that I have been to Johnny Wisebrook's house for formal tea. By the transitive property, I'm a celebrity!"

Plum rolled her eyes. "Okay, yes, you have the bragging rights, but he didn't tell us anything useful."

"He didn't tell us anything useful, but he showed us," said Juan Kevin, a glimmer in his eye.

"What do you mean?" asked Plum.

Just as Juan Kevin was about to speak, the waiter approached and asked what they would like for food and drink. Plum ordered grilled local mahi-mahi filet in a garlic poblano pepper sauce; Gerald ordered a tuna club sandwich on cereal bread with a side of fries; and Juan Kevin had a seafood platter. Plum and Juan Kevin asked for iced tea, while Gerald ordered a banana daiquiri. The waiter assured them that their food would be ready soon.

Juan Kevin leaned into the group when the waiter left. "What I mean is Johnny Wisebrook is notorious for that move—where he throws out his wallet and makes sure everyone sees how much money he has in it. I knew that if I egged him on enough, he would do it..."

"How did you know?" asked Plum.

"It's his, what you would call, schtick. People ask him about women, he throws down the wallet and says they want money, people laugh. Dozens of people at Las Frutas bore witness to that act."

"Why did you want him to do it?" asked Gerald.

"Because I had a suspicion that he confirmed when he threw down his wallet. First of all, he had hundreds of dollars in his wallet. As you will recall, several thousand dollars in cash were found in Arielle's wallet after her death..."

"And she told me that she never had cash!" interrupted Plum. She felt a twinge of excitement. "You think he gave her the money to shut her up or something?"

"I'm not sure," said Juan Kevin. "He may or may not have. But when we are dealing with such a minuscule time frame between her claiming not to have any money on her—which I ascertained when I confiscated her bag—and her death, it does offer up a possibility. And I can confirm that everyone who has seen Johnny's schtick before has reported that he carries a lot of cash. It's all part of his act."

"But they had a high-stakes poker game that night," said Gerald. "Any of the players could have had that money."

Plum felt deflated. "That's true. Remember that Johnny said the stakes were, and I quote, 'big.'"

Juan Kevin nodded and took a sip of his water. "Yes, that is true. And that's why it is not the only thing I found intriguing. Did you see the cards that were in Johnny's wallet?"

"Yes, he had an American Express Black Card, as well as that Dubai card," said Plum. "I've only ever seen one of those Dubai cards in my life, and that was when I did a travel story on the United Arab Emirates, and the man next to me at the hotel was paying for his room with one of those cards. I happened to peep at his bill and balked; it was in the six figures. He must have been royal or an oil baron."

"Yes," said Juan Kevin. "But I'm not talking about the credit cards. Johnny also had a Target card in his wallet."

"Strange to think that a legend like Johnny Wisebrook shops at Target," interjected Gerald. "Oh, here are our drinks."

The waiter placed the teas in front of Juan Kevin and Plum and the giant, foaming daiquiri in front of Gerald. He immediately pulled the spear that was laden with fruit out of the concoction and slid the pineapple off with his teeth before devouring it. Plum watched with disgust.

"I don't think Johnny Wisebrook shops at Target," said Juan Kevin.

Suddenly, Plum remembered the property room at the police station. The contents of Arielle's bag! "Arielle had one of those Target cards also!"

"Yes," said Juan Kevin, a smile forming on his lips.

"But what does it mean, they both signed up for Target cards together?" asked Plum.

"What's the name of Johnny's band?" asked Juan Kevin.

"Moving Targets," mumbled Gerald, before Plum could answer.

"Exactly," said Juan Kevin. "I had been told long ago that Johnny hands out his Moving Target card to women he is interested in. They are specially laminated and some people mistake them as a gift card for the department store, Target. But this one was definitely his, as was the one in Arielle's bag."

Plum sat back in her chair and took a deep breath. "Wow."

"How is it a 'wow' moment?" asked Gerald, slurping down his drink.

"It means that Johnny had met Arielle before and that he had given her the card because he was interested in her," said Juan Kevin.

"But what if he was right, he meets so many women and he gives them to all of them?" asked Plum, suddenly not as excited.

"Remember my conversation with Oliver the bodyguard?

I asked him how many women in rotation. He said fifty and all accounted for. That means that someone was keeping track of who had those Target cards and would have known that Johnny had given one to Arielle. Therefore, Johnny knows that he had met her before, and he's lying to us."

They all paused to ponder this.

"Johnny has a history of alleged aggression with women," said Plum. "Maybe he was aggressive with Arielle and she fought back and then it went too far. Could be a motive."

"We just need proof," said Juan Kevin.

"I don't like this theory at all," lamented Gerald. "Why can't it be someone ugly or poor or a total nobody?"

No one at the table bothered to answer him. Instead, Plum took the remainder of the dinner to brief Juan Kevin on her conversation with Jessica and Max as well as the mysterious coupling of Cornelia and Jeremy. Those interactions now seemed like footnotes compared to the news of Johnny and Arielle's connection. He was looking better and better as suspect number one.

23

PLUM'S REFRIGERATOR WAS IN DESPERATE need of supplies, an assertion that Gerald kept making and one with which Plum concurred. After escalating complaints from Gerald, Plum decided to set off in the early morning to the grocery store in Estrella, where the prices as well as the offerings were far superior to the one located at Las Frutas. The resort store jacked up the prices and primarily targeted tourists or the very affluent who could not be bothered to leave the resort. Not to mention the fact that she had fallen into her old New York ways since Gerald's arrival and had been dining out for every meal. It had to stop, or she would be bankrupt.

Plum had arranged to borrow Lucia's car, as there was no possibility of traveling the dusty public roads in a golf cart—she wasn't even sure how far her cart could go. The setting outside Las Frutas was a marked difference to the fortressed interior enclosed with white walls. The resort was intensely landscaped and lush, full of manicured villas, well-tended flower beds, and emerald grass carpets draping the yards, and had the whiff of the sea salt in the air, mingling with the aromas of spring blooms. The land that stretched out between Las Frutas and Estrella was burnt out by the sun. It was wild and uncultivated, with tangled thickets of thorn, disheveled lawns, and shaggy turf. Years in the harsh, tropical sunlight gave it a tinge of orange and beige. There were crops of sugarcane owned by the Rijo family, a source of both pride and resentment for the natives. Paraisons had benefitted from the Rijo family's largesse, but the Rijos had benefited more. They were controversial to say the least.

Plum often felt when she left the resort that she was thrust into a reality check. Just as Dieter Friedrich's house emitted a theme park vibe, so did Las Frutas, with its immaculate grounds. It lacked the grittiness that had been Plum's way of life until she moved to Paraiso, but she knew now with these murders that there was a sinister element pulsing under the seemingly perfect paradise.

The town of Estrella was dotted with candy-colored buildings ranging in size from one story to four stories. The storefronts boasted striped awnings, and most had gaudy signage advertising ATMs or Coca-Cola. The streets were packed with people, from vendors proferring baskets of bananas, sliced mangos, and water, to locals on their daily errands.

Plum searched for a parking spot in the lot adjacent to La Sirena, the enormous, windowless cinderblock supermarket that was bursting with activity. She slid Lucia's car between a Jeep and a Toyota Camry that had a huge dent on the side. There were racks of grocery carts at the entrance, and after helping herself to one, she entered the store, where she was greeted by a strain of air-conditioning and loud Paraison music booming from the speakers.

Plum spent an inordinate amount of time selecting fruits and vegetables from the plethora of offerings. She had never really experienced the scent of fruit until she moved to Paraiso and now loved to hold a piece of produce close to her nose and sniff it. It unleashed her creative juices, and she had visions of herself as Julia Child, whipping up gourmet dinners with the local bounty. As she lovingly held a warty little gourd, her mind raced to all the ways she could broil, roast, or sauté it. The heart palpitations that followed were intense. Ultimately, her cart boasted a pyramid of jittery, about-to-be-crushed exotic offerings like mangoes, passion fruit, lychees, sea grapes, guavas, coconuts, and pineapple, and this was before she even started in on the vegetables. After squeezing and assessing firmness—and stocking up on basics like rice, beans, meat, chicken, and other less inspiring fare—she checked out of the market, her bill barely grazing the three-figure mark. Take that, Whole Foods!

After loading her bags into Lucia's car, Plum decided to duck into the bank to procure some cash to pay her gardener. The National Bank of Paraiso sported a jazzy orange, red, and black hexagonal rug that Plum felt had been intended for people on acid trips rather than those trying to withdraw or deposit money. The walls were washed in a melon color, and every station had plexiglass separating the teller from the customer, which was inexplicably scratched as if a cat had been held up to the window and wanted out immediately. An orchestral version of the Rolling Stones song "You Can't Always Get What You Want" played softly in the background.

Plum took her place at the front of the red-velvet-roped line that separated her from the ATMs. As she waited, she could overhear the woman in front of her who was having words with the bank teller, in what appeared to be a seemingly endless confrontation. Plum tapped her foot impatiently. Why was everything so slow in Paraiso? But then the words Lucia recited whenever Plum complained about Paraiso echoed in her head: Our way isn't the wrong way, and it will end up rewarding you with a payday. *Hmm*, Plum snorted. That would be wonderful.

Plum stared at the back of the customer, who had what one could only call a perfect figure. She was curvy in all the right places and wore a tight, blue dress with a zipper that went the entire length of her back. Her caramel-colored hair was blown out to perfection and dropped just below her shoulders. She had great legs and wore high heels that accentuated them. Interest piqued, Plum craned her neck to listen to her, as it was apparent that she was agitated.

"I do not understand," the woman insisted. "It is a joint account. I should be allowed access to all deposits and withdrawals."

"Yes, madam," said the bank manager tersely. "And we have given you all the information available to us."

"But why was this amount forwarded to her?" asked the woman.

Suddenly the woman turned slightly to the side, and Plum recognized her. It was Shakira, Dieter Friedrich's "favorite girlfriend"! She looked as beautiful as ever, and Plum marveled that someone could emit the appearance of a supermodel on a meager jaunt to the bank. But her manner was agitated, and Plum was even more intrigued than before. She strained to listen.

"I cannot answer that," said the bank manager. "You will have to ask him. He has signed off on this."

"But I do not want him to know!" wailed Shakira.

"I'm sorry, madam, but that is between you and him," said the bank manager.

More words were exchanged, but it was evident to Plum that Shakira was not achieving her desired outcome. She finally sighed deeply and turned on her heel, where she was face-to-face with Plum.

"Hi, Shakira!" boomed Plum, with faux surprise. She did not want the woman to think she was eavesdropping on her conversation, although she absolutely was.

Shakira surveyed the villa broker with a mixture of surprise and contempt. Plum wasn't sure if it was personal or if she was simply frustrated by her bank interaction.

"Hello, Fig," said Shakira.

"It's Plum."

"Oh yes, Plum," said Shakira in a skeptical tone.

Plum did not want to fritter this opportunity away. "I apologize, but I couldn't help but overhear. I think you are having trouble with your account? You can never trust banks these days."

Shakira scowled, and as if deciding in the moment, spoke. "It's not the bank I don't trust."

"Oh," said Plum in feigned lightheartedness. "Men are also very flighty."

Shakira steeled herself. "Men are not flighty. With some men, what you see is what you get. Those are the ones I find sexy. Others are deceptive. Those are the ones that are dangerous. I'm not scared of danger, though. They should be scared."

And with that pronouncement, she left, her high heels silenced by the thick rug—although they left a trail of poked holes in the plush carpet.

Well, Lucia was right, thought Plum as she entered Lucia's car. Sometimes patience pays off. As Plum shut the car door, a silver Toyota Camry began pulling out, cutting very close to Plum as if the driver didn't see her.

"Hey!" yelled Plum at the oblivious motorist.

He sped past, completely ignoring her. But not before Plum could get a good look at his face. It was Michael, the bartender from Villa la Grosella Negra.

"Jerk," mumbled Plum. But when she got in Lucia's car and put the key in the ignition, she remembered Lucia had seen a silver car that she thought was a Toyota idling outside Plum's town house the night of the intruder. Could it have been Michael? Had Dieter sent him? She shuddered.

When Plum returned to her town house, Lucia helped her unload the grocery bags. It took several trips to the car, and Plum ruefully cursed Gerald for not waking up in time to assist the effort. Surely an assembly line would have been more efficient.

It did give her time to fill Lucia in on Michael and his car. They agreed it was worth mentioning to the police. They stood in the kitchen, replenishing the cabinets and emptying the grocery bags.

"This will all go rotten if you don't eat it soon," warned Lucia, as she pulled out yet another mango from the bag and placed it in the drawer in the refrigerator.

"Obviously. I didn't buy it to languish in my freezer," snapped Plum. "I plan on cooking gourmet meals *every day.*"

She was peeved by the implication, although the truth was, despite her best intentions, Plum was still a lousy cook, and no matter how many tasty ingredients she procured, they usually ended up going to waste. Plum could hear Lucia suppress a chuckle, but when she wheeled around to confront her, Lucia put on a poker face.

"I'm sure you will," said Lucia. "Paraiso has the best fruits and vegetables in the world. It is difficult to resist creating delicious dishes with them." Lucia was no stranger to patriotism. "Nowhere else in the world do you get a mango that tastes like a mango. Or a papaya that tastes like a papaya. Our fruits are succulent and juicy. We are so lucky."

"Preaching to the choir, Lucia," trilled Plum.

They continued to unpack everything until the cupboards, refrigerator, and freezer were bursting. There were enough supplies to stock a Michelin-starred kitchen. The only hurdle remaining was for Plum to don an apron and whip up a gourmet meal. However, when she thought of that, Plum instantly felt demoralized. It seemed a bit daunting. But perhaps with assistance from Gerald she could conquer the culinary arts? She laughed at the thought. There was still the kernel of hope that Juan Kevin might want to help her. Now that would be fun.

Plum told Lucia about her run-in with Shakira.

"Charlie Mendoza's sister-in-law Marta works as head housekeeper for Dieter Friedrich. I should ask her about Shakira," said Lucia. She folded the brown paper bag from which she had extracted boxes of pasta and tucked it in the cabinet under the sink.

Before Plum responded, Lucia moved out of the kitchen.

"What?" exclaimed Plum, trailing her to the living room. "His sister-in-law works for Dieter? Why didn't you tell me this?"

Lucia nodded. "I did tell you before to talk to Charlie, but Gerald dismissed it."

"Never listen to Gerald," said Plum, as she followed her to where their desks were situated and watched as Lucia sank down in her office chair.

"I can give her a call if you'd like," said Lucia.

"Yes, please! And as soon as possible! She may know something."

"She may," agreed Lucia.

Plum sat down at her desk across from Lucia and waited as Lucia called her friend, who was obviously available for a chat. Lucia yakked away in Spanish for a solid ten minutes, making loud exclamations and exhibiting great excitement that initially piqued Plum's interest but then stoked her ire. She did not like to have her patience tried. Initially Plum had interjected with "what?" but was met with a harsh, pointed index finger by Lucia. So she was relegated to tapping her nails on the keyboard, dusting off invisible crumbs from her mousepad, realigning her stapler, moving her jar of pens and notebook to the other side of her desk, and halfheartedly scrolling through emails. Finally, Lucia wrapped up her call.

"I could have gone out for coffee and a cruise around the world in the amount of time that took," whined Plum.

"These things need to be finessed," said Lucia.

"We don't have time for finessing. This is murder. Tell me everything she said."

"She's about to have her first grandchild," confessed Lucia. "They think it's a boy, but the mother is hoping for a girl. That's where there's a conflict, because the father says he only wants a boy, and he wants to name it after his great-uncle who was a war hero. But the mother is very..."

Plum couldn't contain herself. "Are you serious, Lucia?" she demanded. "That is all that you talked about?"

Lucia stopped, pushed her glasses up her nose, and looked momentarily deflated. "No, of course not."

Plum leaned toward her, her hands folded on her desk. "Good. Now tell me the stuff that is pertinent to our case."

"Fine," said Lucia. "But it is bad luck in Paraiso to overlook the good news..."

"Spare me the Paraison rituals for now," seethed Plum. "We can have that discussion *mañana*. For now, give me the goods."

They stared at each other. The standoff continued for a moment before Lucia finally acquiesced. "Okay. She said that the day Arielle showed up at Dieter's house, Shakira had a special meeting with the staff instructing them not to let Arielle in. Shakira explicitly outlined who Arielle was and said that she was a threat to Mr. Friedrich and therefore to all of them. She is unaware who breached her instructions, and that is why she was so irate when she learned that Arielle had gained access to the property and was harassing Johnny Wisebrook."

"Does the housekeeper have any idea who let Arielle in?"

"She's not sure, however, there was one new security guard that night who they think might not have been aware of the mantra, as he was on lunch break when Shakira spoke to the staff. He had worked previously for Johnny Wisebrook as security, and he knew that Johnny handed out laminated Moving Target cards to the women he was interested in. They believe Arielle might have flashed her card to gain access. He would know from working for Mr. Wisebrook that it was the equivalent of having a lottery ticket."

Plum's mind raced. Why would Shakira be so protective of Johnny Wisebrook? Couldn't he take care of himself?

"Did the housekeeper say anything about Shakira's relationship with Dieter?"

"She said that Shakira is devoted to him," said Lucia. "In her words, Shakira is a ferocious animal who will destroy anyone who tries to hurt the people she loves."

"The 'people she loves' being Dieter?" asked Plum.

Lucia picked up her mug of now-cold tea and took a sip. "I suppose so."

"And yet she was very angry about him withdrawing money from their joint account," offered Plum.

"Is that what she said?" queried Lucia.

"She said she didn't want him to know she was looking into it," said Plum.

Lucia sat in silence before responding. "Money always gets in the way of love."

"Unless money is the sole reason for the love," replied Plum.

Plum's ruminations were interrupted by a ping on her computer, indicating that she had received an email. She read it quickly, astonishment flooding her.

> Plum—I'm distraught, devastated, and feel like my life is over. Could you please come to Dieter's at noon to meet me? I need your help to discuss the last will and testament of my beloved wife. Don't worry about your little blowup with Dieter. All is forgotten in this time of epic tragedy. Yours, Gary.

She glanced up at Lucia before squealing, "I'm heading out!"

24

IT WOULD BE DIFFICULT TO pinpoint it exactly, as it always is when something is a sensation rather than a fact, but Plum felt that the atmosphere at Villa la Grosella Negra had shifted into a dark place. She ascribed it to the two deaths that had transpired there in the past week. As Plum was escorted through the grounds to meet Gary by the pool, everything that she had thought frivolous and perky (although, yes, tacky) now seemed gaudy and cheap. The entire ambience had morphed into an abandoned carnival atmosphere, as if everyone had jumped ship and only the losers remained. And even beyond that, there was a definite gloom attached to the estate, sucking the life and enthusiasm out of everyone on it.

Plum was relieved she didn't see Dieter. After his harsh admonishment, she'd hoped she never had to see him again. True, Gary had said all was forgiven. But he had not been there when Dieter reprimanded her.

The white, fleecy clouds skittered along the sky. Gary sat at a table by the pool. He had his computer in front of him as well as a checkered notebook, and his foot was tapping furiously, like a concert violinist desperately trying to keep the beat. His nervous energy was present several yards away, and Plum braced herself as soon as she saw the state that he was in.

"Gary," said Plum pleasantly.

"So good of you to come," he said, rising and kissing her on the cheeks. Plum endured it this time with a stiff upper lip, seeing as he was a recent widower.

They made pleasantries, and Plum gave her condolences, which he took solemnly. They were interrupted by Michael the bartender, who strode over and asked if they wanted anything to drink.

Michael's appearance was dissipated: His stretched-out button-down was half-untucked and peeking out beneath it was a Grateful Dead concert T-shirt. His hair was greasy, and his eyes were bloodshot. The smell of cigarettes engulfed him.

"I'm all set," said Plum.

She eyed him curiously. Was he the man who had broken into her town house and left the knife in Gerald's bed? Could he have been coerced by Dieter to do so? She would never have cast Michael as a villain or serious threat. Frankly, he didn't seem to have his act together. But although his behavior wasn't blatantly suspicious, she did note that he refused to look her in the eye and seemed jumpy. And she remembered the smell of smoke that lingered in the guest room. She kept her gaze on him, but he maintained eye contact with Gary and didn't glance her way.

"Vodka tonic," said Gary. He turned to Plum. "Have something strong. I want to drink to my wife."

Plum turned to Michael. "I'll have a white wine spritzer," she said.

"Sounds good," he said idly, looking down at the table.

Guilty conscience? she wondered as he waddled off in the direction of the bar.

She sighed, hoping that she was wrong—although, that said, better it be a disheveled mess like Michael than a contract Mafia killer from *The Sopranos* who had broken into her house. She wished that it took more than one prompt to encourage her to day drink. But rather than dwell on that, she cheered up by telling herself that it was in honor of the famous Hallie Corona that they were imbibing before sunset.

"I can't believe my wife is not here," said Gary.

"I know. It's shocking. I'm sorry," said Plum. "I've honestly not had that much experience with the death of a loved one, fortunately. I'm not sure what the right words are to console you. But I can tell you that Hallie was really something. Her death will be so upsetting to so many people."

It wasn't a lie; it was just a side step. *Her death would probably be upsetting to some people,* thought Plum. Just not her.

"You hated her," said Gary.

"Now why would you say that?" Plum demanded. Outrage coursed through her veins.

"Please don't pretend right now," implored Gary. "I can't handle that. I need honesty. I need a friend."

He gazed into her eyes with such melodramatic sadness that Plum crumpled. Should she be his friend? Should she admit she thought his wife was annoying? Was there a proper etiquette for consoling people about the death of someone you loathed?

Fortunately, at that moment, Michael brought their drinks, and Plum was allowed to save face by distraction before she answered Gary. He held up his drink, and they both took large gulps.

"Yes, I was not a fan, I will confess," conceded Plum, in what she considered United Nations level of diplomacy.

"She hated you, so you don't have to pretend." Gary laughed.

Plum was seized by a surge of violent hatred toward Hallie. "What? Why did she hate me? The woman used and abused me. She was a hack, and I did everything I could at my magazine to promote her. She was rude to staff, incompetent, a terrible writer, a blowhard, and worst of all, she thought she was God's gift to the world!"

As soon as the words flew out, Plum regretted them. She stared at Gary with embarrassment, wishing she were any place but sitting on the grounds of a multimillion-dollar mansion in one of the most exclusive enclaves in the Caribbean, being waited on by staff.

"Sorry," said Plum meekly.

"Tell me what you really think," said Gary.

"I'm not very good at hiding my feelings," confessed Plum. She would normally not advertise her deficiencies, but as she had backed herself into a corner, this was possibly the only remedy available to her.

"Look, Hallie was a very strong, accomplished woman, like you," said Gary. "And I get how that can cause tension. But I want you to know that Hallie respected you. She knew you could do a lot for her. She had high hopes for you ghostwriting her book and maybe being a background figure to propel her further into fame. She even told me it's people like you who helped people like her make it. And I get it. I want you to feel proud about that."

Plum felt as if she would be sick. Swallowing hard, and taking yet another swig of the spritzer, Plum placed her glass firmly down on the table and looked at Gary angrily.

"Let's not get into this," she said decisively. "I don't care about Hallie's fame. What I want to know is three things: Were you having an affair with Arielle? Did you murder her? And was Hallie murdered?"

Gary gave her a stunned look and then shrank back into his chair. "What are you talking about?"

"Answer the questions, one by one," directed Plum. She had interrupted him, but she had no patience for oscillation. "But before you do, just understand, there are a lot of people working on this. We have a lot of witnesses, a lot of proof, and anything you say can and will be used against you in a court of law, even though I am not law enforcement."

She held his gaze. He tried to look away but ultimately answered, "I was not having an affair with Arielle," he said firmly and with a conviction that would sway even the most insecure jury. "I had met her at a party in New York and was friendly, and I believe she got the wrong idea. I don't—I didn't, cheat on Hallie. Wasn't worth it to me. I'm very ambitious, for whatever that's worth, and I don't want to mess up my career. I will confess, in the early years, Hallie and I had an understanding. But recently, I had no interest in pursuing women because I knew they could wreak havoc on my life. I was happy with Hallie."

"Okay, what about the second question?" asked Plum.

"I didn't murder Arielle. Why would I?" he asked.

"Accusing you of an affair?" offered Plum.

This time, Gary gave a hearty laugh. "You are welcome to peruse my human resources file. You will see dozens of women accusing me of having an affair with them and extorting me. It was one more reason why I was faithful to Hallie. Where there is smoke, there is fire. That type of drama is not at all interesting to me. My aphrodisiac is success, not women. Neither are they my weakness."

"Fair enough," said Plum, her enthusiasm for this line of questioning deflating like a balloon slowly losing helium. She braced herself to restate the last question. "Was Hallie murdered?"

An unexpected look of anguish appeared on Gary's face. Plum saw tears pool in his eyes before he glanced down at the table and concentrated on it with an intensity she had yet to witness. So hard did he examine it that she thought the table might levitate. Finally, Gary glanced up at her, his face sorrowful.

"I did not kill Hallie," he said with conviction. "I don't believe she was killed. I think she slipped on the rocks and fell off the cliff."

Plum held his gaze steadily. She felt like an absolute monster, but for the sake of justice and the sake of those who died, she had to press on. The souls of the dead were resting upon her.

"How is that possible? She just slipped?"

"Yes!" he said, his voice high-pitched and desperate.

"No one pushed her off?" she pressed.

"No," wailed Gary.

"How can you be sure?" asked Plum.

"Because...because...I really think she threw herself off that cliff!" he said. He shrank into his seat, and with his small stature, he looked like a child who had been harshly reprimanded by an unloving stepfather and was sent to the naughty chair.

"Why?" asked Plum frantically. She did not want to allow the momentum of questioning to be lost.

"Because, and this may be hard to believe, her career was stalling. It was hard for her to get work. She was failing as an actress."

"Oh my," murmured Plum, not at all surprised.

"I know," agreed Gary. "Casting agents should have seen how many Twitter followers she had. And read all her witty political posts. Hallie had beliefs. She had her causes. Everything she did was for the common man. She led her life that way; shouldn't that be for something?"

Plum's mind drifted to Hallie's last week of life, spent at a billionaire's mansion on a Caribbean island. Did Hallie think this was the way in which people made reparations? Plum doubted it. Hallie was always in it for Hallie. That was for sure. The question was, was Gary always in it for Gary? And to what extent would Hallie make life better for him?

Gary cleared his throat and pushed the checkered notebook toward Plum.

"This is Hallie's diary. It's where she would jot musings, observations, as well as sketch ideas for her comedy routines. I would love it if you would read this so you can see into Hallie's soul and then make your decision about working on her book."

"I'm not sure."

They were interrupted by Dieter, who came strolling out to the pool area in his bathrobe and bathing suit, holding a ten-pound weight in each hand. As he approached, he alternated bicep curls on each arm. He stopped by their table and stared down at the recent widower.

"Zis is so much sadness, I cannot handle it," said Dieter to Gary. "My heart is broken in a million pieces about zee beautiful wife. She was so much charm and life."

"Thank you, Dieter, I appreciate it," said Gary.

Dieter's eyes moved to Plum. "I have chosen to forgive you. You were very rude. I do not like rude. You were listening to my conversations. But I will be zee bigger person."

"I appreciate that," said Plum disingenuously.

"You were tsk tsk tsk," said Dieter, as he continued curling his biceps.

"Well, it was an accident. I didn't mean to listen," lied Plum. She recrossed her legs.

"I forgive you. Dieter Friedrich is magnanimous. Everyone says, Dieter, how can you be so kind? You are not unlike Jesus. I say, I know," he said.

"You are very generous and kind," concurred Gary in a sycophantic tone.

"I know, my dear friend," said Dieter. He turned toward Plum again. "I am feeling so happy that you have the beautiful friend to help console you."

"Yes, I'm hoping to persuade Plum to write a biography of Hallie's brief but accomplished life," said Gary, staring at Plum questioningly.

So that was the reason he had summoned her, thought Plum. The idea of writing a book about Hallie Corona—even if she had all the time in the world and was destitute—repelled her.

"Zis is a fantastic idea!" said Dieter enthusiastically. "You write on Hallie. Zen you write on me. My life has been incredibly interesting. I have so much money and success. I revolutionized my industry. Every designer in the world has copied me. I'm loved by so many everyday women. I have had permanent success. I am a superpower. Zis will be very intriguing for you."

Plum put her hands up to stop them. "I am flattered by you both, and I have no doubt Hallie's life and your life, Dieter, would make a bestseller. But I'm sorry to say I am not a biographer. I am focused on my new business, Plum Lockhart Luxury Retreats."

Dieter snorted. "Zat is no money. My book will be bestseller. Like Harry Potter, only more. Like the Bible, yes. I sell more zen zee bible."

A commotion erupted behind them, and they saw two men in suits strolling forcefully toward them, with a flustered Jeremy Silver trailing behind and gesticulating wildly. They stopped in front of Dieter.

One of the men—who was bald, late-fifties, and wearing a baggy suit that needed an iron—whipped out identification and thrust it in Dieter's face. His associate, who was in his thirties and attractive with a long, narrow face and closely trimmed brown hair, stood behind him protectively.

"Vat is dis about?" asked Dieter. He pushed away the man's identification. "I see nothing without my glasses."

"I tried to tell them you were unavailable," said an exasperated Jeremy. "But they wouldn't listen. Said they had a warrant from the prime minister himself."

Plum and Gary exchanged amazed looks. What was happening? Was Dieter wanted for murder?

"Mr. Friedrich, I am Romy Gorda, this is my colleague Sebastian Flora, and we are from PEPA, the Paraison Environmental Protection Agency," announced the bald man. "We have compiled an inordinate amount of evidence that you have been amassing land by illegal measures."

This was a curveball, thought Plum. She thought they were here about Arielle.

"Vat?" exclaimed Dieter.

"You have created significant damage to the coastline by your clandestine installation of underwater, sand-collecting barriers. Your acreage has doubled, and this constitutes an egregious and illegal addendum to your property size," added the colleague identified as Sebastian.

Dieter sniffed. "Zat is ridiculous! I do nozing. Zee hurricanes, zee climate change, zat shifted everything. Not my fault I have a bigger beach."

"Your dredging has had substantial impact on the environment, and we finally have proof," said the bald man.

He held out a manila folder. Dieter opened it. Plum strained to see what was inside and had to restrain herself from leaping up and putting her head next to his. She was able to glimpse some typed documents, and as Dieter flipped through, she was able to see aerial photographs taken by a drone. Dieter held up a photo to Jeremy and shook his head.

"Zis is my beach. I do nozing zere," he protested.

"On the contrary," said the bald man. "You installed groins."

"Groins?" asked Dieter. He thrust out his own groin area. "You mean zis? It is illegal to make love on Paraiso?"

"No, we are not referring to that, sir," said the bald man, retaining his cool composure. "We mean the barriers. They are called groins. And they impede the natural longshore transport of sand on an eroding shoreline."

Dieter's eyes narrowed to slits. "Zis is all lies. And I know who is saying zis, it is my terrible neighbor, Charles Nettles. He is so jealous. A jealous man. He wants my happiness. He wants to get rid of me to buy my property for himself. No, zis will not get rid of me."

"This was an order by the government," explained Sebastian. "It was not brought on by a neighbor."

"But surely you know that the Nettles family has done everything to harass and intimidate Mr. Friedrich," said Jeremy.

Plum's eyes widened. What would Cornelia think of that accusation?

"Once again, I want to reiterate: it has nothing to do with your neighbor," said the bald man.

"Absolutely, it does," insisted Dieter. "Nettles is a little man. He has a little mind. He manufactures stories and fabricates lies. I am sure he built zee sandcastles zere himself so that he could get rid of me!"

"I'd like you to come with us right now," said the bald man.

Jeremy Silver became irate. "Mr. Friedrich will not go anywhere with you! This is a totally baseless and incendiary accusation."

The bald man cut him off. "It is by order of the prime minister."

A look of fury overtook Dieter's face. "Call my lawyer, Jeremy."

"I will."

"I go change first," demanded Dieter. "Unless you want me in your courtroom wearing my bathing suit."

"We are not going to a courtroom," said Sebastian patiently. "And yes, you may change. We will be taking you to our offices to answer the accusations."

"I answer nothing without my lawyer!" snapped Dieter. With a flourish, he headed toward his living quarters.

Jeremy turned and glared at the two PEPA officers.

"Please wait at the entrance. I will escort him to you," he commanded.

They did as they were told. Jeremy sighed deeply before heading off after his boss.

When they had left, Plum shook her head in amazement. "This is crazy."

Gary nodded. "Yes, really something. Wow. I wonder who knows about this?" He stopped, lost in thought, and then immediately glanced at his laptop. "Do you mind? I need to send some emails."

"Sure," said Plum, rising.

"Thanks so much," he said brightly. He stood and gave her yet another kiss on each cheek. "Don't forget Hallie's diary," he said, handing her the checkered notebook. "You'll need it for background on the Hallie book."

"Gary, I can't..."

"Please," he insisted, pushing the book into her hands. "Just look at it."

She sighed and nodded silently. Before she had even walked ten feet, Plum was certain that Gary was already emailing his editor to see what kind of exclusive he could get on this information about Dieter. He was such an opportunist.

CHAPTER 25

AS SHE WALKED TOWARD HER golf cart, she pondered the situation with the Paraiso Environmental Protection Agency. When she overheard Dieter and Jeremy discussing what the police might discover on the beach, she had assumed it was some sort of evidence that would link him to Arielle's death. But it must have been the groins Dieter had illegally installed. That made more sense.

She threw Hallie's checkered notebook on the seat next to her. She wanted nothing to do with it, and the idea of perusing Hallie's no doubt pathetic innermost thoughts repulsed her. She vowed not to read it. As she was pulling out of the driveway, a Mini Cooper was driving toward Casa la Manzana. As the car slowed in the narrowed stretch, she saw it was Cornelia Nettles, clad in tennis whites, a visor perched jauntily on her head, and a swinging ponytail falling out from under it. She stopped her car and waved.

"Hi, Plum!" said Cornelia enthusiastically. "What are you up to?"

"I was just meeting with Gary Grigorian," said Plum. "Giving him my condolences."

"Unbelievable! It's so sad," said Cornelia sincerely.

"Yes," said Plum robotically. *Am I really that cold?* she wondered.

"But what was really weird was that people from the environmental agency arrived to arrest Dieter. Apparently he has been moving sand around. Which I suppose is illegal."

"Really?" asked Cornelia with interest. "He's been arrested?"

"I think so," said Plum. "It was really scandalous."

"Listen," said Cornelia, "I'm about to have some lunch. I would love it if you could join me."

Plum hesitated. She should probably get back to the office. But then, this was an opportunity to dive deep into the Nettles family. "I don't want to impose..."

"No, please," Cornelia said ardently. "I hate to eat alone, and Gerta has made my favorite sandwich."

"That's very nice of you," said Plum. "I am hungry."

Ten minutes later Plum found herself sitting across from Cornelia at the same patio table where she had met with her mother and Alexandra Rijo days prior. This time, the table was so beautifully set, it could have been photographed for a magazine. The glass table was adorned with a blue-and-white ikat tablecloth, atop which were wicker chargers, white-bone china, blue linen napkins with the Nettles monogram, and bamboo flatware. In the center was a glass vase filled with languid grasses that moved balletically in the breeze. There was a decanter of flat water as well as one of sparkling and a sweating bottle of rosé.

Cornelia asked Plum to recount every detail about the environmental agency confronting Dieter. As the maid served them, Plum mimicked Dieter's accent and how he asked to change out of his bathing suit. Cornelia laughed heartily and encouragingly.

The sandwiches that Cornelia had referred to were not your average ham and cheese on white bread. Instead, there were paninis with broccolini rapini, pine nuts, and gruyere cheese. Additionally, the chef had made a delicious mango, avocado, and jicama salad dotted with red onion, delicate chicken empanadas, and curried lobster. The abundance of food and options elated Plum.

After gushing over the meal and requesting recipes (that she realized she probably would never make but wished she would), Plum moved to the topic of Arielle Waldron.

"There's something I wanted to ask you," began Plum. "When I was here the other day, I saw a photograph in your living room of you wearing a gold snake bracelet. Do you still have it?"

"I think so," said Cornelia, spearing a piece of mango with her fork. "Why do you ask?"

"It's just that a very similar, if not identical, bracelet was found among Arielle Waldron's possessions."

Cornelia stared at her. "Really? You know, now that I think about it, I'm not sure where it is. I wonder...wait a minute. I was wearing it that day I talked to Arielle by the pool! And I think I took it off to go swimming. Gosh, I forgot about it. Could she have taken it? I mean, by accident."

"Definitely," said Plum. She took a bite of her panini, the soft cheese melting in her mouth. "Arielle was a kleptomaniac."

"Oh, wow," said Cornelia. "I didn't know that. I had no idea."

"How would you?" asked Plum. "You said you didn't know her."

"I didn't know her, and I definitely didn't know she was a kleptomaniac," insisted Cornelia.

Plum noticed that red spots appeared on Cornelia's cheeks and neck. Cornelia was focusing on cutting a piece of lobster as if she were performing spinal surgery. Something was fishy, Plum thought, and not just the lobster. Cornelia was protesting way too much.

"Is there something you're not telling me about Arielle?" Plum asked boldly.

Cornelia quickly glanced up. "What? No, of course not. This is so unbelievable."

Plum had learned that the best way to garner information was to remain silent and allow the other person to start talking. Therefore, she took a large bite of her sandwich, chewed it a dozen more times than she would normally, before following it with a large gulp of rosé. All the while she kept her eyes fixed on Cornelia, who she could tell was struggling with something. Finally, Cornelia put her fork down with a clank.

"Okay, I may have not told you everything," she began.

Plum gave her a fake surprised look and dabbed her mouth with her napkin. "Oh?" she said.

"I did know who Arielle was when I met her at the hotel pool. We'd crossed paths in New York. I thought she was fun and nice when we hung out, but then later that afternoon, I realized that there were some items missing from not only my beach bag but Maia's as well. I was the one who called hotel security to report it. I feel terrible admitting that since she was murdered, and if it weren't for me ousting her from the hotel, she may not have even been staying at Dieter's. I'm responsible."

Cornelia wore a look of genuine misery. Plum felt badly for her. "It's not your fault she was murdered," Plum tried to console her.

"I don't know… I think, what did I care about those things she took? They were just replaceable objects," protested Cornelia.

"Don't overthink it," said Plum. "You wanted your bracelet back. I get it."

Cornelia appeared pensive. She moved her fork around her plate. "I guess."

"Cornelia," began Plum. "I saw you the other day riding on a motorcycle with Jeremy Silver."

She looked up, and again, her face flushed red. "You did?"

"Yes," said Plum. "He's Dieter's right-hand man, and your father and Dieter have a very contentious relationship."

"Not anymore…" interrupted Cornelia.

Plum eyed her carefully. "Are you sure? Because when the environmental agency arrested Dieter, he blamed your father for calling them on him."

"Nonsense," said Cornelia, her face darkening. "They settled their battle."

"Not according to Dieter." *And not according to* Chisme, thought Plum. But she didn't want to let on to Cornelia that Las Frutas staff was putting out a gossip rag. It could be useful to her in the future.

"Well, I know nothing about that," said Cornelia, shaking her head. "And as for Jeremy, we are friendly acquaintances. He's given me a ride a few times on his motorcycle. My parents forbid me to ride one, so it's a secret thrill of mine. But that's all."

"Nothing romantic?" asked Plum, cocking her head to the side.

"No," said Cornelia quickly.

Plum wasn't sure she believed her.

"Really," insisted Cornelia, as if reading Plum's mind. "And please don't tell my parents that you saw me with him."

"Sure."

Cornelia looked nervous. "I know it's childish, and I'm a grown woman and should be making my own life decisions, but my parents really are very against motorcycles."

"Okay," said Plum. "Although I happen to agree with them. They're death traps."

When Plum returned to the town house, she found Lucia at her desk but no Gerald. Lucia was on the phone, and from what Plum could overhear, it was someone inquiring about Villa Tomate, which Lucia was extolling the virtues of. Plum stood by and listened.

"There is a reason we call it Villa Tomate," she said into the receiver. "Because everyone loves tomatoes. You find it in every cuisine. And like the fruit, everyone loves Villa Tomate."

She paused as she listened to the other person on the phone before responding. "Tomato is a fruit... No, it is... Agree to disagree... Are you interested in the property?"

Plum smiled and sat down at her desk. She switched on the

computer and scanned the files that Lucia had sent her updating reservations. When Lucia hung up, she addressed Plum.

"The police came, that Captain Diaz, and asked Gerald to go with them to the station," said Lucia.

Plum rolled her head back. "Gerald will be furious."

"He already was," agreed Lucia. "He went kicking and screaming. He thinks he's here on a vacation."

"There are no free holidays," added Plum.

Lucia rose and walked over to her desk. "Did you have time to check the headlines today?"

Plum shook her head. "No, why? What happened?"

"You should look at them. There is an interesting story about Gary Grigorian. And even more interesting pictures."

Plum quickly opened her browser and waited two solid minutes for her internet to begin working. She was reduced to cursing and moaning. One of the painful aspects of island life was spotty Wi-Fi. Finally, it launched, and she googled Gary Grigorian. She was immediately directed to a page from a salacious website which featured pictures of him in a deep embrace with a girl on the beach. Upon closer inspection, it was obvious that it was Arielle.

Plum's jaw dropped, and she glanced up at Lucia. "He totally lied to me. That little toad."

"What did you expect?" she asked. "He's a celebrity. Doesn't need to tell the truth. Not to mention, wasn't he a weatherman? They get paid to speak, not to be right."

"I guess." Plum turned back her attention to the pictures.

There were several photos, but most of them were basically the same picture with the camera zooming closer and with a slightly different angle. They were definitely taken on the beach at Dieter's house—she recognized the steep staircase with the precarious railing. And in the pictures that were farther away, she could decipher the roof of Dieter's temples.

Gary was wearing shorts and a polo shirt, and Arielle was in a flowing sundress, her blond hair cascading down her shoulders. There was one with her stroking his hair, one where they were kissing, and a few of them walking and hugging. The most revealing was one of them lying on a towel in the sand, Gary on top of Arielle.

"You know what I think is strange about that one?" asked Lucia, pointing to them lying down. "He's staring directly at the camera. He knew these photos were being taken."

Plum squinted. "You're right. Do you think they're staged?"

"Yes," said Lucia.

"But why?" asked Plum. "He and Hallie were putting on this lovey-dovey display everywhere. And he insisted that he didn't cheat. Why would he do this photo shoot?"

"Didn't you say that they would do anything for fame?" asked Lucia. "Maybe this would make some headlines."

"I want to say they wouldn't sink so low, but you could be right," said Plum.

She kept scrolling through the pictures as Lucia stood over her. "Judging by the sun, these were taken either at dusk or in the early morning," said Plum.

"Definitely early morning. That's east. The sun is rising."

"Then since Arielle was only there one night, we have to assume this was the morning that she was murdered," said Plum, turning to face Lucia. "Which would mean that Gary was the murderer!"

"Not necessarily," said Lucia. "It could have been his wife."

"True," conceded Plum.

"Or maybe his wife took the pictures?" asked Lucia, as she made her way back to her desk.

Plum glanced again at the screen. She clicked on the pictures to make them larger. "Oh my God."

"What?"

"It says the photographs were taken by Max Stylo."

Plum and Lucia stared at each other with surprise.

"This is a variable," said Plum. "Jessica told me that she thought that Mr. Big was Gary and Arielle was having an affair with him. But she said Max completely disagreed with her and didn't want her to even mention it to me. But if he took these pictures, he had to have known. Why wouldn't he want Jessica to tell me that he thought they were having an affair?"

"Maybe he didn't tell Jessica?" asked Lucia.

"But why not?" asked Plum. "He and Jessica seem attached at the hip."

"But didn't you tell me that he is suspiciously handsome and Jessica is a baby buzzard?"

"Buzzard?"

"Yes, an ugly buzzard," insisted Lucia.

"You mean an ugly duckling?" Plum clarified.

"What do you mean by that?" asked Lucia. "Ducklings are never ugly."

"Are buzzards?"

"Of course. That's why the phrase in Paraiso is an ugly buzzard," said Lucia.

"In America we say ugly duckling."

"That sounds wrong," said Lucia.

The door banged open dramatically, and Gerald stood on the threshold panting. He placed his hand on his heart, as if he were a damsel having a fainting spell in the 1700s.

"Water," he commanded as he strolled through the living room and collapsed on the sofa.

Reluctantly, Plum went and poured him a glass of water from the tap, which she dutifully brought to him. She had pondered ignoring him, but his whining reached a fever pitch when he was dehydrated, and it wasn't worth the scandal. He glugged it down without even a thank-you.

"Fan me," he commanded.

"Excuse me?" asked Plum.

Lucia came up behind her and was surveying Gerald with a curious look.

"I'm suffering. I need air. Fan me," he whispered.

Lucia and Plum exchanged glances before plopping down on the chairs next to him, without fanning him.

Gerald moaned and groaned, and when they queried what had happened, he put up a finger to ask them to be patient. He ultimately spoke.

"I have been subjected to an entire morning of paperwork and red tape. The police had me do all the official documents on behalf of the Waldron family. I did not even have lunch yet." He swooned.

"But isn't that why you came to the island?" asked Plum. "To tie up all the loose ends?"

"They have asked too much of me," exclaimed Gerald meekly. "I will need a vacation from my vacation."

"You're not on vacation," said Lucia.

Gerald waved his hand in the air dismissively. "Technicalities."

Wordlessly, Lucia and Plum rose and went to their respective desks. Gerald's eyes followed them, and he scowled. Suddenly revived, he propped himself up on his elbows.

"You're not even going to get me lunch? Comfort me through this horrible day?" he sneered.

"Nope," said Plum, staring at her computer screen. She enlarged the photos of Gary.

"Lucia?" asked Gerald. "You have grandchildren. You have the appearance of a nurturing type. Save me."

"You'll have to save yourself today," Lucia retorted.

"You are both cruel," he said.

"Yup," agreed Plum.

"I've never experienced such spiteful and callous behavior," he said.

"Good to know," said Lucia, her eyes glued to her computer.

Gerald's face wore astonishment before he collapsed back into the sofa, continued moaning for another few minutes and, when he gained no traction, finally became silent. His snores blazed through the town house within minutes.

26

PLUM AND JUAN KEVIN HAD a long phone call where she filled him in about Dieter's arrest as well as the photographs. He said he would find out what was going on with Dieter, but in the meantime, he was very eager to have another unofficial conversation with Max and Jessica. Through his security access, Juan Kevin had searched the hotel bookings and ascertained that Max and Jessica had not yet checked out, and furthermore, they had reservations at Las Casitas, a restaurant located in the hotel, that evening. Juan Kevin booked a table next to them for himself, Plum, and Gerald, who, once roused, insisted that he accompany them because he was entitled to a fantastic meal after his hard work and lack of recognition that morning.

Lucia offered to drop them off at the restaurant on her way home so they wouldn't have to take the golf cart. Juan Kevin said he would drop them off after.

Las Casitas was positioned on a balcony overlooking the hotel pool. It was a completely open-walled and whitewashed restaurant, with rattan pendants hanging from cavernous ceilings and modern tables with crisp, white table linens adorning them. Thumping music leaked out of the speakers, and waiters in button-downs with ties catered to the sleek clientele. It had more of a Mykonos vibe than a Caribbean vibe, with both the staff and the customers assuming haughty and condescending airs.

Juan Kevin was seated in a chair in the corner booth when they arrived, and he stood until Plum was ensconced in her seat. Gerald plopped down on the bench next to Plum and snapped his fingers so that the maître d' would not leave until Gerald ordered a drink.

"I need a fruit punch," he demanded.

"I'll tell your waiter," she assured him. "Anyone else?"

Plum ordered a white wine, and Juan Kevin got a club soda. "Don't you ever drink?" Plum asked.

"When I am off duty," he replied.

Plum felt his eyes drift over her body, and she burned with pleasure. She had taken extra care with her outfit tonight, donning a pale-blue floral dress that cinched at the waist and her favorite aquamarine and diamond earclips. They had been her first splurge when she made editor-in-chief of *Travel and Respite Magazine*, and she wore them on special occasions. Although tonight wasn't exactly a special occasion, she had felt compelled to wear them.

"I checked up on Michael, the bartender at Dieter's house," said Juan Kevin.

"Oh? Was he the intruder?"

"I brought him in for questioning," said Juan Kevin. "He wouldn't confess, but I am fairly certain that he was the one who left the knife. He's not a good guy. Turns out he is a bit notorious. He is not only a bartender but a cocaine dealer."

"That's probably what Gary was getting from him the night we saw them," said Plum.

"Exactly. I banned him from the resort. Told him I never wanted to see him on Las Frutas property again, or I would have him arrested," said Juan Kevin.

"Boss move," said Gerald with respect.

The waitress came and took their food orders. Plum ordered

warm, yucca-crusted goat cheese mâche followed by lobster fricassee with a lime and sauterne sauce. Gerald opted for the hearts of palm avocado salad followed by the filet of sea bass with a salsa verde. Juan Kevin had salmon on crispy rice followed by a beef stew with a side of mashed green plantains with salami, onions, and eggs. There was excitement all around in anticipation of their scrumptious meal. But Plum also could hear Lucia in the back of her head telling her that she was spending too much money dining out and she better be careful. She did feel guilty splurging.

They were halfway through their appetizers when Max and Jessica sat at the table next to them. Plum feigned astonishment at the coincidence, but so horrible was her acting that Gerald kicked her under the table. She had opened with "fancy seeing you here," which she had thought sounded candid and genuine, but by the terse grimace on Gerald's face, it was obvious she would have failed at the American Academy of Dramatic Arts.

Max and Jessica, while not enthused by their proximity to their acquaintances, were polite and friendly. Max looked as handsome as usual, his blazing good looks enhanced by the light-blue V-neck shirt he wore, which brought out the color of his eyes. He held hands with Jessica the entire dinner.

Lighthearted banter continued through the cocktail hour, but then Plum became bored and went in for the kill.

"I saw the pictures you took of Arielle and Gary in the *Daily Mail* today," said Plum.

Although he tried to be nonchalant, it was clear that Max was unsettled. He shifted his weight in his chair. "How'd you know I took them?"

"They had your name in the credits, emblazoned on every picture," said Plum.

"If you can't do the time, don't do the crime!" squealed Gerald.

Juan Kevin cleared his throat. "I'm sure you have a reasonable explanation for why you did not inform me or the police about these photographs."

Jessica shot Max a panicked look of concern and stared up at his Adonis face while he debated how to respond. It was evident to everyone at the table (except maybe Gerald, who kept checking his texts) that Max was conflicted. Finally, he answered.

"I did take the pictures," he said. "And look, I didn't want to hurt anyone..."

"Max is a very good person," said Jessica firmly. "He always does the right thing."

"Thanks, babe," he said, looking at her with adoration. He stroked her hand, and she purred underneath his glances. "It's true. I always do the right thing."

"And what is the right thing in this situation?" asked Plum.

With a dramatic sigh, Max disentangled himself from his girlfriend and put his hands on the table then leaned in. "Arielle asked me to take those pictures of her and Gary Grigorian. It was all arranged. She told me to meet her at eight a.m. at Dieter's house. She said it was the only safe time, when Hallie would be off on her walk, and I could get some great shots. She told me she would pay me two thousand dollars in cash."

"And did she?" asked Juan Kevin.

"No," said Max with annoyance. Plum instantly thought of the two thousand dollars found in Arielle's bag.

"Gary was in on the whole thing. I think he gave her the money, but I can't be sure," said Max.

Oh, I can be sure, thought Plum. But instead, she said, "Why was Gary in on it?"

"His image had become dull," said Max. "He was a mere game show host. I mean, those guys are not exactly on the front lines of society or fame. And the kicker was he was in a seemingly happy marriage. They had maxed out their celebrity as a unit. Gary was gunning for the big time. He thought it was time that he spiced up his image, had a more salacious reputation. I can't help but think that was Arielle's idea…"

"She could be super persuasive," added Jessica.

"It's true," agreed Max. "We were all hanging together a few nights before, and Arielle told him as much. He was pretty drunk and got excited and agreed. But Hallie heard the tail end of the conversation and shut it down. She was, understandably, very possessive and didn't like any of it. So, when we decided to proceed, it was all on the down low."

"When Arielle went to Dieter's, it presented a perfect opportunity," said Jessica.

"Yes," said Max. "We decided to take the pictures without Hallie knowing. But for some reason, she cut short her run that day and found us and freaked out. I was asked to leave the property immediately, and I never got my money."

"When you left, it was just Hallie, Gary, and Arielle on the beach?" asked Plum.

"Yes," said Max. "I didn't want to deal with the drama. And honestly, I felt guilty. But then Arielle died."

"And after Arielle died, Hallie reached out to Max and asked him to take her pictures for *People*," said Jessica. "We thought all was forgotten."

"Yeah," said Max. "Hallie and I had a great photo session. And then she died. Then I was like, what? In a total meltdown. And honestly, initially, I wasn't going to do anything with the pictures of Arielle and Gary. I thought that would be cruel. I had promised…"

"That's why he didn't want me to say anything to you," said Jessica to Plum.

"Did Gary try to buy back the pictures after Hallie died?" asked Juan Kevin. "Did he try to stop you from releasing them?"

"I reached out to him and sent my condolences. I said, of course, those photos of him and Arielle would never see the light of day," said Max. "But his response really surprised me."

"And me," added Jessica. Her eyes widened and flitted from Juan Kevin to Plum to Gerald.

"What did he say?" asked Plum.

"He told me to sell them to the highest bidder," said Max. "Make money."

Max sat back in his seat and took a long drink of his Diet Coke through a straw. Jessica grabbed his hand across the table. Plum glanced at Juan Kevin to gauge his reaction, which was one of confusion. Gerald was useless, tapping at his cell phone, only half engaged.

"What do you make of all this?" asked Plum.

Max paused before speaking. "I don't know," he said.

Jessica said, "I know. Maybe it wasn't such a happy marriage. I think he was happy to be rid of his wife. He obviously didn't want to protect their legacy. Maybe she had done something to really piss him off."

"And what about Arielle?" asked Plum. "Do you think he could have killed her?"

"I don't know why anyone would kill her," said Jessica, loyally.

They discussed other things for the rest of the dinner, but one thing Plum still had to figure out was Max's relationship to Arielle. After all, the Polaroid found in her belongings was of her in a compromising position with a man who had a tattoo on his butt cheek. The same tattoo that Max had. There was no possible way it could be anyone else.

Plum texted Gerald, even though he was sitting right next to her—it seemed to be the only way to get his attention. She asked him to run defense on Jessica and make up some fake social conversation when they walked to their cars so that she and Juan Kevin could talk directly to Max.

When they left the restaurant, the night was still humid, and the air was fresh.

"Can I steal you away from your hot boyfriend for a minute to chat with me?" Gerald asked Jessica. "I bet we know a lot of the same people, let's play the name game!"

He took Jessica's reluctant arm (she gave Max a despondent look as if she were being separated for life) and linked his arm under hers. Gerald winked at Plum, who took the opportunity to sidle up to Max. They all walked along the lighted path to the parking lot. Plum, Max, and Juan Kevin led the way, while Gerald and Jessica took up the rear. Within seconds, Gerald had Jessica laughing hysterically at something he said.

The moon was high in the atmosphere, and every possible star and planet was scattered across the sky like a Van Gogh painting.

"In New York, there is so much fog and light pollution that we don't even see these stars," said Plum.

"That would make me crazy," said Juan Kevin.

"It can," admitted Max, craning his neck upward. "It's really beautiful here."

"You should photograph it," suggested Plum.

"Good idea," agreed Max.

She waited a beat, trying to make sure she posed her questions in an offhand manner. "I'd love to ask you something, but it's probably too intrusive," she whispered in a low tone that she had used on clients when she wanted to bait them.

"What's that?" asked Max.

Plum gave Juan Kevin a look, and he understood and slunk back to walk several feet behind Plum and Max.

"No, forget it," said Plum. "I'm just a nosy barker."

"No, it's okay," said Max. "I've told you so much already, I don't want to hold back."

Plum continued walking the path, sidestepping a couple returning to the hotel. Patience, she had found, worked well with Max's age demographic. They were not used to having to wait for anything. Everything in their life could be ordered or delivered at a moment's notice. The only currency to use against them was delay. She said nothing until finally Max spoke again.

"Really, what is it?" he implored.

"Well, I noticed that you had a tattoo on your, you know," she said.

"My butt? Yes, I do! It's an arrow," he enthused, happy that she had ultimately spoken what was on her mind.

"Right," nodded Plum. Then she stopped and turned to him. "I saw a Polaroid of you and Arielle naked!"

Max's face became surprised. "Not possible," he said firmly.

"Don't tease," she said.

He stopped dead. "I'm not teasing. I never hooked up with Arielle. I mean, a long time ago, but not recently. And we definitely didn't take pictures together."

Juan Kevin, Jessica, and Gerald came upon them and stopped as well.

"Everything okay?" asked Juan Kevin, arching an eyebrow and giving Plum a curious look.

"What's up?" asked Jessica.

"Plum said that she saw a picture of me and Arielle naked," said Max. "Which is not at all true."

They all stared at each other in tense silence.

"Plum, are you goofing?" asked Gerald, trying to break the mood.

"I'm not," said Plum. "I saw you entangled with Arielle…"

Suddenly, Plum was not so certain. She shot Juan Kevin a desperate look.

"Could it have been you and Jessica?" asked Juan Kevin, in a Hail Mary.

Max and Jessica, who had stood erect with recriminations, suddenly softened and looked at each other with both love and embarrassment. Even in the dark, Plum could see Jessica's blush.

"If you mean there was a naked picture of a man and a woman, then yes, it was us," confessed Jessica.

"But she had blond hair!" insisted Plum.

Jessica gave Plum a pitiful smile. "Sometimes I dress up. I have lots of wigs, and Max and I like to spice it up."

"Jessica is wonderfully creative," said Max, as he kept his eyes glued on his girlfriend.

"Aw," said Jessica.

"But how did Arielle get the photograph in her possession?" asked Juan Kevin.

"Yeah, was she some sick voyeur?" asked Gerald.

For the first time, Plum witnessed Jessica's face become harsh and angry. There was a glint of rage that flashed in her eyes.

"Arielle had to take something from everyone. She thought it would complete her, but all it did was illuminate how shallow and hollow her life was."

There was stunned silence. And then just as suddenly, Jessica softened. "Sorry, I don't know what I was saying. I'm just tired. Can we go, sweetie?" she asked, gazing up at Max.

"You bet," he said, taking her hand.

CHAPTER 27

AFTER THEY HAD LEFT MAX and Jessica, Plum thought they would call it a night, but Juan Kevin had other plans. He had instructed his staff to be on the lookout for Johnny Wisebrook, and he had received a text during dinner that Johnny was currently at the tapas restaurant on the marina, having drinks with his crew. Juan Kevin believed a further conversation with him was warranted, therefore they agreed to head to the marina. Gerald was the most ecstatic, as he was ready to continue his hobnobbing with the aging rock star.

The marina was heavy with the scent of sea salt and jasmine. It was buzzing as usual, tables full of tourists and regulars, the sounds of voices and cutlery echoing through the piazza and bouncing off the walls of the three-story buildings. The tapas restaurant was on the edge of the square in the marina and did not abut another restaurant, so it afforded some privacy. Johnny sat at a small table littered with half-eaten plates of food and cocktail glasses. His group was a motley crew: there was a man about Johnny's age, who had a fleshy nose, a face full of broken blood vessels, and wispy hair. He had a very robust laugh that he used frequently, and Plum thought either he was listening to a stand-up comedy routine in his head or he was a bit daft. There were two very young women in their early twenties, both of whom were smoking cigarettes and wore a lot of makeup. One had dark hair pulled back in a sleek ponytail, and the other was blond with feline features. They wore little clothing. Standing off to the side was Oliver, the bodyguard, who was watching his boss carefully. His eyes tracked Juan Kevin, Plum, and Gerald as they approached.

"Juan Kevin!" said Johnny. "How are you, mate?"

"I'm good," said Juan Kevin. "What a surprise. We were coming for a drink."

"Join us," said Johnny.

A waiter brought over additional chairs to the table, to the dismay of the two women, who appeared unenthused to have to share the attention of the legendary rock star. They pinned fake smiles to their lips when introductions were made. The man with the hearty laugh was Daniel, and he was a business associate of Johnny's. Plum wondered if he was paid to laugh at everything Johnny said to make him appear more amusing.

"Johnny, please tell us when your next album will be released," begged Gerald.

"Yeah, not sure, mate," said Johnny. "Still working in the studio. Hope to get it out beginning of next year."

"I'm sure it's amazing!" gushed Gerald.

"It is," said Johnny with confidence. "Best one yet."

The two girls began inundating Johnny with requests for a sneak preview, but he demurred. The waitress distributed drinks, and Plum kept giving Juan Kevin sidelong glances, wondering when and if he would ask Johnny any questions about the Target card found on Arielle. Was he waiting for the right opportunity?

It came about ten minutes in. Juan Kevin adeptly and subtly steered the conversation to women and what they want from Johnny. Then one of the girls made some flirtatious comment to Johnny, and he fell into the trap. Almost immediately, he stood, flung out his wallet, and did the same routine that he had done at his house. "This is what you want from me," he said as he threw his wallet on the table.

The girls laughed, as did Daniel (who probably laughed the hardest, despite having witnessed the act many times before, no doubt). Juan Kevin stood to help Johnny gather the cards and money that had fallen out of his wallet.

"Ah, the famous Target card," said Juan Kevin, holding it between his fingers.

"Yeah, mate," said Johnny reaching out his hand. "The golden ticket to entry *en mi casa*."

Juan Kevin held it in his fingers for a moment before gingerly handing it back and saying casually, "You know, Arielle Waldron had one of those in her belongings when she died."

Johnny didn't react. "Is that so, mate?"

"I thought you said you never met her," Juan Kevin said.

"I thought I hadn't, but I also told you I meet lots of ladies," said Johnny.

"But you only give out a small number of these, so you must remember her," Juan Kevin pushed.

Johnny's face became harsh. "I don't like what you're insinuating, mate."

Juan Kevin looked at Plum, and she understood that he wanted her to enter the conversation. She could ask the hard-hitting questions.

"Did you hook up with Arielle?"

Suddenly, Plum had the strong sensation that danger was approaching. She glanced around the marina. There was a couple strolling down the dock toward the yachts in front of them. To the side, a big group was taking selfies. A yellow-and-white striped cat slithered past the bicycle rack and down an alley. What had caused Plum to feel nervous?

"What's she doing here?" boomed a voice behind her.

Martin Rijo.

Plum turned around.

He wore a belligerent look on his face and had adopted an aggressive stance. Plum stared at his face and noticed that his eyes were dilated and flicking around, as if he were on something.

"Ah, Martin," said Johnny. "I have invited friends to sit with us."

"She's no friend of mine," said Martin.

"It's all good, mate," said Daniel. He pulled a chair out next to him, on the other side of the table from Plum, and motioned for Martin to sit down. "Come 'round here."

Martin folded his hands. "Johnny, we have business. I don't want her anywhere near me."

"Martin, this is really unnecessary," said Juan Kevin.

"I don't trust this dog one bit," said Martin.

Plum's face flamed with mortification that swiftly turned into rage. She stood. Her stature worked for her benefit in this situation as she towered over the tiny tyrant. "Now listen here, you bully. You are rude and inappropriate. I think it's you who should scram."

Martin moved toward Plum, but just as he did, Juan Kevin leapt up and got between them. He pushed Martin back.

"No reason we can't all be civil," warned Juan Kevin.

"No reason to be civil," said Martin.

"What's his problem?" asked Gerald, taking a sip from his drink. "This guy needs a chill pill."

"I need you to get out," demanded Martin. "I own this place, and I don't want the lot of you around."

"Martin, you can't do that," said Juan Kevin.

"Yes, I can," insisted Martin.

"We're having a nice time, mate," said Johnny. "Why don't you get a drink?"

For some reason this caused Martin to explode. He turned to Johnny, and as he raged, little specks of saliva came spewing out of his mouth. "Listen here, you old perv. Don't tell me what to do.

I'm tired of cleaning up your messes. Tired of covering for you. I don't need your crap."

Johnny shook his head and turned to the two women, who were watching wide-eyed as the drama unfolded. "Don't mind him, ladies, he's a drug addict."

Martin picked up Juan Kevin's empty chair and threw it. A hush came across the piazza as everyone turned to witness what was going on. Oliver stepped forward and stood in front of Johnny, blocking him from Martin's wrath.

"Drug addict? Who the hell are you?" demanded Martin. "You're a degenerate gambler who owes money all over the island. You washed-up, old has-been!"

Everyone was stunned. Juan Kevin and Plum exchanged gapes. The two women appeared confused, and Daniel was horrified. At first Johnny looked like a deer caught in the headlights, but then he turned and chuckled.

"Oh, mate, you are a jokester," he said, laughing it off.

"I'm not joking. And I'm not your mate," seethed Martin.

"Let's go," said Johnny. He snapped his fingers, and Daniel popped up. The two women looked at each other as if to ask if they should follow suit, but Johnny ignored them. Oliver began to shield Johnny as they walked toward the exit.

Martin moved toward Johnny. "You can't walk away, old man. You got debts to pay."

Johnny stared at him but didn't say anything.

"Let's talk about this later," said Daniel. "In the morning."

Martin blocked Oliver, who was blocking Johnny. "We talk about it now."

Johnny's temper flared. "Listen, you little bastard, I owe you nothing. Remember who you are—just a street urchin that some rich people scooped up. You are scum."

Martin lunged at Johnny, but Oliver caught him. Juan Kevin rushed over to hold Martin back. Plum glanced around the courtyard and could see people filming the interaction with their smart phones. This would not look good. While Juan Kevin and Oliver held on to the flailing Martin, who was desperately trying to get free, Daniel quickly shielded Johnny from the crowd's view and ushered him out of the square. Only when they were sure he was long gone did they release Martin.

He dusted off his shirt and glowered at Juan Kevin. "You are finished now, Juan Kevin. Toast."

To avoid escalating the situation, Juan Kevin didn't respond. He kept his eyes on Martin, until the scion skulked away.

When they returned to the table, the women had left, and Gerald remained. He drained his fruit punch, popped the cherry in his mouth, and grinned. "That was epic."

Juan Kevin's office was located between the marina and Plum's town house, and he asked her if she wouldn't mind stopping en route while he drove them home. The entire resort had security cameras everywhere, and he wanted to make sure that he took the footage of what had transpired at the tapas restaurant. Although he was no fan of Martin's, he explained to Plum that it was his job to protect Las Frutas as well as the reputation of the Rijo family, therefore he had to make sure the footage didn't get into the wrong hands. Even though he trusted his staff, this was too sensational and could provide a big blackmail opportunity for someone. Plum didn't want to mention that everyone at the marina had filmed the scene on their phones, as she was sure that Juan Kevin knew that, but she figured he had to do his part to control it.

By the time they reached the office, Gerald was snoring in the back seat. They decided to leave him, and Plum went inside with Juan Kevin. There was a young man sitting in the front where Patricia usually sat, and he and Juan Kevin had a brief exchange in Spanish before moving together toward a back room Plum had not been in before. Much to her surprise, there was an entire wall of screens, revealing almost every public corner of the resort.

"Wow," Plum gasped. "Big Brother is watching."

Juan Kevin nodded. "Yes."

Her eyes flicked from one monitor to the next. There were cameras on the golf course, the beach, the marina, the restaurants, the hotel pool, reception at the front gate, the tennis courts, the heliport, the shooting range, as well as the polo fields. Due to the late hour, some had little activity, but others—like the bars and restaurants—were busy.

Juan Kevin sat down at the desk where a monitor was placed. He pulled up the footage from the camera on the corner of the marina where the tapas bar was located and rewound it. When he found the recording of Martin exploding and lunging at Johnny, he watched it slowly before copying it to a flash drive. He then erased the footage on the monitor.

"That's it?" asked Plum, who was leaning over him.

"Yes."

"Did you ever look through the footage the morning that Arielle was killed?" asked Plum, her eyes flickering between each screen.

"Dozens of times," said Juan Kevin. "I had my entire team do so too."

"What about when Hallie fell?" asked Plum.

"We did as well. Unfortunately, there are no cameras along that cliff."

"Could you humor me and show me the shots from that morning?" asked Plum.

Juan Kevin glanced at his watch before conceding. "All right."

He typed on the keyboard, and suddenly all the cameras blinked and changed their picture. The light immediately transformed, as they were looking through events that transpired in the early morning, and visibility was much improved.

"I'll put them on a slow fast-forward, otherwise we will be here for two hours, as it is in real time," said Juan Kevin.

Plum walked up to the screens and glanced at each one. She paid little attention to the tennis courts and shooting range, as they were on the other side of the resort from Dieter's villa. Her eyes moved along until they rested on a familiar villa.

"You have a camera on Alexandra Rijo's house?" asked Plum.

Juan Kevin came up behind her and nodded. "Yes, it is the only villa that we watch. Most people have their own security systems or don't use one. In general, the resort is very safe, we have no crime, so people don't need it."

"No crime except murder," said Plum.

"Unfortunately, yes," he admitted.

Plum watched Alexandra's villa before moving on to the footage of Coconuts, but she saw something out of the corner of her eye and quickly looked back at Alexandra's villa. She squinted, unsure.

"Look, Juan Kevin, can you blow that up?" she said.

"I can try." He went back to the monitor and increased the picture.

"That's Johnny Wisebrook!" said Plum. "And that's Alexandra Rijo!"

Sure enough, although obscured by the palm trees in front of the villa, Johnny and Alexandra were embracing before she led him into her house. The time stamp said 8:07 a.m.

"Johnny and Alexandra are lovers?" asked Plum.

Juan Kevin was astonished. "I had heard rumors, but I dismissed them," said Juan Kevin.

"That's probably why he didn't want to tell us where he was. If they are top-secret lovers."

"Could be," said Juan Kevin. "How did my team miss this?"

"He probably didn't park in the driveway and went in through the side," said Plum.

"I suppose," said Juan Kevin.

"I wonder why Alexandra would go for him."

"Maybe she likes danger," said Juan Kevin.

"But she seems so respectable. That said, her son is a monster. I wonder if he knows mommy is sleeping with the man he called a degenerate."

"He probably does, and that's why he was so enraged," said Juan Kevin.

Plum was suddenly tired. "I guess we have to remove him from our list of suspects," said Plum, somewhat deflated. "Which is a pity because I really wanted him to be the killer. He's an ass."

"We just have to keep looking," said Juan Kevin. "I feel as if we are getting closer."

28

THE NEXT MORNING PLUM FOUND a message from Alexandra Rijo, who said she would be having an early lunch at the restaurant by the golf course and would like it if Plum stopped by. The missive felt like more of a command rather than an invitation to Plum. She instantly wondered if Alexandra knew Plum had discovered her relationship with Johnny. But how could she? Juan Kevin wouldn't have told her. Plum had no choice but to find out.

"I read your diary, and it makes no sense," said Gerald as he wandered into the kitchen for coffee.

"You read my diary!" exploded Plum. "How dare you? You little..." Then she stopped. "I don't have a diary."

Gerald poured himself a large cup of coffee and added milk. "Then what was that sad, handwritten book I read?"

"I don't know what you're talking about... Wait, you mean the checkered book? That's Hallie's."

Gerald took a sip of his coffee. "Oh, that makes more sense. There was a lot of stuff about a husband and TV roles. I thought you had some sort of double life."

Plum took her cup of coffee to her desk. "No. Gary gave it to me, and I refuse to read it. That's why I left it on the coffee table. Anything interesting?"

"Well, I have to think," said Gary, plopping down on the sofa so aggressively that his coffee slopped over the rim of his mug. "Now that I know it's Hallie's, I have to completely revise my impressions. She did say that the person who killed A—I assume that's Arielle—did it because she was blackmailing him and knew about what was going on with 'The Girl.'"

"What?" asked Plum. "Let me see that book."

"It's next to my bed," said Gerald.

"Quick like a bunny," commanded Plum, using the phrase that Gerald had used on her days before.

He sighed deeply and went to retrieve it. Plum didn't have time to scan the entire book, but Gerald was correct. Hallie said she knew who it was. Gary was right when he said that in his TV interview.

Plum slammed the book shut. "Good work, Gerald."

"I know," said Gerald.

The restaurant was located between the driving range and the eighteenth green of the La Cereza Golf Course. Golfers were setting out to play or coming in off their rounds. Caddies scrambled to hoist golf bags onto carts and polish the clumps of mud off the heads of clubs. Plum had briefly considered taking up golf but then had been deterred by how much time and effort was involved. It was such a tiny ball and caused such consternation to its players, she wondered if it was really worth the stress. Although she liked the idea of more outdoor exercise, it was more of a theoretical impulse rather than one she would put into practice in the near future.

She found Alexandra and her associate Giorgio Lombardi

seated at the best table in the dark-wood paneled restaurant, which had a panoramic view of the golf course. Alexandra had the remains of a cobb salad in front of her, and Plum surmised that Giorgio had ordered the hamburger, judging by the half-eaten pickle and red onion circle that remained on his otherwise empty plate.

"Plum, good of you to come," said Alexandra when Plum appeared at the table.

I didn't really have a choice, did I? she wanted to say but instead said, "Of course."

Giorgio chivalrously rose and waited for Plum to be seated. "So nice to see you again, Miss Lockhart," he said smoothly.

"We are just finishing up. I'm sure you've already eaten," Alexandra said.

As if on cue, Plum's stomach rumbled. "I'm all set," she lied, but the truth was she was famished. The pickle was looking pretty darn good right now.

Plum looked at Alexandra under a different lens now that she knew she was a part-time lover to a full-time lothario. Was the sophisticated lady bit all an act? Perhaps she was wild underneath her designer golf clothes and expensive jewelry.

They briefly discussed the golf course and the round that Alexandra had just played. Plum feigned interest as they analyzed the various holes and the shots that they felt were successful. There were a lot of references to various "lies" and references to how the greens were playing ("fast," they both concluded) as well as a few debates about erroneous club selection. Plum had to stifle a yawn. By the time the reason for the summons was revealed, Plum's nerves were stretched thin. Was this about Johnny? Or Martin?

"Plum," said Alexandra, for the first time turning completely in her direction. Her delicate gold and diamond earrings flashed in the sunlight. As usual, her makeup was impeccable, and her chocolate-brown eyes were both inquisitive and knowing. "I am aware that you were friends with Hallie Corona, and I would like you to help us during this tragic situation."

Plum shifted in her seat. A waitress came and poured her a glass of water, and Plum took a sip to stall for time. "I would not call myself friends with her, but I had worked with her."

"Details," said Alexandra dismissively. "As the owner of Las Frutas, it is very important to me that we maintain a stellar reputation. I cannot have scandals occurring here."

"It is terrible for business," Giorgio added.

Alexandra nodded. She rubbed her finger along the rim of her water glass. "Therefore, I am looking to you to aid me in containing this mess."

"How so?" asked Plum.

"I'm not exactly certain," said Alexandra. "But I know you are building a life here and establishing your own business. It is important for you to have the support of the community. To have my support," she said, her eyes lingering on Plum an extra second to make sure that she was comprehending her meaning.

"Of course," said Plum.

"Therefore, I need for you to confirm your allegiance to your new home, Las Frutas. And assist your new neighbors if something arises," said Alexandra.

"What Mrs. Rijo is saying, Miss Lockhart, is that if things become salacious or—worst-case scenario—litigious, we can count on your help to round out the full picture," said Giorgio.

"What's the full picture?" asked Plum.

Alexandra gave her a half smile. "No need to be coy. We are both businesswomen and know what must be done to succeed in this world. Often it means getting your hands dirty. As of now, we are very happy with the story that Hallie Corona slipped and fell to her death. A sad tale, but an accident. If it was a suicide, that's also very sad. But there are those sniffing around, suggesting it might be something more insidious. And that is not good for Las

Frutas. Therefore, I will count on you to make it obvious to the world that it was either an accident or suicide. Do I make myself clear?"

Before Plum could respond *crystal* (which she thought was probably a bad idea), Giorgio quickly added his version of a threat. "We want your company to do well here on Paraiso. But we will need your cooperation to make sure that happens. Otherwise, Plum Lockhart Luxury Retreats will face an uphill battle."

Plum gave them her most winning smile. "Absolutely."

"Wonderful," said Alexandra, turning back to Giorgio and taking a prim sip of her iced tea.

It was obvious that Martin had not yet shared his anecdote of what happened the previous night. Nor had Johnny, for that matter. Plum decided she had to do damage control before they turned Alexandra against her.

"In fact," said Plum, making sure she had Alexandra and Giorgio's attention. "I am so committed to Las Frutas and the community that I am working hard with my press contacts to suppress the story about what happened with Martin and Johnny Wisebrook last night."

Plum could see Alexandra grow pale and her face become drawn. "Oh? What happened?"

"They got into a fight, and Martin wanted to beat Johnny up. There was a lot of name-calling."

Alexandra shot Giorgio a look. He cleared his throat. "And what instigated this fight?"

"Funnily enough, me. Martin really dislikes me for my business association with his stepmother. It's becoming a problem," said Plum. "And I'd really like your help with him. Maybe you could ask him to cut me some slack."

"I can't control his behavior, sadly," said Alexandra. Some of her resolve was slowly returning.

"True. That is true," said Plum. "You know, he really seemed to hate Johnny, and I wondered if there was another reason. Maybe it has to do with a woman?"

Plum and Alexandra locked eyes, and Plum could see understanding in the latter's. She knew Plum was telling her to get her son to back off or else the world would know about her relationship with Johnny Wisebrook.

"I'll see what I can do," Alexandra relented.

"That would be wonderful."

Plum decided to stop by the taco truck to pick up a quick bite before heading back to her town house. Her conversation with Alexandra and Giorgio hadn't fazed her, despite the fact they were basically threatening to destroy her business unless she went along with their program, and she had to threaten them in turn. The sad reality was that she had made similar overtures and intimidations during her publishing career in New York City. And she was not eager to expose Hallie's death as anything other than an accident. In fact, she really wanted very little to do with the lingering specter of Hallie Corona at all.

Plum ordered a shredded chicken taco with adobo, fire-roasted tomatoes, and salsa verde, and because she was ravenous, she also added a chargrilled shrimp taco with chipotle sauce and jicama. When they were ready, she walked to a little high-top table off in the shade and began devouring her meal.

The day, like all days so far, was sunny, bright, and flawless. As the months became warmer, she thought that perhaps she would have to take to wearing a hat full time, and perhaps long-sleeved shirts with built-in sun protection. She couldn't risk continuing to expose her chalky-white flesh to the elements.

Plum happily finished the last bite of her taco, took a sip of her mango iced tea, and was about to leave when she saw Shakira pull up in a convertible Mercedes. She quickly exited her car, slamming the door behind her, and stormed toward an elderly woman in a maid's uniform, who was standing with a friend at another table a few yards away. Shakira wore a tight wrap dress that plunged to her navel, stilettos, and aviator sunglasses. She looked badass and ready for business.

Shakira spoke to the woman fiercely, gesticulating wildly and pointing a finger at her, and the maid's brown eyes widened. Plum ducked into the shade, pressing herself against the gum trees to avoid detection. Unfortunately, they were speaking in Spanish, and although Plum fancied herself proficient in the language, she had no idea what they were talking about. It was a lively exchange, where Shakira appeared hostile and the maid defensive and uneasy. It ended with Shakira stomping off, returning to her car, and taking off.

"Hello, Plum," said a male voice behind her, and Plum almost jumped out of her skin.

It was Charlie Mendoza. The middle-aged man with bushy eyebrows and a friendly, round face was Lucia's friend and the director of Las Frutas Resort Entertainment. He had helped Plum book Gerald's boyfriend's dance troupe at the resort.

"Charlie, you scared me," gasped Plum.

"I'm sorry," he said. "I didn't mean to."

"I have to confess, I was eavesdropping, or attempting to," said Plum. "Dieter Friedrich's girlfriend Shakira was just here, and she was yelling at that woman over there. I was trying to figure out what she was saying."

Plum pointed in the direction of the maid.

"I think I can help you out," said Charlie. "That's my sister-in-law Marta. She's the head housekeeper at Mr. Friedrich's. Let's go talk to her."

Brief introductions were made, but Marta looked warily at Plum, unsure whether or not she should betray the confidence of her employer. But with Charlie's assurance that Plum was a colleague of Lucia's, and not to mention that Plum was a good donut (a Paraison saying, equivalent to a good egg in English), Marta agreed.

"She's mad at me because she thought I had been indiscreet," said Marta softly. "But it is untrue."

"What did she accuse you of?" asked Plum.

"Señor Friedrich was recently arrested for moving sand. He learned that someone who works for him gave the information to Señor Nettles, his next-door neighbor, who called the authorities. Shakira knows I am friends with the Nettleses' housekeeper and accused me of telling them. But I had no idea about this at all. It was not me. My friend and I do not share information about our bosses as we know they do not like each other."

"Dieter told me they were friends," said Plum.

Marta shrugged. "Sometimes there is peace, and sometimes there is war. I never know."

"Who do you think leaked the information?" asked Plum.

Marta hesitated.

"Go on, tell her what you think," prompted Charlie.

"I feel disloyal, but then he is disloyal," said Marta.

"Who?"

"Mr. Silver."

"Jeremy?"

"*Sí*. I believe he told the Nettleses. He is trying to... What's the word?" She said something in Spanish to Charlie.

"Ingratiate," translated Charlie.

"Yes, ingratiate himself to the Nettles family."

"Why?" asked Plum.

Marta looked as if she would rather do anything else but answer these questions. "I have heard...that he is romancing the daughter and her father disapproves. Señor Nettles has forbidden it. Jeremy must prove himself, his loyalty to her."

Plum nodded. "I see," she said.

Marta leaned closer. "And we heard that he was doing something…funny with the money. Jeremy controls the accounts, and our friend at the bank said Shakira was mad some money was moved around."

Plum remembered Shakira raging about a man, but she had assumed it was Dieter. Could it have been Jeremy?

"Interesting. And Marta, why didn't Shakira want Arielle Waldron at the villa? Was it really to protect Johnny Wisebrook?" asked Plum.

"She said that her friend had been at the hotel pool and overheard Arielle telling her friends that she had a plan to destroy Señor Friedrich so he would have to move and the Nettles could buy his property," said Marta.

Plum pondered this. Would Arielle have been talking to Max and Jessica about this? They didn't mention it. But then she remembered something. Cornelia had met Arielle at the pool when she was with her friends. Could they have mistaken Arielle for Cornelia? Something else occurred to Plum.

"Marta, did Jeremy misplace his computer?" she asked.

Marta's face became animated. "*Sí*, he told you? He was searching for it everywhere. But we didn't see it. No one on my staff took it. We are very honorable," she said, standing upright.

"I'm sure you are," said Plum. "And did it go missing around the time Arielle was at the villa?"

Marta nodded. "Yes. He was asking us about it, and he was very mad. Then they found the girl on the beach, and we were interrupted."

CHAPTER 29

"IT'S JEREMY SILVER," SAID PLUM breathlessly into her phone. "He's the killer."

She had darted back to her golf cart and hastily called Juan Kevin.

"How do you know?" asked Juan Kevin on the other end of the line.

"I'll fill you in. Cornelia Nettles might be in on it with him, I don't know. But let's go confront him."

"I should tell Captain Diaz," said Juan Kevin. "And where are you? I'll pick you up."

Fifteen minutes later, they were at the gates of Dieter Friedrich's villa. She had apprised Juan Kevin of all the information, and he agreed with her theory. Captain Diaz was not available, but Juan Kevin left a message. Plum was relieved, as she assumed Captain Diaz would tell them to stand down.

"I knew that charger meant something," said Juan Kevin.

"Well, you would never have known if not for me," insisted Plum. She would not allow him to take away any of her glory.

When they pulled into Villa la Grosella Negra, Plum bounded out of the car, and she and Juan Kevin rang the doorbell. The

French maid that she had met upon her first visit answered the door.

"We need to see Jeremy Silver," said Juan Kevin.

"In his office," she said, opening the door wider to accommodate them.

"And where might that be?" asked Plum.

The maid sighed as if she could not believe she was being asked to do anything other than open the front door. Reluctantly, she led them down a corridor, her stiletto heels clacking along the way. They exited the house and walked over a bridge and along a mossy stone path that cut through a large swath of trees. It was notably hotter and buggier here without the sea breeze. They made their way toward a small log cabin tucked away on the west side of the estate, close to the large stone walls that separated Dieter's property from the Nettleses' villa. It reminded Plum of an illustration of the witch's house in the copy of Hansel and Gretel she had read as a child.

"Voilà!" the maid said dramatically, rolling her eyes at them.

"Thank you," said Juan Kevin.

She quickly clacked away, and Plum wondered what she was rushing off to do.

It felt eerily quiet on this part of the estate, and maybe just in general, thought Plum. Through the window, they could see Jeremy sitting at a neat desk, writing something in a large notebook. Juan Kevin rapped on the window, and Jeremy glanced up. He motioned for them to enter.

"Sorry to disturb you," said Juan Kevin. "We have a few questions to ask."

"Of course," said Jeremy politely.

Plum gave him the once-over. If he was nervous, he certainly didn't show it. His beard was neatly clipped, his hair tidy, and if anything, he appeared more relaxed than when she last saw him. That was about to change.

His office had a seating area, and Plum and Juan Kevin sat on the celery-colored sofa, while Jeremy took the armchair across from them. He folded his hands, leaned forward, and said, "What's up?"

"We want to discuss your computer," said Juan Kevin smoothly.

A glint of suspicion appeared in Jeremy's eyes. "What do you mean?"

"The computer that has all of the information about Dieter's illegal activities. Building groins and amassing land," said Plum. "We know that you had proof of all of it and you were supplying the information to Cornelia Nettles."

Jeremy gave them a small smile. "I have no idea what you're talking about."

"I think you do," said Juan Kevin patiently.

Jeremy paused. "I found my computer. I had misplaced it, but then I remembered where it was." He motioned to the computer on the desk. "I thank you for your concern, but I'm good."

"If we were to take your computer to the police, would we find Arielle Waldron's fingerprints on it?" asked Plum.

"It's possible. It may have accidentally been in her room," said Jeremy.

"It wasn't accidental. But I think you know that. Arielle was a kleptomaniac. She stole the computer, found out that you were working against Dieter in conjunction with the Nettleses, and tried to blackmail you. She wanted to remain at Dieter's and continue her pursuit of Gary Grigorian and Johnny Wisebrook. But you had to get rid of her, or she would ruin your plan," said Plum.

"And you killed her," added Juan Kevin.

Jeremy stared at them as if frozen, his close-set eyes startled. But then he immediately started laughing. A long, deep cackle. He laughed hard and then walked over to his desk.

"You are too funny. You're a better comedienne than Hallie Corona!" He chuckled. "But you have no proof of what you are saying. And if you did, where are the police?"

"They're on their way," said Juan Kevin.

"Then it's time I'm on my way," said Jeremy.

Suddenly, Jeremy flung open the top drawer of his desk and pulled out a pistol. He aimed it at Juan Kevin and Plum.

Plum felt a litany of emotions—shock, horror, but ultimately, terror. Juan Kevin instinctively stepped in front of Plum to shield her.

"You don't want to do this, Jeremy," said Juan Kevin.

"You shouldn't have meddled," said Jeremy. "Everything was on track. Dieter is gone, I proved myself worthy of Cornelia, and her family was finally ready to embrace me. Do you know how long Charles Nettles has wanted to enact revenge on Dieter Friedrich? He never liked that Dieter had been with Wendy before him; he was always jealous. And I was able to give him evidence that will send Dieter to prison and force him to sell his villa. You should have left well enough alone. You're just like Arielle."

"Is that why you strangled her?" asked Plum.

"That brat wouldn't keep her mouth shut. She was going to ruin everything. I did everyone a favor. She was chasing both Johnny Wisebrook and Gary Grigorian—or 'Mr. Big,' as she called him. Everyone wanted to get rid of her."

"I'm sure they didn't want to kill her," whispered Plum.

Jeremy seethed. "I had to stop her. I took back the computer. I made sure to shut down all of the cameras on the property."

"I thought that was an electrical outage?" asked Juan Kevin.

"No, I did it," boasted Jeremy. "I control them."

"How did you get the power to go out at the Nettleses' place also?" asked Juan Kevin.

Jeremy looked momentarily flustered. "Coincidence."

Plum didn't believe him. Had someone from the Nettles estate helped him? Cornelia perhaps?

"Why did you take Arielle's phone?" Juan Kevin asked.

"She had pictures of me and Cornelia on it. From the hotel pool. I got rid of it," said Jeremy.

By smashing it on the Nettles property, thought Plum, again wondering how involved Cornelia was.

"Did you kill Hallie also?" asked Juan Kevin.

"She found my computer before I did," he snarled. "And she was going to expose me. I had to get rid of her."

He made a move toward the door, keeping the gun pointed at them the entire time. Suddenly, the door burst open, and Captain Diaz stood on the threshold. Juan Kevin took the opportunity to lunge at a startled Jeremy and tackle him to the ground. Jeremy fought back, but Juan Kevin overpowered him and pinned him down. Plum ran over and retrieved the pistol then gingerly handed it to Captain Diaz. It all happened in a flash, and it was the most heart-pounding minute of Plum's life. Captain Diaz ultimately handcuffed Jeremy with the assistance of his deputy.

"Are you okay?" asked Juan Kevin, his face awash with worry.

"I think so," said Plum, before she collapsed into his arms. *Like a damsel in distress,* she thought to herself. Dammit.

Captain Diaz had heard the confession and brought Jeremy to the police station to book him. Jeremy wouldn't say anything further without a lawyer, but he was insistent that Cornelia had nothing to do with Arielle's murder. He would remain true to her until the end.

After Juan Kevin and Plum made their statements, Juan Kevin was allowed to bring the rattled Plum back to her town house. Lucia made Plum drink a cup of brandy that had materialized out of nowhere, and Juan Kevin tried to fend off Gerald's questions until Plum had stopped shaking. She never wanted to be this close to getting murdered again. She felt as if her heart had jumped out of her body and done a little dance and was now agitating to keep jigging.

"I can't believe you put your life on the line," Gerald said. "You really went above and beyond to help me out. Don't worry, I'll make sure to give you credit."

"I don't think it's credit that Plum is after," said Juan Kevin. He was sitting next to Plum on the sofa and rubbing her back in lazy, warming circles.

"No," agreed Plum.

"Excellent! So, then, you don't mind if I kind of inflate my role to Mr. Waldron?" asked Gerald. "Pretty please?"

"Do what you have to do," said Plum with a smile. "I'm just happy it's over and happy he's caught. Now we can try to return to normal."

"Ugh, that means I need to go back to New York," lamented Gerald. "I barely had a vacation. Although on the bright side, New York is so beautiful in the spring. I love the cherry blossoms in Central Park and along Park Avenue. Don't you wish you were going back, Plum?"

Plum scanned Lucia, Gerald, and Juan Kevin's faces, her gaze remaining on the latter's. "Honestly? No," she said.

"But you're a true New Yorker!" protested Gerald.

"Maybe not anymore," said Lucia with a smile.

30

PLUM HAD NEVER BEEN SO thrilled to be behind the wheel of a car. It didn't matter that it was a secondhand Toyota that had already logged forty-two thousand miles. And for someone who appreciated status, Plum was undeterred that it had been advertised as a "*near* luxury automobile" (though she wondered who in their right mind would think that was good marketing). The bottom line was it was the first car that she ever owned, and she was thrilled to no longer have to rely on borrowing Lucia's sedan or making long journeys in her pokey golf cart.

It also meant something else to Plum: she was putting down roots. She may not yet have found her dream house (or even her *near* dream house), but she had made an investment, which meant she would be in Paraiso for the future. Or at least the *near* future.

As she steered the car along the dusty road toward Estrella, she felt liberated. Instead of blasting the air-conditioning, she rolled down all the windows and let the hot wind blow in her face. And despite the fact she was headed to Juan Kevin's house, she didn't think twice that her hair was beginning to coil up into boing-boing curls and she would arrive at his doorstep with wild and crazy locks. Okay, perhaps she would run a comb through it when she arrived, but a few months ago, she would have doused her head in a gallon of hairspray and tortured herself to make sure it was pin straight.

She was excited. Juan Kevin had invited her to lunch. At his house. And it had not been an on-the-fly, offhand offer. He had sent her an email, with "an invitation" in the subject line. It was as close to a date as she'd had in eons. Ever since she had received the invitation, she tried to imagine what his house looked like. Was it supermodern? Was it run-down? Was it generic and characterless? She couldn't envision it.

When her GPS (yes, the new car had navigation!) led her down a quiet, shaded road toward the water, she felt her anticipation grow. The bossy British voice instructed her to make a right, and she turned down a pebbled driveway flanked by a row of thick tamarind trees. As she moved closer, the house came into view, and Plum smiled. It was perfect.

The two-story cottage was made of white coral stone, but the shutters, metal awnings, iron railings, and latticework were all sage green. There was a Juliet balcony on the second floor, right above the entrance, which was opened by French doors. On the right side, Plum saw a shaded veranda with potted ferns and wicker furniture. It was romantic without being fussy or pretentious. Everything about the house made her want to stay there forever.

Juan Kevin opened the door with a grin.

"Welcome to *mi casa*," he said.

"*Gracias*," she said.

She saw him eye her appraisingly, and she did the same in return. He wore a soft, powder-blue shirt and white pants, and instead of his usual loafers, he was wearing moccasins. It was nice to see the relaxed and off-duty Juan Kevin.

"Please come in. What can I get you? Wine? Prosecco? Lemonade?" he said, leading her through the entryway.

"Whatever you are having," she said, padding along the dark mahogany floors.

"Let's have prosecco," he said. "We have a lot to celebrate."

It had been two weeks since they had scuffled with Jeremy Silver, who was currently behind bars and awaiting sentencing. He had initially pleaded guilty, but Captain Diaz had informed Plum that he thought Jeremy would end up retracting his confession and trying to stay out of prison, now that he had a sense of how awful it was to be incarcerated.

"That we do," said Plum.

They passed through the living room—which was comfortably decorated with plump, slipcovered sofas and armchairs—out to the veranda. Plum saw that a skirted table had been laid out for lunch. There was a beautiful platter of poached herb chicken with sliced avocado, tomatoes, asparagus, and diced jicama, as well as a green salad, yucca-crusted goat cheese, and fresh bread. He had really outdone himself, thought Plum. Juan Kevin held out her chair, and she sat down while he popped the prosecco cork open.

She stared out at the view. There was a small dark-bottomed pool, framed by beautiful wildflower bushes. She couldn't see the sea, but she was close enough to smell it. Music drifted through the speakers that hung by the balustrades, and an overhead fan lazily turned in circles.

"This place is paradise," she said.

He smiled. "To me, it is," he said, pouring her a glass of the fizzy wine.

"I never want to leave."

He poured himself a glass and then clinked it with hers. "To solving crime," he said.

"Hear, hear."

Once they had a taste of the bubbly, Juan Kevin filled their water glasses then sat down and offered the plates to Plum.

"Have you heard anything else about Cornelia Nettles?" asked Plum, scooping a large portion of salad onto her plate.

"She has been elusive and impossible to talk to directly," said

Juan Kevin, serving himself some chicken once Plum had taken a bit. "She lawyered up and left the island, and they say she knew nothing about Jeremy's involvement in the murders."

"Yeah, right," said Plum.

"Jeremy is still loyal to her and has also insisted that she knew nothing," said Juan Kevin.

Plum took a bite of her chicken. It was delicious. "We'll see how long that lasts. Maybe if he wants a plea deal."

"Of course, I think she was complicit, but there's no real proof linking her to the crime," said Juan Kevin.

"She did conceal evidence," said Plum.

"Hard to prove," insisted Juan Kevin.

"Speaking of crime, any word on Dieter?" she asked. She tucked into the yucca, and the creamy goat cheese came oozing out. "How is he liking prison?"

"You didn't hear?" asked Juan Kevin, dabbing his mouth with his linen napkin. "He also left the island before they could get to him. Packed up and went to his house in Germany. If he returns, he will be incarcerated, so looks like he won't be back anytime soon."

"Wow," said Plum. "Although you can only imagine how he spins it in his mind." She began to imitate Dieter's accent. "'I am in Germany in zee best house in zee world, better zan anywhere else.'"

Juan Kevin laughed. "You do that very well."

"Do I?" asked Plum, smiling.

They kept their eyes on each other for a beat before Plum looked down at her food. "This is delicious, by the way."

"Thank you."

She smiled, and again, they stared at each other. Suddenly there was a buzz from Plum's phone. She quickly reached for her bag.

"So sorry, I forgot to turn it off," she said, quickly retrieving it and clicking the sound off. When she glanced at the screen, she saw that it was a text from Gerald, and she quickly scanned it. "Oh, not to be rude, but this is from Gerald. He is reporting that Gary

Grigorian was offered the job hosting *Access Hollywood*, and he's now the most in-demand celebrity around."

Juan Kevin sighed. "I suppose the stalwart widower wants to extend his fifteen minutes of fame as long as possible."

"Hallie's death was gold for his career," said Plum, returning her phone to her bag and placing it on the ground. "Gerald said that Gary even got some cameos in upcoming films."

Juan Kevin shook his head and refilled their prosecco glasses. "How is Gerald?"

"He's fine. He's back with Leonard and, of course, taking all the glory for solving Arielle's murder. I think he's even getting a raise."

"Somehow that doesn't surprise me," said Juan Kevin.

"Oh," said Plum, taking a large sip of water to wash down her mouthful of chicken. "He also told me that Jessica and Max are engaged and planning a huge wedding."

"Good for them."

"Yes, and they even want to come back here for their honeymoon, can you imagine?" asked Plum.

"Paraiso is beautiful. Why wouldn't they?"

"Oh my, you and Lucia are the most patriotic people I know," she said, wagging her finger at him. "I mean, yes, it is paradise, but her best friend was murdered here."

Juan Kevin shrugged. "But the murderer was caught. And the island has returned to its magical self."

"I suppose," she said. "But it's good for me, because they booked Casa Tomate, my newest property, which is finally up and running. It's quirky and charming now, and it fit their budget."

"Win, win," said Juan Kevin. He offered her more salad.

"I'm just devouring this food. It is so good. You need to teach me how to cook!"

"I will," he said.

Suddenly a song came over the sound system, and Plum's ears perked up.

"This is a Moving Targets song," she said.

Juan Kevin frowned. "I used to like his music and have it on my playlist, but now I'm not so sure."

"I still like his music," she said. "Just not him."

"Actually...and I don't like to gossip," said Juan Kevin with hesitation.

Plum leaned in eagerly. "What?"

"I heard he had a falling out with Alexandra Rijo. Apparently, he has left Las Frutas for at least the near future."

Plum sat back in her chair. "Interesting. He is a scumbag."

"Alexandra finally figured that out," said Juan Kevin. "I guess we all did."

"There are a lot of bad people around," said Plum.

"There were," corrected Juan Kevin. "Now only the good ones are left."

She smiled. "I hope so."

Juan Kevin put his hand on top of hers and pressed firmly. He looked her straight in the eye. "I know so."

Plum's heart did that fluttery thing again. She suddenly felt as if she were about to jump off a cliff without a safety net. But she knew that there was someone who would catch her and make it all worth it. She smiled back at Juan Kevin.

Looking for another tropical mystery to sink into? Check out an excerpt from the Trouble in Paradise! mysteries:

1

PLUM LOCKHART SAT AT HER desk on the twenty-sixth floor staring down at the blaze of neon lights illuminating Times Square. It was only four thirty, but it was already dark outside and as cold as it could get without snowing. *A pity,* thought Plum. At least snow would have made the filthy streets look pretty. The endless frigid winter days had blended together, and it felt to Plum like it was the forty-seventh day of January, yet it was only the first week. The weather matched her mood: gloomy, negative, and uninspired.

It had been a particularly grim afternoon. Plum had been forced to lay off Gerald Hand, her art director, and he had made a scene (predictable) and accused Plum of being "an opportunistic cold-hearted wannabe" (uncalled for) and was escorted out by security (not her idea). The entire editorial staff was now on edge and regarded Plum with weariness and suspicion, which she resented. She felt they should be grateful to her for keeping them employed in this treacherous market. It was no secret that *Travel and Respite Magazine* was hemorrhaging money—the entire publishing industry was collapsing—and downsizing was inevitable.

There was a knock at Plum's door, and she swiveled her chair around and espied Steven Blum through the glass wall. She motioned for him to come in, although he was already halfway through the door. Seeing as he was her boss, he really didn't have to wait for permission.

"How did it go with Gerald?" asked Steven, taking a seat across from her.

"Brutal."

Steven nodded. He was squat, bald, overweight, and hardly fit the profile of head of the magazine group at the glamorous Mosaic Publishing, but he was a numbers guy who had been promoted from accounting.

"It couldn't have come as a shock to him. The magazine is doing terribly."

"He has an inflated sense of self," sighed Plum, taking a sip of her white chai latte. "But people are delusional."

"Yes, I have often found that."

"He really didn't have to take it personally. He was very catty and churlish. He could have at least left with dignity."

"Yes, that's the way to go. Take your leave graciously."

"Well, what's done is done," she said and began flipping through some of the files on her desk. "The good news is that I finalized the feature on Mongolia. I'll actually be heading there myself for ten days. I ordered all of my horseback riding paraphernalia online. If you look over there, you can see a box of whips… Just to clarify they are for riding, not—"

"Plum…"

"Yes?"

"We need to talk."

"What's up?"

"*Travel and Respite* is basically a pamphlet these days."

"And I choose to see that as a positive. It is easier for people to pop in their suitcase and bring with them when they travel."

"We are shutting it down," Steven announced.

"Completely? Not even turning it into a website?"

Steven shook his head. "It's done."

Plum had suffered enough disappointments in her thirty-five years of life to quickly adapt and turn setbacks into opportunities. She folded her perfectly manicured hands and placed them on her desk. Once, she had skipped a manicure and a nasty editor at a competing magazine asked if her nails were jagged because she had scratched her way to the top. While it was true that she was ambitious and had succeeded, she had done so through hard work and plunging ahead when the chips were down. She was proud of her efforts. And she had kept her nails perfectly polished ever since.

"All right, then. What's the plan?" she asked brightly.

"No plan. As of this afternoon, everyone is released."

Plum glanced sideways out the glass doors at the remaining skeleton staff.

"We can't move them over to another magazine?"

He shook his head.

"How about *Panda Love*? I heard the plushie market is brisk."

"No. When we shut down *Mansions and Hovels*, we put the editors there."

"Steven, if there is one favor I ask of you, and only one, it's to find them jobs. My team means a great deal to me. I want to do what's right by them."

"Okay, but it's unlikely."

"This will be a blow," she said. "Where will you move me?"

Steven stared at her without saying a word. His mouth formed into a sort of flat line, the crude type that a child would draw when first putting pen to paper. "Nowhere."

"Nowhere?" asked Plum. "Enough joking. Seriously."

Steven didn't respond.

"I thought you were grooming me to take over one of the bigger magazines?"

"You thought wrong."

"Are you telling me that I'm…laid off?" she asked, her voice rising.

"Yes."

A thought occurred to her. "Steven, if you were going to fire me, why did you have me fire Gerald? Why didn't you do it?" she asked, looking up and blinking through her trendy fake eyelashes.

"I knew he would make a scene. I didn't want to deal."

"He hates me now!"

Steven shrugged. "Calm down, he'll get over it."

She glared at him. "I find it very insulting when men tell women to calm down."

"Just act like a lady."

"I am a lady, and this is how we act."

"Now, don't you make a scene," cooed Steven, as if speaking to a toddler. "Didn't we just say not to be churlish? To take your leave graciously?"

Plum felt as if her head were about to spin off and go flying all the way down to Broadway. She imagined it splattering right at the feet of some tourists from Des Moines who were on their way to see *Phantom of the Opera*. Then they would really have something to tell their friends back home.

"What does grace have to do with this? This is my livelihood we are discussing. I have financial responsibilities."

"Like what? You're single, no kids."

"True," she conceded. "But I sponsor an animal shelter in Long Island. I don't know what they would do without my assistance. There are a lot of abandoned older dogs, hard to find homes for…"

"You're whining about animals? Let's not be a drama queen."

Oh, really, thought Plum. She would show him a drama queen.

She instantly recalled the way women on reality shows handled their rage, which was flipping over tables, so she rose and put both of her hands under her glass desk and tried to hoist it on Steven's lap. But sadly, the desk was so heavy that she couldn't even lift it an inch and merely exerted a tremendous amount of useless effort in her attempt. After awkwardly huffing and puffing while trying to lift the table—while Steven watched with amusement and contempt—Plum finally sank into her chair, certain she had caused blood vessels to pop in her brain with her futile endeavor.

"Just go," she said sadly. "I need to process this."

"Unfortunately, it is you that needs to go."

Plum glanced up and saw that two security guards had miraculously materialized at her door. "You're throwing me out?"

"You can take your whips and riding helmet with you."

ACKNOWLEDGMENTS

Thank you so much to the fantastic Sourcebooks team, Anna Michels, Jenna Jankowski, and Shauneice Robinson, and copy editor, Manu Velasco. I also would like to extend gratitude to my amazing literary agent, Christina Hogrebe, and my excellent film and TV agent, Debbie Deuble Hill. I appreciate Carol Fitzgerald's continuous support and cheerleading! And once again, this book could not have been written without my sister Liz Carey, who is my sounding board, editor, and confessor. Love always to Vas, James, Peter, Nadia, Mopsy, Dick, and Laura.

ABOUT THE AUTHOR

Photo by Tanya Malott

Carrie Doyle is the bestselling author of multiple novels and screenplays that span many genres, from cozy mysteries to chick lit to comedies to YA.

A born and bred New Yorker, Carrie has spent most of her life in Manhattan, with the exception of a six-year stint in Europe (Russia, France, England) and five years in Los Angeles. A former editor-in-chief of the Russian edition of *Marie Claire,* Carrie has written dozens of articles for various magazines, including countless celebrity profiles. She currently splits her time between New York and Long Island with her husband and two teenage sons.